THE SCHOLAR OF MOAB

Steven L. Peck

Torrey House Press, LLC
Utah

First Torrey House Press Edition, December 2011
Copyright © 2011 by Steven L. Peck

Published by Torrey House Press, LLC
P.O. Box 750196
Torrey, Utah 84775 U.S.A.
http://torreyhouse.com

International Standard Book Number: 978-1-937226-02-2
Library of Congress Control Number: 2011939466

Front cover photos by Guy Tal, Guy Tal Photography, www.guytal.com
Back cover photo by Nicholas Bailey
Cover design by Jeff Fuller, Crescent Moon Communications

Dedicated to the original members of the Gala Cotillion Club where this work was given birth: Steve and Jaylyn Hawks—true and graceful Moabites, and Lori of course.

THE SCHOLAR OF MOAB

REDACTOR'S PROLOGUE

The memory of Hyrum Thayne is fading among those undaunted souls who continue to make their home in the Moab Valley. Only a remnant of his abandoned statue remains. This reverently erected monument established to honor the Scholar of Moab is now in ruins and languishes abandoned in the small, neglected park uphill from the Mormon chapel on Locust Lane. Should you find the vestiges of that once grand idol, and pull back the verdant fescue ringing the red-rock base out of which two hollow, broken brass shins protrude boldly (like some perverted twist on an Arthurian legend), a plaque can still be read:

Hyrum LeRoy Thayne
Scholar and Scientist
The Lord's Chosen Servant and Defender of Moab
1950-1977

In 1982, the statue was chained to a pickup hitch by a group of prom-night revelers and yanked down. The giddy celebrants, two of whom had just lost their virginity, dragged Hyrum's simulacrum down 4th East in a blaze of sparks. Unobserved by the distracted police (who in their defense, had their hands full with other prom-night shenanigans), the teenagers heaved the bronze memorial into the tamarisk-infested slough that lies along a slow bend on the Colorado River, just east of the State Road-191 Bridge, where now a beautiful wetlands reserve has been established. For years Hyrum's head and one of his arms, pointing not into the future, but straight into the sky, could be descried struggling to rise from the thick, muddy quagmire. By 1985, just as Moab's mountain biking excellence was about to launch it as a tourist Mecca, the last tip of his noble upraised hand slipped from view.

By a series of strange coincidences, I have come to be The Scholar's chronicler. It started when my uncle invited me to help him go through the combat zone of my grandfather's papers. My grandfather was a bitter old man who had alienated himself from the rest of his family after he had cut himself off from the Mormon Church. He told everyone to leave him the Hell alone. They did.

In the old curmudgeon's trailer was a mountain of filth and garbage: old newspapers, reams of computer printouts, paperback books, 20 years of junk mail, car parts, food packaging, and the shabby remains of old Kenwood trailer furniture. Cat hair was abundant, and feline urine raised such a stink as to leave the impression that the sulfury gates of Dante's Inferno had just been opened. I opined that the whole mess ought to be burned to the ground, but my uncle insisted that there might be some genealogy buried in the refuse and insisted we go through the stacks of papers with some attention, carefully and methodically. Thank goodness for his insight and olfactory endurance, or the tale of Hyrum Thayne might have been lost forever. How my grandfather came upon these documents, I cannot guess. Their provenance has been beyond my talent to discover, but they were set aside with some care, if that word can be used for anything in my grandfather's trailer. They were hidden in a box marked simply: *Keep*. In it were: Thayne's journal, an account of the events leading up to his saving the town from the Gadianton Robbers; a reprint of his article on bumblebee faith, published in the *Bulletin of the Ecological Society of America*; a photo of William and Edward Babcock, the conjoined twins who cowboyed for the Wixom Cattle Company up in the La Sals; a photocopy of a picture of Dora Daphne Tanner (taken from her book *Red Rock Flows through My Veins*) standing beside what she claims are the remains of the crashed alien craft, which secured her fame as both unbalanced and as a nature poet; a few of Ms. Tanner's letters; Thayne's library card; a photo of Hyrum and Sandra Thayne on their wedding day, standing by their white Ford Mustang (she with her foot on the bumper, hitching up her dress, he removing a garter); a poem by Sandra titled, *Our Forever Love my Hyrum Dear*; a clipping from the *Times-Independent* on the book burning vandalism at the library; and lastly, one half of *Webster's Third New International Dictionary* 1971 ed. (specifically "manifest" through "Zs").

Of course, the obvious feature of the contents of this box is that it is certainly not a random collection of memorabilia. It all pertains to Hyrum's saving the town from the notorious Gadianton Robbers—and his martyrdom.

In what follows I have tried to tie these things into a coherent story using his own words and letters, interviews with the people who were involved, articles from various sources, and my own investigations. In particular, the late Babcock twins were essential in reconstructing this story. Marne Law, Hyrum's former Mormon home teacher, reluctantly shared many details of the story, but, unfortunately, died before I could complete the interviews. These have not been included here because Hyrum's journal contains most of this, but they do add some collaborative weight to Hyrum's story. Like Sandra,

Law shared the conviction that the Gadianton Robbers and communists were real and he maintained stoically the received view of the events. Dora's letters came from her evidence file collected by her state-appointed legal defense team and from the Utah State Mental Hospital. I would like to thank the Moab branch of the Daughters of the Utah Mormon Pioneers for helping me track down Hyrum's genealogy. In the narrative that follows, not all documents are included, but I've incorporated those that seem to give the clearest picture.

I prefer to remain anonymous. I refer to myself throughout what follows as *The Redactor*. Hyrum's journal begins in June or July 1977 and continues up until his death in August. I have broken it up into several parts, and have embedded the other more or less contemporaneous source documents with the events he describes. I corrected most of his spelling, except where it seemed to authentically flavor his voice or where it was important to understand the events. Leaving all his original spelling distracted from Hyrum's voice. I left the original punctuation and capitalization because that seemed to capture something of his personality. All documents have been deposited in the Utah State University Library archive, however, should one wish to consult the originals.

Poem, Our Forever Love my Hyrum Dear, *by Sandra Thayne.*
Written just before their marriage. May 10th, 1966.

Hyrum Dear I love you well
And oft my heart you make to swell,
(And now it seems my belly as well)

This babe of ours will deep love keep,
As we watch its face when it's asleep
(Of you and me its features reap)

The night wherein we made the child,
The Monkees played all the while
("I'm a Believer" soft and mild)

Our love will last eternally,
and from each other we will never flee,
(and together we will ever be)

Hyrum's journal, hand-written manuscript.
Written between June and August, 1977.

I Hyrum having been born of goodly parents am from Moab. This must be distinctly understood if any sense is to be made of any of this my Dickensian life. Am I learned? Not as much as you might be led to believe by my use of numinous locutions. Yea, I graduated as many ordinary souls do from the auspices of Grand County High or I should say I would have graduated had I passed Mr. Wondells History class but without the 4th of a credit he should have provided I was forced to sit upon the dewy lawn in front of the High School whilst my graduating class graduated in their festive finery without me. Sandra was Pregnant sitting there with me on the cool green grass but only months along & not yet showing. I am sad to report that it would be her one & only pregnancy & the baby would not be born into this world. Its spirit she says awaits our reunion when Christ comes again & reigns for 1000 years in the Millennium. She lost it at the beginning of the third Trimester. She has never recovered I think & as of yet pines away in Sorrow. There are many sorrows in this the story of my Scholarly life many of them having to do with Babies.

How do I begin? How indeed. The rise from my beknighted state to one of mighty & true erudition will stand credibility on your hoary head. You will see me ascend from a miserly laborer with the USGS verily the united states

Geological survey to a flagship Scholar invited to stroll among the high & mighty & publish landmark Science in the prestigious periodical the <u>Bulletin of the Ecological Society of America</u>. Why did I underline that? Because titles are underlined in works of Scholarship. Verily verily you will learn much more than this. Much more indeed. For I. Even I of my own Labors have engaged with the profoundest heights of Science & Literature. It is from the peaks of these high Heights that I first found entanglements both Wide & Deep.

It started in the cool summers of the La Sal Mountains. Behold these great behemoth mammoths can be glimpsed from about anywheres in Moab but most wonderfully from flats north of town up past the Cowboy bar on the South end of town on Highway 191. They rise from the Canyonlands like a great Coyote set to howl just before it strikes at a new born baby sheep fresh from its mamas hips. Of which I have seen many in my younger days. The names of these great mountains roll off the tongue like the prodigious Mt. Peele & tremendous Mount Tukuhnikivatz & mighty Mt Mellenthin & the wise Mt. Waas. Some say they rose only after the days of Peleg as mentioned in the Bible when Noah fresh from his Ark spied the rainbow rising like a Trout from among the clouds of which their moisture was emptied of water like the dugs of a newly milked cow because of the forty days of rain & the Windows of Heaven being opened & such. Geologists tell a more unlikely tale about Continents floating around like foam on a beer which as you know a Mormon ought not to drink.

Up in the La Sals I was gregariously working for the government in the form of the illustrious USGS & I had been assigned to work with The Bob. He was a mean spirited SOB if you will excuse my bringing to your mind swear words. His grizzled face was like that of a Grizzly bear & he arose on his haunches to over 6 feet. He had long claw-like fingers with which he clenched in frustration all his sorrows & failings. And of those he had no lack. The story told around the old trailer that we stayed at up in the La Sals during the week was that The Bob had got himself a Phd in English at Harvard & then tried to write his self a <u>Novel</u>. Trouble was that even his own mother would not read the pitiable thing & so he returned to get a degree in Geology so as he could keep himself a real job. Trouble was that meant that he had to work with me. I never did anything to deserve this & so this was a clear case of Evil in the world or as Scholars know a Theodicy which is a <u>Words of Power</u> word about which KBYU just broadcast a panel of experts talking about it which is the evil Underarching & Overflowing the world & the fact that God has his own ways & keeps his own council. Of course we Mormons know why there is evil in the world. Its because God in his wisdom send us down here to get Tried & Tested but the rest of the world thinks that evil is like holes in the goodness of God. The show on KBYU had a gaggle of Religion Professors saying whats what about this. We know moreover & nevertheless that Heavenly Father allows evil so as to put us through the wringer to show if we were up to being a God ourselves or not as the case may be. You will find that I have Messed this chance up royally.

Anyway. Well perhaps I should tell what we did up on the Mountain. What indeed. We were making underground maps of the way things were in the different Strata & Stratum of the many layered Earth. We would draw up to an a priori arranged spot & and find some bedrock to set up some sensing equipment that essentially were Seismographic seismographs. Some other guys a posteriori & miles away would set up some explosions & we would watch the tectonic wave propitiate to the very spot we was set up on. Of course in describing this it sounds exotic & greatly interesting. You are probably thinking that we would never get bored doing true Science like this but the facts must be told it was pretty slow most of the time. So while you may think that Science is thrilling & full of advanced kinds of things it was mostly alot of waiting around doing nothing but watching the recording Machines drum roll along like a scroll turning under a little pin hooked up to listen for the explosion that was to go off a posteriori to our setting up the equipment. We were in ennui & languor. And you will be surprised to learn that really this scientific work had little to do with my becoming a Scholar & scientist of note in the field of bumblebee Studies. They were known to Dickens as Humble Bees. We scientists call them Bombus of course which is the name that was derived from the Greeks or the Latins & which was taken by Science to be the name by which these beasts will be known when we talk about them for reasons we keep to ourselves. But I will talk about this later after I tell you how The Bob who by no forethought in himself sent me on an intellectual journey & launched my career as a great Scholar of world Renownededness & entered me back into full fellowship of my Church in outward appearance but inside like many Scientists I was an unbeliever & only Machiavellied many people of which now I'm a bit sorry. It is now causing me much problems whereof I will speak of by & by. But I write this for my conscience & to squash those lies that are told about me here & there. I say unto you O Sandra if you are reading this any rumors about me are false. I was True as I was Blue.

Well I've fallen into digressions. Yea such Dichotomies dwell in the hearts of those who write & philosophize about the deeper matters of Scholarship. If you are not ready to follow where the datum leads than I am sorry for you. Very very Sorry. Wherefore & Moreover I will continue with my story of The Bob. I will start on that clear Fall day in autumn which we rode merrily along. The Bob was in a foul mood. So it came to pass that here I was bouncing along a dirt road heading up along the South face of Tukuhnikivatz looking for a good Outcropping of Bedrock so we could set up. I was sitting with this most bitter of men. I spotted a likely spot & pulled off the road into a small meadow surrounded by aspens. He got out walked over to a tree left his mark & then got back in the truck. I did'nt see much use in disturbing him so I set about setting up the Sensing Station. I had done it a 100 times so there was'nt really any need for him to be there at all. Yet at the time I was not seen as a man even learned enough to be trusted to set up what I knew how to set up better than the man who was Given charge. Such is the nature of hierarchal hierarchies which is a way of saying someone is over you even though they do'nt deserve it.

Truth is he was a first class idiot. On the way up there I spied a Coyote running through some of the brush oak on the right side of the road & it paused to look at us. I slammed on the breaks & as white dust gathered around us I threw open the door & reached around & grabbed the Winchester 264 my Dad bought when he got home from the War. I kept it laid on the backseat floor of the cab just for such occasions. Its a beautiful gun that shoots like a dream & do'nt require much pampering & I aimed across the top of the truck & as the dust cleared I saw the Coyote was still staring at us. Just then The Bob opens the door & steps out of the truck & if I had'nt been paying attention I would have plugged him in the back of the head. Excuse me I said & he turned round to see me sighting the gun right down into his face. Shit he said & I'm quoting so its ok for me to say that & he jumped back into his seat. I was back on the Coyote & just as I was pulling the trigger he slams his door shut & the Coyote bolts. The Shot went bad & instead of a nice lung shot I hit it in the back just above the hips. It gave a sharp angry yap & whipped around in a crazy jerking way like he was trying to nip a horsefly or whatever had Panicked his backside. I ran down to it jumping over the sage like a Wildman cause I was pretty overcome with the Buck fever that comes when you shoot something. It was hit bad & hard but it was doing a pretty decent job of crawling forward dragging its back legs those being as dead as a doornail. It was trying hard to get away but not making much headway. When I got up to it it tried to turn on me Snarling & Snapping but I leaped back & laughed cause I knew it was'nt going to get me. I pulled the rifle up & popped it in the head to put it out of its misery. Soon The Bob was standing there frowning at the killt beast. He was wearing on his hip one of those giant useless tourist Bowie knifes in an Indian looking sheath covered in Turquoise beads & I said Let me see your knife so I can cut off the Bounty & he said You are'nt using my knife. So I hiked back up to the truck & grabbed a little sheathless Buck out of the toolbox. It was as dull as a butter knife cause no one cared to sharpen what everybody used & I had to saw off the ears & tail with that useless Thing. I put them in a paper bag & The Bob just stared at it & then said What a waste. I pointed out that there was a $20 Bounty on coyotes & that what was one mans waste was another mans dinner. He just shook his head all condescending like & we got back in the truck & continued up the mountain. Sandra for one would be glad for the Money.

It came to pass on this day long long before the gloaming commenced I took out my army knapsack fished around & pulled a hardback copy of a Lewis Lamour novel I had borrowed from the Library. I think I had better point out here when I say borrowed from the Library I mean borrowed. I never check them out. It is too much work & I hate having to remember my library Card. Mostly I hate having someone else know what I'm reading & then there was the facing of Sister Goodsons so judgmental & condemning looks. Her brows always wrinkle just enough to say Brother Thayne is'nt there something a little more uplifting you could be reading. She was in my Church Ward the Moab 4th too so I could'nt check out half the books I might like to anyway. So I took them cart blanch. I just slip them into my shirt & then when I'm done drop them back into the night Dropbox. It works out better for everyone.

I was just starting into chapter 2 when suddenly I noticed that The Bob was staring at me. And what a look. He might as well have just said out loud Hey boy I am soap & your dirt.

But instead he said what do you do around here when your not on this mountain picking your nose.

Quickly I gulped for air. It is amazing how the mind in a tight situation can in the blink of an eye flash through a 1000 ideas. Play them in an instant & then put out all the possible answers to such a loaded question & at the speed of light pick the worst one of the lot & send it to your mouth to blurt out. And I was not yet a Scholar. And I had not yet bought a copy of Words of Power: 30 Days to a Better Vocabulary therefore the power of my words was compromised by inexacteditudeness.

Well I like to bowl I said. Well the truth is I hate bowling. I do'nt know how it came out except that I had bowled a 150 the other night & was glad because I beat our neighbors the Macks. Somehow that sense of pride had snuck out of my mouth & come out as an admission of all The Bob wanted to hear. He roared. He laughed. His scorn to this day rings in my ears. Like the sound of the devil in a Hell of strange laughter laughing Hellishly. He cackled so hard I thought I was going to have to administer first aid. Somehow he managed to get himself under control & quieted down to a thoughtful chuckle. He was clearly of the school of thought that bowling was like life in a town like Moab slow & not much action.

Actually I started feeling pretty good inside. Even then my Scholar nature could discern the heart of the matter. I realized that I had made the poor miserable man for just a moment glad he was alive. Somehow it made me feel in control. Sort of how an actor on a stage must feel when he gets the audience feeling just how he Aims them to feel. Scholars call this an exploitation. I decided I had an advantage in this & played it up for all its worth.

Sometimes I said me & the boys like to play checkers at the barbershop. I had seen enough of Andy Griffith to know what he was looking for. He started to giggle & snort.

And I said with subtlety & without Guile or remorse Every once in awhile when things are really cooking we'll invite the folks over & barbecue some chicken & play horseshoes. He was in a full blown laugh at this time & I was starting to feel really good.

One time me & the boys got some old truck inner tubes & floated down Mill Creek from the Power Dam to the Colorado. For some reason this did'nt have the effect I had hoped & he stopped laughing & looked Thoughtful. I was racking my brain trying to think of something to say when suddenly he looked at me & said.

You live in a trailer do'nt you boy. He said it sort of softly like he was talking to a child or if I was an ape. Or like you do your dog after you kick it for jumping on you.

No I lied.

Where did I pick you up this morning? Was that your wife in the door?

I had forgotten that he had picked me up.

Well we're just living there until the house we are building up Spanish Valley Drive is finished. Its just a Rental.

I could of kicked myself for saying that because we Own that trailer outright. It brought a smile to his face & this time it did'nt make me feel in control. It seems however that once the floodgate is open there is no stopping it. Locution on the run.

Yes sir we would not live in a trailer on purpose. No we are just living there for a week or two. It is my brother who is dirt poor. He's nice to put us up & all but it would be Terrible to have to live there a long time with all those other trailer trash folks hanging around & leaving their cars around & stuff like that. So verily I said in the entrapment of my soul by this conniving man. Why did I say this? I did'nt mind living in a trailer park at all. I had done it most of my life. I knew there was some of the town folk in high school that looked down on it & one Cheerleader especially that was always throwing it in my face but they were not down to earth folk anyway so I never gave them no thought. But here I was making excuses I did'nt care about to a man I did'nt care about Either.

I knew a bunch of the kids in high school that lived in the trailer parks & I can tell you that if I had kids thats not where I would like to live. Why did I say that?

A wave of bitterness passed over The Bobs face like an explosion showing up on a seismograph. He looked down at me for a second & then as if realizing who he was talking to said to himself.

Man! What a Dickensian life you lead.

I had no clue what he meant. At first I thought he might have been waxing a bit profane but something in the way he said it made me think he was just talking over my head. I must have Looked as puzzled as I was because the next thing he said was.

Look it up. That ended the days conversation.

I could hardly read my <u>novel</u> all that day. Now I was not completely ignorant even at that time I did like to read & I knew that we only pass through this life for an ephemeral time. But Dickensian had got me good. I looked all through the Sackett book I was reading to see if I could catch it in being used but Lewis Lamour had neglected to use it in that particular book. I almost thought of asking The Bob but that would not do at all so I thought I would just bide my time until I could get back home & Look it up. I guess I had sort of taken it personal he used the word right when I was lying about my life & the timing was such that when he said it stuck on me like a cheat grass seed to a sock.

All that afternoon I kept hearing him say Man! What a Dickensian life you lead.

Man! What a Dickensian life you lead.
Man! What a Dickensian life you lead.
Man! What a Dickensian life you lead.
Man! What a Dickensian life you lead.
Man! What a Dickensian life you lead.
Man! What a Dickensian life you lead.
Man! What a Dickensian life you lead.
Man! What a Dickensian life you lead.
Man! What a Dickensian life you lead.
Man! What a Dickensian life you lead.
Man! What a Dickensian life you lead.
Man! What a Dickensian life you lead.
Man! What a Dickensian life you lead.
Man! What a Dickensian life you lead.

Man! What a Dickensian life you lead.
Man! What a Dickensian life you lead.
Man! What a Dickensian life you lead.
Man! What a Dickensian life you lead.
Man! What a Dickensian life you lead.
Man! What a Dickensian life you lead.
Man! What a Dickensian life you lead.
Man! What a Dickensian life you lead.
Man! What a Dickensian life you lead.
Man! What a Dickensian life you lead.
Man! What a Dickensian life you lead.
Man! What a Dickensian life you lead.
Man! What a Dickensian life you lead.
Man! What a Dickensian life you lead.
Man! What a Dickensian life you lead.
Man! What a Dickensian life you lead.
Man! What a Dickensian life you lead.
Man! What a Dickensian life you lead.
Man! What a Dickensian life you lead.
Man! What a Dickensian life you lead.
Man! What a Dickensian life you lead.
Man! What a Dickensian life you lead.
Man! What a Dickensian life you lead.
Man! What a Dickensian life you lead.
Man! What a Dickensian life you lead.
Man! What a Dickensian life you lead.
Man! What a Dickensian life you lead.
Man! What a Dickensian life you lead.
Man! What a Dickensian life you lead.
Man! What a Dickensian life you lead.
Man! What a Dickensian life you lead.

Man! What a Dickensian life you lead.
Man! What a Dickensian life you lead.
Man! What a Dickensian life you lead.
Man! What a Dickensian life you lead.
Man! What a Dickensian life you lead.
Man! What a Dickensian life you lead.
Man! What a Dickensian life you lead.
Man! What a Dickensian life you lead.
Man! What a Dickensian life you lead.
Man! What a Dickensian life you lead.
Man! What a Dickensian life you lead.
Man! What a Dickensian life you lead.
Man! What a Dickensian life you lead.
Man! What a Dickensian life you lead.
Man! What a Dickensian life you lead.
Man! What a Dickensian life you lead.
Man! What a Dickensian life you lead.
Man! What a Dickensian life you lead.
Man! What a Dickensian life you lead.
Man! What a Dickensian life you lead.
Man! What a Dickensian life you lead.
Man! What a Dickensian life you lead.
Man! What a Dickensian life you lead.
Man! What a Dickensian life you lead.
Man! What a Dickensian life you lead.
Man! What a Dickensian life you lead.
Man! What a Dickensian life you lead.
Man! What a Dickensian life you lead.
Man! What a Dickensian life you lead.
Man! What a Dickensian life you lead.
Man! What a Dickensian life you lead.
Man! What a Dickensian life you lead.

Man! What a Dickensian life you lead.
Man! What a Dickensian life you lead.
Man! What a Dickensian life you lead.
Man! What a Dickensian life you lead.
Man! What a Dickensian life you lead.
Man! What a Dickensian life you lead.
Man! What a Dickensian life you lead.
Man! What a Dickensian life you lead.
Man! What a Dickensian life you lead.
Man! What a Dickensian life you lead.
Man! What a Dickensian life you lead.
Man! What a Dickensian life you lead.
Man! What a Dickensian life you lead.
Man! What a Dickensian life you lead.
Man! What a Dickensian life you lead.
Man! What a Dickensian life you lead.
Man! What a Dickensian life you lead.
Man! What a Dickensian life you lead.
Man! What a Dickensian life you lead.
Man! What a Dickensian life you lead.
Man! What a Dickensian life you lead.
Man! What a Dickensian life you lead.
Man! What a Dickensian life you lead.
Man! What a Dickensian life you lead.
Man! What a Dickensian life you lead.
Man! What a Dickensian life you lead.
Man! What a Dickensian life you lead.
Man! What a Dickensian life you lead.
Man! What a Dickensian life you lead.
Man! What a Dickensian life you lead.
Man! What a Dickensian life you lead.
Man! What a Dickensian life you lead.

Man! What a Dickensian life you lead.
Man! What a Dickensian life you lead.
Man! What a Dickensian life you lead.
Man! What a Dickensian life you lead.
Man! What a Dickensian life you lead.
Man! What a Dickensian life you lead.
Man! What a Dickensian life you lead.
Man? What a Dickensian life you lead.

I started counting & every time I thought it I threw a rock at a tree. When it was time to head down I just walked over to the tree & counted up the rocks. That is exactly how many times I thought it between the time I ate my lunch & the time we packed up to go back to the base camp. I wanted to let you get a feel for my afternoon ruminations.

On the way down from the mountain The Bob did'nt say a word. And it was a long drive being as we were working up near Miners Basin & our camp was down near Dark Canyon Lake. I drove up the dirt road to the front of the double wide where we stayed during the week on the mountain. The Dynamite Crew was already there & had started making Spaghetti. A staple out here. The Bob did'nt say nothing to nobody. Not even the head Geologist so I felt a little better maybe they lived Dickensian lives too but still being called something that I did'nt know had not set very well with me & that night I did'nt feel much like playing cards with Rick & Dave. I had better tell you about Rick & Dave. They had been working on this job for as long as I have. There just a couple of local boys like me who happen to know something about Explosives they learned in Vietnam & got hired on to set most of the charges. Daves about 40 & is sort of a late blooming hippie. He always wears a ponytail thats pulled up sort of high to hide the bald spot in the middle of his head. It does'nt work.

Dave loves to talk & if you do'nt get down right rude he wo'nt stop. If you start looking around & turning your body so as to be obviously trying to end the conversation he just ups his Voice & moves closer. After 10 years you learn how to say Well Dave I've got to go & walk away. Abscond if you will. He'll keep talking so you usually have to head to the John to get him to shut up. But after you come out its easy to ignore him & keep him from getting going. He's like Smoking just do'nt start.

Rick is half Indian & is probably the best friend I ever had except for one other that has been as good a friend as is possible in this world of woe. But Rick was a good one till the other friend came along. I've never been to his house & he's never been to mine but we've had some talks that have made us some sort of Blood Brothers like they say the Indians do. We did'nt become friends like in the city if you can call Moab a city where we all just pop over to someones house & watch a game or go hunting & fishing together but never get inside one anothers Head.

I remember one December late. Rick & I decided to escape a couple of Geologists that were fighting over some Fossil one of them had found. One swore it was a Brachiopod & the other was convinced that it was a hunk of Bivalve. My heck it was just a slash in the limestone. It did'nt look like nothing to me. These are things you learn about from geologists & are Fossils that got laid down in the flood if you are to believe my Sunday school teacher. Which I do'nt because I am a Scientist. But I pretend mostly for the sake of not causing hard feelings.

It was getting heated in there & even Dave had gone to bed to escape some of the bad feelings flying about. Rick & I decided to take some fresh air. There was no moon & the cold December night was as black between the stars as a birds eye.

The Milkyway looked clear & full & the stars as bright as the cars on the Salt Lake freeway from the 6th South overpass look. Now the La Sals are the only mountains I ever been in so I do'nt have much to compare it to but its hard to imagine that the sky could be any darker or more Mysterious. Fact is some of the geologists who have been up in the Rockies & one that has even been in the Andes says the stars from Geyser Pass are the most clear & beautiful stars on Earth. Thats not hard to doubt.

We started walking through the inch or so of snow into the desert & talking about the Mysterys. You know those talks that take you further & deeper then you've ever been before. The kind of talks that require a full sky the desert & a sense of wonder. We talked about the Anasai & how they just up & disappeared & nobody knows what happened or where they went. We wondered if they might of been taken up by UFOs or if maybe they went off with the lost 10 Tribes of Israel. We talked about the universe & how maybe we are really just an Atom on somebodys big toe. We talked so long & so deep I thought I was going to burst into tears. Well soon the sun came up & even though we were pretty dog tired we shook hands before we went into the cabin & in that shake somehow we became Brothers. Maybe its something only the Indians know how to do but after that many a fine talked followed.

Even though Rick is'nt a Mormon he does'nt drink. I've suspected that he's smoked a joint or two but he do'nt drink. His dad died of liver disease. His Dad was a full-blooded Navaho & when he was dying in the hospital in Flagstaff he made everybody leave the room but Rick. Then he pulled him close. Rick remembers every word cause he rehearsed it again & again in some Indian way.

I copied it down. It was this.

Listen to me. Your mother was White & even though she left me she was good. You take care of her. I have disgraced my Ancestors. I have washed away all my peoples blood with the White Mans drink. It has poisoned our people & I will not see my Ancestors in that better place. Never drink. Never. The day you do you are no longer of my people. You are a White Man. One drop & you have washed away the blood of my People. You are not of my People if there is ever found even a beer in your blood. Do you understand? Come closer & I will bless you. I bless you that the White Mans blood will not overtake the blood of the People. I bless you that you will have a great mission to perform for the People. Remember my People. He said he blessed him like the Mormons do by laying his hands on his head because his dad had been a Mormon for a time.

Now this next part is really spooky if he tells it late at night between the walls of a the red rock canyon under a full Moon like he did me. But he swears it is true.

Just then his father jumped to his feet. He pulled all the tubes right out of his arms. He stood on top of his hospital bed & started to sing in Navaho. Rick said that all the sudden after just a few seconds of singing his father started a conversation with the wall in Navaho. He would say something. Look earnestly at the wall & then say something else. All of the sudden tears started running down his face & a big Peaceful smile spread across his face. Rick had never seen his father cry before & it really unnerved him. Then he spoke to the wall very strictly & pointed at Rick. He did not like what the wall said because an argument started. He said his father started pleading with the wall & all the time was pointing at him. Rick was about 13 at the time & was at this point huddled in the corner hugging his knees. Suddenly his father Shouted in joy & triumph & sat back down on the Hospital bed. He looked at Rick with clearer eyes than Rick had seen in years & said They will honor my promise. Never drink. He closed his eyes & laid back down & started singing again. Rick says a Chill ran down his spine so cold he almost passed out. He managed to run out of the room & get his grandparents who were waiting outside. When they came back in his father was dead.

Rick had always kept his promise. He has a big Scar from his lower lip to his chin where a bottle of wine broke on his teeth when in high school some kids tried to pour it down his throat. Rick still has all Indian Blood & always will as far as I can tell.

I think this story is interesting cause my other friend had strange things happen too. There are weird things in the world. Strange even for a Scientist & Scholar like me.

Well I've gotten a little away from the story but like I was saying I did'nt even feel like cards that night & I went strait to my bunk & laid down knowing full well that there was no way I would ever get to sleep. Its funny the effect that a single word can have on you. I hear new words all the time that I do'nt understand & just plain do'nt pay any attention to. But somehow when they are directed at you it Changes everything. You need to find out if it is true or if it is false or what. You just cant sit around not knowing if you really do live a Dickensian life or if it is bad or blessed to live such a life.

I was called the name Monday & I lived for Friday so I could find out what I had been called. I also lived for Friday because I could not stand another day with this awful creature we called The Bob. He had insulted me twice more during the week but at least the other times I knew what he meant. Lowlife & Redneck I have heard before. Friday finally came but just as we were heading up to the mountain for our last day of work before the weekend something Terrible happened. The head geologist came up to us as we were loading the truck to go. He was obviously upset about something.

Bob. He said. Denver called last night & they want you to spend another week or two with us. You can stay here over the weekend or you can get a Motel in Moab. It is up to you.

I did'nt know whether to cry or hit something. I could'nt stand it. It was'nt fair. Another week with this guy & there would be a Murder. All the way up the mountain I was furious. The injustice & cruelty of life just served to fuel my conviction that the Lord was much further away from this World than the folks at Church were letting on. My inactivity was well justified. Just as these thoughts were taking hold an Idea struck me. A wonderful terrible Idea as the Grinch might say. Maybe there was a God & I got to thinking maybe one of these weeks I would go to Church & give thanks for the Blessing that had just come.

All day long The Bob would do not a thing. From the time we pulled in until the time we pulled out he just would smoke his pipe & walk around in the Splendor of the La Sals. Except when he was tired of roaming around thinking deep PHD thoughts then he would come over by where I was reading or resting & find Fault with my life. He blasted Mormons. He cut down Indians & said they lost their way. He yelled about working folk farmers & the guys out at Denver & everyone that had done what he had'nt. I would'nt do anything but grunt at him & I think he took me for quite the ignoramus. I did'nt much Care about what he thought. He was one of these people so low in life they are more like Gnats than people. They just buzz around bothering those of which they have no reckoning. The only time he bit was in that comment about a Dickensian life & that had done nothing but peak my Curiosity. Well it more than peaked my Curiosity. It had got under my skin & started me Itching so bad it would'nt go away until I got it Scratched.

As I said he Never lifted a finger to help me set up. He never helped or commented in choosing a site. Nothing. This was to be his downfall & doom & it worked Beautifully.

That morning the Idea came to me I pulled off the road & started examining the map to see where they were going to be doing the Blasting. The Bob did'nt even look my way. They were going to be Blasting up near the west end of Fisher Mesa. I figured if we turned left when the Castle Valley road split at the Loop road & drive up to Jimmy Keen Flat we'd have both Castle & Mary Jane Valleys between us & the Blasting site.

I was as happy as a child at Christmas. Dr. Bob did'nt suspect a thing as we turned south instead of north & skirted the west ridge of Horse Mountain cause he never paid no attention to anything. He did'nt bat an Eye as we wandered past Porcupine Draw & up onto the flats & pulled into a spot just off the Loop that obviously did'nt have any bedrock in which to anchor our equipment. Getting the chance to stick the sensing equipment into 5 feet of soft foothills loam was more than I could have hoped for in a 1000 years. But the proof of the existence of a Heavenly Being came that afternoon.

I was just starting to take a snooze in the shade of the truck. Dr. Bob was sitting in a fold-out chair holding a parasol in one hand & smoking his Pipe in the other contemplating the mysteries of red ant hills. Little did he suspect that he was sitting with someone who would write a scientific Paper on a cousin of the ant the Bombus Bumblebee. These are both under the scientific head Hymenoptera which to scientists who study the Greek origins of names means something about Wings. Suddenly I heard the sound of a truck. I stood up & brushed off my backside. I would of been less surprised & delighted if Santa Claus had driven up with the Easter bunny & the Tooth Fairy pulling his Sled. There was Dr. Wes Crowden our site geologist who I was hoping would come by but he was with Dr. Amy Loyd the Chiefist geologist of the Utah-Western Colorado Mapping project. She was second in command of all the big wigs over in Denver. I had seen her lots of times. But to be here now well it was almost a Spiritual experience. I tried hard not to smile. I tried real hard. It was only with an effort like The Brother of Jared had in exercising the Faith that lighted the ships across that Great Deep with stones made to glow like light bulbs that Kept me from laughing with delight.

The Bob jumped to his feet. He was almost comical in his change in aspect. He went from King of the World to sniveling servant. Indeed Obsequious is the word <u>Words of Power</u> recommends.

Dr. Loyd! He almost bowed. What a pleasant surprise. He weaseled. Wes you should of told me she would be in the area.

Dr. Crowden looked cold. What in the HELL are you doing here! What do you mean by being here!

The Bob glanced nervously over at me.

I thought you said they were Blasting up on Fisher Mesa? Dr. Loyd seemed genuinely confused.

They are! Someone has made a terrible mistake. Dr. Crowden looked like he was going to punch someone as he said the last words Slow & Low.

I could'nt resist acting like Daffy Duck. I almost started talking like him too.

I tried to tell him but he Insisted. It was'nt really a lie because I did'nt really say what I had tried to tell him.

You little Bastard he said looking at me.

Kruchfield! Look at this you've got the sensor stuck in 20 feet of Sand. He whined the last part like a man who cant believe something his kid has done.

Never been told to stick it in dirt before I commented in a Perplexed sort of way. It was'nt a lie either because I had never been told to stick it in dirt.

Dr. Loyd looked at me. Do you think you can pack this up & get it back to base camp by yourself- Hyrum Thayne is'nt it?

You bet. Yes. Thanks. Dr. Loyd.

Call me Amy. Kruchfield let's get you out of here before any more Damage is done. I want you on the next ride out of here. You're Finished here. Or anywhere She whispered to me.

He was Mumbling & Stammering trying to blame me a poor uneducated Moabite for setting up a complex geological sensing station at the incorrect location and in Sand. His trying to send the problem my way did not go well. They all pulled off together leaving me a happy man & The Bob sitting in the back of the pickup like somebody's just whipped Hound. I fully intended to go to Church the next Sunday.

Note from the Redactor

I've confirmed that the man Hyrum called "The Bob" was Robert Kruchfield. Hyrum was off on a couple of details. Dr. Kruchfield did obtain a PhD, but it was in Comparative Literature from Yale, rather than English from Harvard. His master's in geology was actually prior to his doctorate, and was from the University of Wyoming in Laramie, with a technical writing minor. After being fired from the USGS, he became a successful apiarian, and followed the almond orchard blooms through the San Joachim Valley in Central California. He currently owns about 2000 hives that he trucks himself. He staffs a small Mexican crew, which he keeps on year round. I caught up with him near Merced, California, but he refused to be formally interviewed about his summer working with Hyrum, though he did answer a few of my questions. He was not unhelpful, but claimed not to remember any of the staff he was working with that summer, and did not want to pretend he did. He admitted that it was a dark time in his life—his dreams of an academic career were fading with every shortlist he failed to make in his application for faculty tenure-track positions. Currently, he and his wife of thirty years have two daughters and three grandchildren. He spends his winters near Santa Fe, and occasionally leads a tutorial on Proust at St. John's College.

As I was packing up the Equipment I saw the Babcock twins. He is a 2 headed man the first head being called Eddy & the other Billy. I run into alot of the cowboys up on the mountain most of them running around in pickups but the twins are always mounted up & riding their Gelding. They are pretty friendly but when these events were transponding I had not yet made there acquaintance. It is strange to contemplate these wondrous Siamese twins. Both heads are college Educated. They are a sight to remember up here in the La Sals riding about on their painted Appaloosa a quarter horse as perfect as they are an Abomination. When I use that word I do'nt mean to use it of myself but I am recalling the words of Berta Dallon & Betty Lassiter who considered the twins to be cursed of the Lord although neither sister would never say it to there faces. The sisters held the world to be a place where people get what they deserve in this life by the way they acted in the Primordial Existence. Negroes being restricted from the Holy Priesthood & all had been the worst of the lot up there & had been sitting on the fence in the war between Jesus & Satan when we all had to decide one side or the other. You were made into a Demon here on earth if you chose to follow Lucifer. Chinese were only a little better but had gotten off the fence before the Negroes. Whites clearly followed Jesus Plan to let us have free agency rather than Satans plan to make us all tow the line in a kind of Communist way. But if you were born a Mormon then you were a Warrior & Leader in the War in Heaven. One of the Generals even. Roberta thought the twins must of just barely made it into choosing Jesus in the nick of time over Satan to be born so Accursed. But Betty figured if that were true they would have been nigger Siamese twins. So they could have been a little worse although clearly very close to have been chosen for Demonhood. This Religious debate was a constant topic of discussion with those 2 women according to Sandra who lunched with them often. They were quite impressed her husband had Seen the 2 headed beast personally.

I once met a Negro. While they are ubiquitous in other parts of the Palatinate we have made into this the US of A & I have seen them on TV often enough these children of Ham or so they are called seldom make their way into the Moabesqueish land. This Negro was from the Denver office & had come to take an Accounting of our books. He had lunch with us & seemed little different in the manner of our jokes & polite conversation. He did not seem like Bill Cosby at all though which was pretty Surprising to me. I told him that I had 2 Bill Cosby records but he was not impressed even after I did the Noah part every bit in the voice of Bill Cosby. I cannot tell you how this Astounded me. It seemed he took a Dislike to me when I asked him what the Ghetto was like but the mood passed quickly & our conversation started up again. When he found out that I was a Mormon he asked why he could not have the Priesthood. I told him the theory of Betty & Berta that he had been a fence sitter in the Primordial Existence & he laughed deeply. He told me that his father had been a Baptist minister & that if he had heard what we said about how they had not chosen Jesus he would have gotten a lawyer friend to sue the Church all the way to Hell for teaching such Nonsense. Jesus was his life & Nobody had better say differently. He told us he had a wife & family at home & this too seemed out of place from what I knew because I had read a book by Elder Peterson one of the Mormon Apostles in which he said that indeed the Negro race was Cursed because of the way they acted in the War in Heaven and Betty and Berta held that that made them Lazy and prone to wanton lasciviousness. He did not seem like that to me. These are my impressions. To me I could feel that he was Different. But it did not seem to be a matter of smartness. I would of said seeing as he was an Accountant that he was Smarter & less lazy than me.

Anyway the twins passed. I wanted to say something but I was packing up. I would of liked to tell them about The Bob. They met him a couple of days ago according to Rick who was there & They did not think much of him. They asked him about his PHD work & he laughed & said Like you'd know what I was talking about. As I said both heads are college educated but they just said Likely you are right. Then Rick & the 2 heads talked about Lewis Lamour who they said they quite enjoyed. All the while The Bob was huffing & snorting. Have you read him? Eddy asked him. He snorted & said Not a chance. Then those 2 started speaking a different language & laughing. The Bob turned red & Marched away looking scared. Ass They said in English. Rick said he laughed & laughed at that.

SOURCE DOCUMENT #3:

Letter from William Babcock to Redactor.
Vienna, Austria. May 18, 1997.

Dear <Redactor>:

It is a pleasure to make your acquaintance. We would be delighted to give whatever information we can to support your quest to understand the unsettling events surrounding the death of Hyrum Thayne. Your candid letter did much to assure us that your intent was not malicious and that you were motivated only by a benign desire to situate the facts of the matter. We will therefore try to return your candidness with our own. We are quite grateful that you have decided to reopen this long overdue inquiry into this strange and affecting fragment of our past. We have been reluctant to explore it even among ourselves, and your letter has launched us into new conversations, reminiscences, and explorations. Even Marcel seems to have become more animated. He has propelled us on lingering walks along the paved trails flanking the *Donauinsel*. These strolls have been especially conducive for reflecting on our time in Moab and the La Sals. Over the last year Marcel has seemed afflicted with an unusual melancholy, and has led us to the opera or the State Theater, more often than perhaps Edward or I really want. Your letter has been a godsend since it seems to be providing a distraction for all three of us. So attending to the matter of your inquiry: How did we meet the Scholar of Moab?

To give you context for our interaction with Hyrum, there are a few things that you ought to understand about our states of mind during those years. We were in a hard place. Oxford had rejected both of our DPhil theses (I was gratified to hear that you had taken the time to read these humble offerings, so I will not bore you with a discourse about their contents). We felt angry and slighted. They had clearly been misread. This was a common problem in our academic programs. While intellectually our tutors and professors understood us to be two people, we were often lumped together and taken *as if* we were a single entity.

If you'll allow me to indulge in a small aside to illustrate this—I remember a lecture given by none other than Gilles Deleuze in the Sorbonne. We were visiting Paris from Oxford sniffing through some unpublished papers of Bergson on consciousness, which Deleuze, the stormy French philosopher, had rooted out in his research for use in the great metaphysician's biography. The lecture was on "multiplicity" and was attended by a *Who's Who* of the French intelligentsia. Even Derrida was there, sitting in a corner, looking bored and morose, sighing, snorting, and chewing on his finger. René Thom, the topologist, was visiting from the *Institut des Hautes* Études *Scientifiques* and began, quite suddenly, deep in the lecture, to argue with Delueze about the "actualization of repetition." Suddenly, Delueze pointed at us with his long-nailed finger and said, "There! There is repetition caught in the moment between virtuality and actuality, between possibility and the unification of multiplicity, between the qualitative and the quantitative. There! There is 'différance' screaming towards existence, existence sluicing through potentiality, and potential itself skating unforgivingly towards emergent unity." Thom called us a topological manifold of singularity, a "projection" resisting reduction in complementary planes of asymmetry.

Everyone was looking at us, and soon everyone was arguing about our "unfolding into a universe of emergent relevance." "Hoist them up here," Deleuze suddenly called, and several students moved as if they would lay hands on us in order to do just that. I smiled and gave my head a small shake to gently warn them away, and the students backed off. But Edward screamed. Then, in tears of anger, fear, and frustration, he whispered in a deliberate, measured cadence, "We are not an illustration of anything." The place went as still as one of those clear icy winter dawns in a snowy alpine meadow. After the rush of Edward's emotion, I suppose I expected respect, or even pity, in the tension of that moment of silence. But nothing of the sort was forthcoming from the crowd. I glanced at Derrida—he looked amused. Thom looked nonchalant and would not allow his gaze to wander our direction. But Deleuze exploded. This embarrassment was a personal affront that he would not stand for—we were there from Oxford at his invitation, after all. And, I must admit, I was a little embarrassed at Edward's outburst. But the French bastard did not rail against Edward for his intrusion; he sputtered incoherently in outrage at both of us! For all his talk of multiplicity and difference, we were yet just one thing to him. Forgetting all propriety and good manners, he called us a "sinister flagitious wart." Marcel was offended enough to march us in a huff from the lecture. I was livid, both at Deleuze and at Edward. I did not speak to my brother for a week, and ever since both of us have despised all French philosophy, which we agree is overrated and uninsightful (except obviously Merleau-Ponty, as our dissertations must have suggested to you).

Back at Oxford, we had expected trouble with our theses. Writing about consciousness is always perilous. The differences between our theses were subtle. Even so, a nuanced reading would have revealed that we were in disagreement about fundamental aspects of consciousness—not in agreement. However, taken together, *as if* from a single author, the two papers seemed to broker incoherence, rather than divergence of thought. To make matters worse, the long shadow of the "linguistic turn" still seemed to haunt the halls of the academy there and even to talk about consciousness-as-such was seen as bad form. Nagel was yet to ask, "What is it like to be a bat?" and although what we talked about then would seem mundane today, at that darkened period it was perceived in stiff Oxford as a loose and flighty subject, something the French or Germans were talking about, and unfit for serious work on the nature of mind. "Had we just ignored Russell and Popper?" seemed to be the major complaint (and yes we had). So we were not passed.

After both of us were failed at our *viva voca* examination by our respective examiners, we were devastated. There seemed to be a conspiracy against us. How could we *both* fail our final examination? Looking back, I'm quite sure there *was* a conspiracy. How could Oxford graduate a freak (I use the singular article purposefully here, as I am convinced that that is how we were perceived)? A freak writing about consciousness of all things? Such absurdities were beyond the imagination and tolerance of even the most free-thinking don.

We wandered aimlessly for a good while. Edward bitter; I depressed. We put on weight and independently thought of suicide. Nevertheless, neither of us dared broach the subject, nor wanted to carry out such an act, when it would snuff out the life of two other beings (the revelation that we were both contemplating ending our life came out on our recent walks along the Danube). It's a wonder Marcel did not just plunge us into the sea, since he knew both our thoughts (and which provides independent evidence that he or she is not just an extension of our combined wills).

In early Spring 1972, we were slumming in Wyoming, staying at the Frontier Inn in Evanston, when we came across an advertisement in the *Rock Springs Rocket* for ranch hands—no experience necessary. We applied. I think the Moab rancher who hired us had in mind to make a little money running a small carnival sideshow act. However, oddly enough, after some initial training, we turned out to have a knack both for the saddle and for finding elusive lost cattle hiding stubbornly in the thick scrub oak of the summer range. "Two heads are better than one," the foreman used to joke as he came to appreciate our skills at bringing in the last of the herd, even if it meant a little more work for the hands to saddle us up. Of course, we could never rope or care for our horse properly, but we could keep the dull white-faced beasts together, and get them off the mountain as well as any of the best cowboys. As you might suspect, the rancher only paid us as one person, but we decided not to take offense—money was never the reason we were doing this.

The five years spent cowboying up on the Colorado Plateau summer range are among our fondest memories, which seems ironic now, given what we know about cattle and the ecology. But there, riding among the cool aspens of the La Sals, Edward and I seemed to find ourselves again. That strikes one as clichéd perhaps, but so it was. The adventure brought a measure of satisfaction and peace that we had not experienced as students. Even now, as we ride the U-Bahn from our apartment near the Sperl Café to the University of Vienna, its swaying motion reminds me of the easy back and forth gait of our horse, Starry. I still dream of the calming sound he made when he pulled a wad of succulent grass from the meadows ringing Dark Canyon Lake's lush offerings. During those moments when we would pause in our ride, he would chew loudly, his mouthy back and forth grind mashing the grasses rhythmically in a deep methodical chomp that spoke of purpose and satisfaction.

We first met Hyrum in the most peculiar of circumstances. Jung would have called it synchronicity (you must wonder at my referencing Jung from Freud's city!). Or as Hyrum might have found more appropriately stated: in an almost Dickensian plot twist. The unlikeliest of coincidences converged to bring us together. We were looking for strays up near Taylor Flats on the west side of Mt. Waas. The day was gray and darkening as the afternoon wore on, and we had wrestled ourselves into a rain poncho just in case one of those thunderstorms for which the La Sals are so famous broke. I had just warned Edward that we should head back to camp, when an unearthly but very human wailing seemed to rise with the wind. The hair on my neck and arm rose. Marcel gave the horse a forceful kick in the flanks and, undaunted, Edward wheeled us toward the sound. My urge had been to run away, but Edward has always had more courage and raw fearlessness than I (he just scoffed at this, but it is true). About a hundred meters into the aspens we came upon a woman as naked as a Valkyrie, raving on a gray igneous boulder rising from among the white-barked trees—the rock about the size of a Volkswagen. She was howling and weaving her body in wild undulations, screaming for the "return of the monsters" and crying viciously that she would "do again" what she had "done before." Standing opposite her was Hyrum Thayne, eyes wide and apparently recently drawn there by the commotion as well. He was in tight straight-legged jeans, a blue cotton work-shirt, and wearing a well-worn felt cowboy hat. She had obviously not seen any of us. Her eyes were closed, and there was an intensity and purpose to her dance that demanded a complete abandonment of self-consciousness.

Suddenly her eyes opened. She turned, looked at us, and screamed in surprise and terror. In a panic, she leapt off the rock and bolted right into Hyrum, apparently not seeing him. She was in a state of unbelievable excitement and agitation and pushed him back with enough violence that he tripped to the ground. She looked down at him with such wrath and venomous wildness that I almost panicked, and I reined Starry so hard to the right that the poor animal's head was forced almost back to his neck, wheeling him around completely. When we brought Starry back to face the scene, the woman looked at us with the same fierce enmity. We stood frozen in her gaze. Edward was starting to find his voice, when suddenly her eyes rolled back into her head and she passed out onto the soft aspen leaves. Hyrum looked at us. We stared at one another, then at the woman on the ground, then back to one another. Hyrum, coming to himself, ran over to her but seemed unsure whether to touch her naked body or keep away. Even from our perch on Starry's back, we could see she was breathing, so Hyrum stood and considered us. He then bowed formally and offered that we must be the Babcock brothers (I'm sure the rumor of the cowboying Siamese twins had spread far and wide in the region). As we told him our names, he did something quite unexpected and rare among those meeting us for the first time: he shook each of our hands, acknowledging our individuality and thereby immediately endearing himself to both Edward and me.

When we finished these oddly timed introductions, we looked back only to find that the unconscious woman had disappeared! We rode around the area in widening circles, but could find no trace of her. After calling for her for close to an hour, trying to assure her we meant no harm, we resigned ourselves to her unwillingness to be found. After the fruitless search, we rode back and found Hyrum sitting on the same rock. He said a small pickup he'd seen parked up the hill from us was gone, and he figured she had cleared out. He opined that she was a writer-poet named Dora Daphne Tanner who lived in Moab—her picture was a common sight in the *Times-Independent*, and she was one of Moab's most famous residents. It turned out to be so, but at the time he could not be sure. We had never heard of her (we are not fans of American poetry, I'm afraid). We found her clothes and a few belongings not far from the rock outcrop that she had been standing on to stage her dance. We decided to return to camp. Hyrum gathered up her things and took them with him. The weather seemed to be worsening, and by this time the sky was nearly black with roiling clouds. The blowing trees were shaking and convulsing in a wilder and wilder rampage. On the right and left, the aspens were repeatedly pushed almost halfway to the ground by the occasional irate gust. Leaves and other plant debris were racing through the trees like ghosts. We thought a soaking rain imminent, and I admit to some growing anxiety at the Wagnerian sound of the wind. Or was it excitement? Being without access to the legs in such events always seems to generate and exaggerate a mixture of emotion because I am not in complete control of my fate.

We offered Hyrum a ride back to his truck, and he gratefully accepted. From the same rock that had played such a convenient stage for our *danseur noble*, he adroitly mounted. He endeared himself again. Most people find us repulsive, or even monstrous, upon first meeting, but as soon as Hyrum obtained purchase on Starry's back, he wrapped his arms around us and held on as we galloped back down the road. It started to pour. We quickly found the place where Hyrum had set up his little seismic station. One of his coworkers was sitting in an idling pickup—windshield wipers banging out time on full speed. Hyrum dismounted and after giving us a hurried thanks, climbed quickly into the truck. It was only a twenty-minute ride back to our camp, and Starry seemed willing enough to make a swift run for the tin-roofed stall attached to the mobile trailer that served as our summer range home. He raced back as quickly as he could carry us, but in the end we were all soaked through. I was disappointed to find I was given access to the legs when they were good for nothing but shivering. Still, we had met Hyrum, and who would have guessed what that would mean to us in the long run.

I hope I have not been over long in answering a simple question about how we met the Scholar, but that is the tale in full. Please, if you have any more questions, feel free to contact us as often as you wish. During finals, of course, I am swamped with grading exams and might be a little sluggish in my response, but please do not interpret any delay as a lack of interest. We are getting older, and things seem to be taking longer every year that passes, but your project intrigues both of us deeply. Edward offers his blessing on your task (you may be interested to know that his homily today, taken from Matt. 25:40, contained a reminiscence of Hyrum's initial kindness and acceptance—all thanks to your forcing us to recall our first meeting with the Scholar).

With greatest gratitude,
William Babcock

SOURCE DOCUMENT #4:

Letter from Dora Daphne Tanner to unknown correspondent.
July 21, 1975.

My guide said I must write. It is my gift. This muse's voice, a voice that strums my damaged soul, leaving me to carry these tones from another world, or from nowhere, or from everywhere. I cannot tell. I cannot speak to the sources upon which I draw anymore. I can't think. How can I write when my head screams in broken and scattered sentences? When the focus of my mind slides this way and that—holding nothing, locking onto bitter nothings that roil and boil and bleed? I draw from a poisoned well. I need healing, she says. I need to recount these events. These events no one will believe. Even the photos convince not a soul. I am laughed at. Scorned. Shorn. Mourned. Alone. A bone skull left to dry in raging red desert yellow sun. A sun on edge of a galaxy. A galaxy in a universe where monsters live. Where malicious ghosts stalk the edges, edges without reason, reason without meaning, meaning without hope. I was a woman. I lived alone in a trailer, a trailer without neighbors. A woman alone in the Lisbon Valley. Alone. Had any been there then, would the vampires of spirits that haunt the spaces of those untoward and shadowy dimensions, those that abut our four, have loosed their grisly purposes on me? Who can say what the intentions of such shadow beings are?

I remember the stars were out that night. Bright. Shimmering. Shining from burning orbs so far away that humans evolved to this form were just a thought, or a dream in a toddler universe when those dancing waves of light left their mothering sun. I slept some that night, content and easy on my cot. My cot laid outside. Laid so that the night wind might calm and sate my ancient soul with its song, a song that joins my own, a song in a chorus of praise for whatever Goddess there might be. Then, I could believe in a Goddess. A kind, close Goddess. Not a God, certainly, but at least a feminine deity. Now she too is gone.

They came instead. Secret, silent things. Things without souls. Without heart or mind. Without regard. Without love. Without doubt. Bathed in certainty and calculation, these large-eyed creatures froze me. Damned me. Body and soul. Numbing my existence down to a core of fettered consciousness. I was not allowed to sleep. Oh no. Left with eyes wide and open and seeing. Ears to hear. Heart to feel. Terror. Horror. Alone. Dread without voice. A silenced violence.

The table was cold. Obsidian black. They minced about, handling this and that—things that glowed and others that did not. Long I lay on that frigid alter, as if an accoutrement of the room, as if something found, something put aside, something to consider at leisure, something that matters little, to be ignored, something without rights, without meaning, something second-rate, without dignity, shabby, common, disposable, something ill-favored, that should be pitied but is not, something fenced out, without friends, worthless, helpless, damned, something to disregard, to silence, to use, then leave, then abandon crumpled and broken. In the desert lost.

Then, I was not ignored. There were two demons. Four attentive eyes focused on me. Their gaze burrowing into me like a worm into soil. Suddenly. Without reason. They crowded me and with adept fingers dexterously plied tools fashioned from the same cold blackness as the table. From its icy malevolent aspect I could see their instruments were made without doubt or question. Made for purposes unknown and unkind. Ethicless things. Some tools were long thick cylinders, like vacuum attachment hoses, some as thin as a bee's stinger. There was not an orifice that they did not probe. No space they did not violate. They were violent. Intemperate. Efficient.

And their eyes. Without malice. Or concern. They were not from a universe where love existed. I was nothing. I was everything. They were something outside of a God's or the Goddess's purview. Their eyes exposed a hole in the universe and there was nothing that could fill it. No, not even a deity could find their way in that darkness. Could even a Goddess rescue me? No. In those eyes, I knew I meant nothing and I was absolutely and utterly alone. They say that even a gravitational black hole bleeds some radiation. These reflected only void. Nothingness without being. Existence stopped where their black eyes began. Eyes more empty than death. Devoid of both space and time, they could destroy even a soul.

How long? Hours? Days? Years? In real time I lost three days. They found me far up Coyote Wash. Wandering. Babbling. Crying. Wearing a nightshirt. No panties. No shoes. No memory of those three days would emerge until years later. I would find the pieces of their craft up on Island Mesa almost in Colorado. And that would bring it all back. Everything. There on the sagey desert floor I found it, obsidian black, as light as air, thin as paper. It had crashed. Clearly the apparitions were not invincible. Did I fight them? Was I responsible for this debris field? Did I wake from their lightless paralysis and crush their heads in a fit of desperate revenge? I do not remember. I like to think so.

There Faewolf. I've written. It didn't help. I cannot escape the memory of their eyes.

Hyrum's journal, hand-written manuscript.
Written between June and August, 1977.

I was at the Library when it opened at 10 Saturday morning. The night I got home I had gone for the Dictionary before even giving Sandra an I'm home kiss. I ran to our bedroom where we had paperback copies of the Webster Desk reference set sitting on our chest of drawers. We had gotten it free one time for subscribing to <u>T.V. Guide</u> or some such thing & from its stiff feel I realized that it had never been opened before. I went through the ds like a esurient man frantic with lycanthropy. Sandra had Followed me into the bedroom & was standing in the doorway as I went through the d-i-ks; dikdik dike diktat. Not d-i-k.

Honey how do you think you would spell Dickensian. The blasted trouble with a Dictionary is you have to know how to spell most of the word just to get started. It has always been the starting that kills me.

Try d-e-c-k. I did. Nothing.

Try d-i-c-k. I did. Nothing.

Try d-i-c. like in Dictionary. I did. Nothing

What does Dickensian mean any way?

Thats what I'm trying to find out.

Why?

Because someone said it to me & I want to know what they said.

How did they use it?

They said I had a Dickensian Wife.

Try d-a-k. I did. Nothing.

It soon became apparent that there was'nt anything in this Cheap thing about what that word meant. We sat down on the edge of the bed in despair. It was'nt Saturday night so I did'nt lay a hand on Sandra even though sitting next to her on the bed had started my Manliness stirring.

Who said you had a Dickensian wife? Was it that Lamanite your always hanging around with? She had always been a little worried about my hanging around with Rick & every time she had a chance she would put in a little Dig about it.

No. It was a Geologist. Whats for supper? She got up & started moving toward the kitchen talking louder & louder as she got closer to it & further from me.

You know I ran into Brother & Sister Oakenberry at City Market yesterday & it seems that Brother Knight is being released as the Second Counselor in the Elders Quorum. He said that it was a Shame that you had'nt been to Church lately because he remembered that you were about the best Leader the Elders Quorum ever had & he would of liked to see you take his place. Do want Tabasco sauce on your spaghetti too?

I was slipping toward the shower hoping that she'd get all her talking out of her while I was in the shower.

Yes. I like Tabasco sauce on everything.

Well anyway I've been doing some thinking. That was always proceeded with Its time you got Active in the Church. So I just turned on the shower. There are fewer pleasures in life then washing a weeks worth of mountain off your body. Especially if the weathers a little Chilled & the waters warm. There are showers up at the base camp but no one but the GS 10s & above use them. There must be something particular about gaining an education that makes you feel like you needed a shower every day. I enjoyed the shower & the mountain running down the drain with days of hard works sweat & grime disappearing. When I turned off the water Sandra was standing in the doorway talking away. I suppose that subconsciously I had known she was there but my head does a Good Job of taking care & shutting down what I do'nt want to hear & I was sort of surprised to see her standing there talking away.

Anyway. She was saying with the Millennium starting any time now theres no harm in getting yourself & God getting right with each other. There was a long pause as I dried my hair then she said.

So what do you think?

I'll think about it ok? Is dinner ready?

Like I said the next day I was at the Library when it opened. Miss Goodson gave me a friendly wave.

Morning Brother Thayne. Hows Sister Thayne doing? She keeping the show on the road? She really did'nt expect an answer so I did'nt offer her one. I just Smiled & nodded.

New issue of Flyfishermen in.

Really? I tried to act excited.

She opened the door & I went straight for the Unabridged Webster Dictionary sitting on a little podium all by itself.

D-i-k. Nothing.

I was thinking maybe I just ought to ask Sister Goodson if she knew how it might be spelled but I was afraid that she would know what it meant & that it would be something Vulgar or nasty & I'd Shock the poor woman to death. But I kept at it & suddenly there it was!

Dickensian (dɪˈkɛnzɪən) ajd. 1. Relating of or to Charles Dickens.

That was it. Of course I had heard of Charles Dickens. You couldn't go through a Christmas season with out hearing his name a 100 times & seeing at least 15 versions of <u>A Christmas Carol</u>. What did The Bob mean though saying I had a Dickensian life. Did he mean I was a Scrooge? That did'nt feel right. Maybe Bob Cratchit? I did'nt have any kids. I puzzled & Puzzled. Finally realizing it was safe to question Sister Goodson on the subject I interrogatived her.

Sister Goodson have you ever heard of the word Dickensian?

No. I have'nt young man but you are Welcome to look it up.

I did & it meant something about Charles Dickens.

Ah of course. I should have guessed. He's one of my favorite Authors. Have you ever read <u>Great Expectations</u> or a <u>Tale of Two Cities</u>? Wonderful books. Just wonderful.

What if someone said you lived a Dickensian life. What do you think that would mean?

She looked Thoughtful for a moment & said.

You know he lived an exemplary life & I suppose it would mean that you lived a life of sobriety & Temperance.

I knew that was dead wrong.

Then she said Charles Dickens was a man much like Abraham Lincoln. He always looked for the best in others & in life. He started in poverty & disgrace & through hard work & Perseverance & by simply pulling himself up by his bootstraps he won success & the things that come from a life well spent.

This was going nowhere & called for Desperate action.

Oh! look theres the new <u>Flyfisherman</u>. Excuse me Sister Goodson there is an Article on tying flies for the caddisfly hatch that I've just got to read. Will you excuse me please.

I went back to my thinking. What did that son of a heathen mean? Suddenly Inspiration struck. It seemed odd even then that I would get 2 such Grand impressions on 2 consecutive days one that took down The Bob & then this one. I renewed my temptation to go to Church. I walked over to the book stacks & headed for the Ds. In Moab they only keep about 10 aisles of Books on hand but if you do'nt see what you want you can ask them to send for it from the public Library up in Price. It takes about 3 weeks & if you still want it after that time you only have about a week before they want it Back. I only did it once when there was a book on hunting Antelope that I wanted to take a look at before the big pronghorn Hunt in the Fall. It was overdue (I was'nt used to hurrying with my books when I just borrow them like I said) & they charged me $3.65. It was'nt the money that bothered me so much as the feeling that I was a common Criminal. I was being fined like I had been stopped by the police & given a ticket. Very exacerbating.

I found what I was looking for. <u>The Major Works of Charles Dickens</u>. As I picked up the book there was an almost Sacred feeling. Sort of like when you walk on the grounds of the Salt Lake temple. My stomach felt the same way it felt back in high school when I asked Sandra to go Steady with me. My hand was actually shaking. The book was an old one & the cover was made of leather. I opened it slowly with the feeling that great Mysteries were contained Within. On the inside front cover was written this inscription.

Donated to the Moab City Library by the Grand County Ladies Literary Society on this the second day of August in the One Thousandth Nine Hundred & Twenty Second Year of our Lord.

It was written in a flowing Script with each of the words beginning letter overflowing with elegance & locution with the words that followed neat & even & rounded. I was almost Moved to tears. I almost slipped it under my coat but thought

This book deserves to be Checked Out. Then I thought that there was no way I could read this book in 2 weeks or even 6 weeks if I used all my renewals & I went ahead & slipped it under my coat. I did however Resolve that I would be more careful with this book than with any of the others I had Ever taken.

At last I had the secret of the word Dickensian. Within these Pages I would soon be able to decode what that overstuffed geologist had called me. No more would I be the victim of my Ignorance. I rushed out of the Library & into my '71 Mustang & headed for the Dump. The Dump was situated in a valley right behind the large valley in which Moab lies. The ridge that separates the 2 is one of the most peaceful Places on this earth. Since the Dump is the only thing out this way the tourists do'nt go up there & the local folks only come to empty their Pickup loaded with trash so all & all its a good place to look over the city cause you can drive nearly to the top & get a little peace & quiet. Fact is this is the very Spot that caused Sandra & I so much trouble when we were teenagers.

The place had a bunch of kids shooting 22s so I just drove back down to the Trailer. My heart was still beating like a Drilling Rig about to lose a bit & as I ran inside I almost knocked over the Ceramic bull out front we had bought on a trip to Tijuana one summer. My only trip Abroad. I ran into the living room gave a quick yell to see if Sandra was home & then pulled out the Book from beneath my coat.

Thats how this whole Mess started. It took 1 year 7 months & 3 days to read: <u>Great Expectations</u> <u>A Tale of Two Cities</u> <u>Hard Times</u> <u>Oliver Twist</u> <u>Bleak House</u> <u>David Copperfield</u> & 21 short stories including <u>A Christmas Carol</u>. It seems funny but while my body was high in the La Sals my spirit was in London. While the cool wind blew the aspens making the leaves dance I was walking barefoot on Cobblestones on foggy mornings. Instead of seeing the soft white clouds sailing in the deep blue behind the hard rocky face of Tukuhnikivatz I was being used by Pickpockets in an English countryside. Rather than being a sensing station technician I was the Apprentice of some cruel artisan. Nothing as ever grabbed me like those Books. Why had'nt anyone ever told me about these stories? Except of course a <u>Christmas Carol</u> which I watched every year. I thought at the time that I could never go back to a <u>western</u> again. Lewis Lamour or Zane Gray did not have the perspicuity I now was embroiled with.

It was Saturday night when I finished the book. I knew I was going to finish that night so I had kept reading even though Sandra was hinting around that it was Saturday night & that we ought to GO TO BED. I read until 3 & suddenly it was all over. That last word had been read & the <u>Collected Major Works of Dickens</u> was at an end. As I closed the cover of the book after the last page I felt like someone had just died. For over a year I had lived for this moment & now that it was here I felt overwhelmingly sad. Sadder then I think I had ever felt in my life. I have thought since that I felt like I did when I was a kid & Tarkus my dog died. Who would I play with now? Or really what would I do tomorrow at work? What would I read? I had been on so many Adventures in the last year. Experienced so many Things. What will become of me now I thought. I picked up the book slowly & thumbed through all the paths that I had walked through in this book. Bits of sentences crossed my view & brought up images so real I could'nt tell them from pieces of memory or from remembrances of some Past Life. I'm not a Hindu reincarnationist mind you but thats what it felt like. I read the words & Remembered Miss Havisham & how mistaken I'd been about her role in my-Pips life. I read &

Remembered the horrible Fagen Bill Sikes & dear sweet Nancy so coldly Murdered. It could'nt be over could it? I started to cry. I had'nt cried for nearly 10 years not since the night I found out the baby in Sandra died. Once I started it would'nt Stop. It was like I'd put a tiny hole in an irrigation break that once the water starts more & more mud just keeps falling away until finally the ditch is just Running at full. I sobbed & sobbed & the whole while felt pretty darn Foolish about it & kept thinking its only a book for Heavens sake but it did'nt help & the tears kept coming. It may sound sad to cry about finishing a book. In fact you might think that I should have been happy. And I was. Its hard to explain but as a Scholar I should try I suppose. When something becomes Apart of you. When you've put in alot of time with a group of people a place or a way of life it gets Inside you. Well not just inside you it becomes You or you become It or something. Rick my Indian buddy could tell you more about this. Maybe thats how we become what we call Ourselves. Maybe Rick is an Indian because he has hung around Indians & their ways & Indian stuff has filled up his Soul. Maybe if I had done the same I'd be a Lamanite too. It seems that the stuff of life is like campfire Smoke. If you hang around it you start to smell like it & there is little you can do to get it off even if you want to. Well enough aggrandizing philosophizing the point is that something in me had Changed. Something about reading those books had made me into a new person. And the funny thing was I still did'nt have a clue as to what the word Dickensian meant. Then it Happened. The event that without occurring this thing would have never been written you are now reading. You would have some other thing in your hand & I would be somewhere Else.

Have you ever had one of those experiences where a strange Coincidence makes you stop & feel like God is telling you something? Nothing big but like when you are reading a magazine & someone on the radio will say the 2 words your reading at the exact same time you are reading them? Or like when your eating Cereal for breakfast & watching TV & suddenly you notice the guy on the television is eating the same kind you are? Sometimes I think something Big is behind these sorts of things & I cant help but stop & take notice of where my life is heading when things like that occur. If I were'nt a Scientist I might think it was God Himself. Well that night the Biggest of the Big occurred.

I knew I would not be able to sleep because of the Emotions that were filling me up after having finished the book so I decided to watch a little television & eat a TV dinner to sort of help me get my head back to Normal. We had a nice TV 25 inch screen & all the works. Sandra had sort of insisted on it seeing as how she had to spend every Weekday night alone watching it. She thought it important that a TV persons head be of a Realistic size otherwise her television pleasure was obnubilated.

Well most of the Channels had signed off, but something was on KBYU the educational station broadcast by the Lords own University. It was a public TV station on Chanel 11 & they were in the middle of one of those drives. I always try to give a couple of bucks because I do watch the fishing shows on Saturday & Marty Stofers Wild America on Wednesday nights. Well anyway the lady was just pleading for all us late night Viewers to give a call & that we would be returning to Michael Dickens World Views in just a moment.

Verily the name Michael Dickens hit my ear like a semis honk on a foggy morning. How strange I Thought. A Dickens doing a show on the very night that I had finished reading the works of Charles Dickens. There was something to this.

Something Cosmic. Something of Universal proportions. For some reason I was supposed to watch this show. Despite my Tiredness I had to be indefatigable.

It took me a while to figure out what there was in this Program that I was supposed to fathom. He was talking about 18th century Jewish peasants in Germany. Well I did'nt know much about the topic & I was starting to nod a bit when suddenly It hit me. The reason God had led me to read Dickens. Why I finished on the very night that a Dickens would host this Program was all suddenly Clear. He said & I wrote down these words at the time & I've carried them with me ever since. Alot like Ricks last words from his dad. Words that have been by this time written on my Heart.

To the Jewish mind the attainment of Wealth was not the highest principle that a man could attain & I mean man as we know little about womens perceptions of this era. There was alot of Bla bla bla about something & something Materialism that he said while I was scratching down that part. But then he said Scholarship was seen as the highest good & the Appendix of achievement. To be a rabbinical Scholar was the closest man could attain in becoming like God. To be a Scholar was to be Everything.

The words sliced me in 2 like a 4th of July Watermelon & it all came together for me. The reading of Dickens was just a Beginning. God wanted me to become a Scholar. At that moment I resolved that I would someday be the greatest Scholar to graduate from Grand County High. I turned off the television & a Calm swept over me as I went to bed with visions of hosting the Hyrum Thayne Scholars Hour on Public television. From here on it was only a matter of Time.

Folded paper found in book belonging to Dora Daphne Tanner.
Scrawled in pencil across top: "notes for two or three poems."
Likely written summer of 1976.

I am walking. The sun sets over the edge of the discrepant western rim casting downtown in a welcoming valley shadow that lingers over the city patiently until that ancient orb sets more completely over the bend of our mother planet's graceful curve. The heat relaxes only a little in that shading. I am walking. I pass the Apache Inn. A complaining semi rolls by roaring in a guttural ungodly voice forcing gazes to turn to and attend to the discord and disruption. Faces pass me. I know a few. I nod. There is Katie Brandon who interviewed me for the *Times Independent* a year ago, holding her daughter's hand, about to go into the hardware store. There, across the street, I see standing in the doorway of her empty tourist shop Liz Laney. She features my book by the cash register. She waves. I wave back.

I pass the bridge over Mill Creek. Now I am passing by the Walker's Drug, a car of teenage girls goes by "dragging main." I hear strains of Dr. Hook's Medicine Show from their 8-track. As they pass, they whoop and laugh greetings at some boys lekking on the pavement by their Mustang, its ripe red paint and dazzling chrome oozing éclat, ennobling the space and marking it as a place of virility and status. I feel its tug. I feel its tug. Pulling. Drawing me. Not to them. To another.

I am walking away from downtown along the highway South. I've passed Miller's Supermarket. The light is slipping away more quickly—nearly all is in shadow, even the edge of the eastern ridge. Only the La Sals, spectacular and silent in the distance, are tipped with golden sunlight. I turn on Fourth South and head down Bittle Lane. It is quiet and the fields that stretch on either side carry the scent of alfalfa. Sweat trickles down my face. I pass a row of trailer houses, then a small low brick house with large gorgeous sycamores arrayed in front stretching up to the blackening deep blue of the cloudless sky. In the house, strains of Elton John bleed from the brick walls, then suddenly cease. I hear a singsong voice calling from the back yard, calling someone in for bedtime. A white muzzled vizsla on the front lawn sees me, raises its head, stands, and watches. I can see it is chained, an elephantine corkscrew metal anchor twisted into the ground fixes its orbit, and a ring of dead grass marks the limits of the dog's patrol. It does not bark but remains vigilant with an unreadable canine attentiveness.

I turn toward the highway and pass the bowling alley. I stop to replenish what has drained away in the heat at the drinking fountain within. The deep rumbling clatter of pins. The cannonade of the rolling bowling balls. Pin ball machine flippers, clack, clack, clacking way amid a clamor of bells and rings. The gentlemanly breaking of billiard balls. Cheers. Announcements over a loudspeaker publishing the availability of a lane or an admonition to visit concessions. A gum-chewing middle-aged woman sensuously drawing a slow drag from her mentholated Kool, dressed in couture bowling ally chic, laughs. Twice-risible men, many unemployed with the death of uranium mining, bedecked in absurd shirts and bicolored shoes, showing how it is done. The cacophony of humans fleeing boredom and endless, listless, crushing, stiffening ennui. I flee back into the night. I breathe.

It is dark enough for early stars but the streetlights block the view. I cut over to Holyoak Lane and wend my way past houses now awash in soft yellow lights leaking into the night. I turn left onto Mill Creek Drive. I know my destination now. I will go to Lefthand and swim in the cool night waters of that hidden pool. I pass the body shop junk yard. Old cars scatter into the distance of the field stretching upslope to the rear of the car repair bays. From behind a fence two large surly pedigreeless dogs bark viciously as I pass. Still too much light to glimpse my heavenly guides and guardians. The first hint of cool appears. Then is gone.

I pass the drive-in theater. I gasp. There he is with a face sixty feet high. His jaw clean and hard and fixed. His hat pulled down low deeply shading his eyes, each iris a disarming blue and as deep as a galaxy. I see teenagers jumping out of a pickup. They run to the side of the road, disappearing into trees. Sneaking in, no doubt, as the driver pulls in the truck, the cab still full of youthful bodies. It slides up to the paybooth then through the main gate.

I look up at the screen and see him again. I follow the disembarked teens on a path through the trees. A tear in the chain link fence guarding the large parking field with its rounded berms and rows of speaker posts lets them slip in. Again I follow, but my eyes are on the man on the screen and I cut my bare leg just below my cutoffs as I slip through the jagged opening of torn wire and metal. But there he is. So alike, as if he leapt from the mountains into a Spaghetti Western. I watch as he mounts a horse to give chase. Long of line. Strong. Lean. The outdoors exuding from him like an elemental force, like an animal that knows no fear and questions nothing of his existence. He is more handsome than even this actor, I think. I thrill. My chest feels light and the breath in my lungs seems to glow with a rush of heat that cannot be explained by the dry Moab summer swelter, and I picture him standing there holding out my abandoned clothes and his eyes meeting mine without reservation or judgment and his hand shaking mine and then his smile that speared me like the deep thrust of an ancient hoplite Greek warrior dragging me to a kind of death or a kind of life with the Gods. I was undone. Figuratively and literally.

I walk over to the concession stand and buy a Seven-up and get a napkin to press against my bleeding leg. I can hear the movie over the boxy metal speakers attached to the hundred or so odd cars aimed at the giant screen. I walk slowly to a place away from the lights of the fountain counter. I stand before the screen watching. Longing. I cannot help but notice the car before me. I see the silhouette of heads against the illumination of the screen and as I watch they move closer, and closer, then they turn facing each other, then they are gone as they sink into the seat, the movie abandoned.

I am walking again. Up the Power-dam road. I pass occasional cars parked for those that need more privacy than the drive-in provides. The fall of Mill Creek as it pours over the forsaken dam creates a roar and a mist that rises above the slot canyon pool into which it falls. Are those voices I can hear in its tumult? I pass by, following the trail up to Lefthand. I know the way by heart. The stars are visible now, the city lights hidden and masked, though their glow rises from the west. Their starlight fills the sky with a kind of magic and for moment I forget the terror that dwells in such reaches. I look around. Was that a noise? My breath comes quicker. I push it down. I remember to breathe.

Lefthand.

I am floating in a pool. Surrounded by stars exposed through a keyhole of sky left visible from between the small red rock canyon pool nestled between low cliffs. The waters cradle my naked buoyant body. My head is laid back and my ears underwater catch the occasional tink of a stone pried loose and cast over the small waterfall that marks the entrance to this sanctuary. The water tumbling into the pool delivers to my submerged ears a low rush and comforting bubbling. There is sentience all around me. Presence. Being. Power. Will. A vitalism that enlivens the pool. I can feel the fish, the insects, the moss carpeting the rocks over which this cool water from ancient comets flows, I can feel the tiny leaches clinging with their seta, they are living. Aware. Aware of me. Aware of me being aware of them. We are joining at vibrational levels where consciousness finds purchase. I can feel us all. Floating I am not one thing. I am everything. I am becoming the water. I am becoming the rough sandstone rock that protects this small basin. I am becoming the air and the stars and everything that marks the waves and structure of existence. I am not a separate thing and that realization heals, if only for a moment in this occasion of consciousness of being. And strangely in every vibration that marks the stuff of this place I sense... him.

DOCUMENT #6:

Abstract from The third mind: unconscious control by a neural
mass in a set of Siamese twins, *by William Babcock,
Edward Babcock, and Heinrich Bergstien.
Mind and Brain 1970, 6: 458-479.*

Two of the authors are conjoined twins with a shared
neural mass located ventrally of the L3 Lumbar vertebrae. The
mass is an ovoid structure (confirmed by x-ray) 5x9 centimeters
and seems to control lower limb movement, sexual activity,
and digestive function. Neither Edward Babcock (the right
persona controlling right arm), nor William Babcock (the left
persona controlling left arm) have constant conscious access
to this region of their body, but alternatively share access to
this nerve bundle and the areas, such as the legs, it controls.
The neural mass seems to make decisions about where the
legs will take the body based, in part, on the urgency of the
individual twin's needs or desires. It also seems to have a sense
of "fairness." If one of the twins wishes for movement and he
has been granted access several times in a row, the neural mass
will give the other twin a chance to "use" the legs or sexual
organs and the neural 'feeling' associated with those lower
extremities. At times, the neural mass acts according to the
desires of neither twin—e.g., to run from ambiguous danger
(one, say, that neither twin has noticed) or to seek out sexual
activity. Some activities require coordination of both the
neural mass and the twins. For example, bathroom functions
require the integration of all three personalities with the neural

mass alone detecting, for instance, the need for urination. In such cases, the lower extremities are used to orient the twins' body in such a way that they recognize that they are positioned to urinate, by moving them in front of a urinal. Then one of the twins must use his hand to facilitate the implied goal of the neural mass. Which twin gains control or feeling in such cases seems largely arbitrary. When the neural mass is acting independently, neither twin can anticipate which one will get the feeling of the legs or be granted access to their control if given at all. The examples discussed in this paper imply that the neural mass has access to the brains of both twins. This includes their visual cortex, thoughts, feelings, and their desires. However, the mass can make decisions independent of either. What this implies about the nature of consciousness is discussed, including whether this neural mass is an independent and separate consciousness. Thoughts on what that means for personhood are explored.

DOCUMENT #7:

Poem by Dora Daphne Tanner, published in Shenandoah
Spring 1977.

Earth Stains

You came unexpectedly,
returning things lost, things left behind,
things I thought forever gone.
My salty tears always pooling,
were suddenly dry,
wiped by the playful
twist in the corners of your mouth.
Your loamy brown gaze,
redirecting mine, away from inwardness,
toward the desert, toward the landscape,
both barren and rich,
healing in its undulations.

Your soul is stained with red rock
in ways that come only by breathing in,
over and over again Navajo
Sandstone and Chinle Formation rock.
Your eyes reflect morning canyons,
your lips spotted with sores burned from high
altitude sun and ancient wind—
palms rough from handling earthy things.

You babbled about rabbis and London,
blasting caps and seismographs,
But all I knew was you were there,
bringing the desert mountain laccoliths
into me.

Hyrum's journal, hand-written manuscript.
Written between June and August, 1977.

So it came to pass that I was back on the Mountain &
Jim asked Wheres your Book? Verily I had been working with
Jim Frankle now for over a year. We did'nt talk much. He had
allowed me to read my Dickens books & I had allowed him
to read his Geology journals. We had sort of a silent mutual
Agreement. We would talk only on the way up to set up the
sensing station. After that we were allowed to be by ourselves.

I finished it.

Really. Good for you. There was a long pause as we went
through some bumpy holes that the rains had Gouged out. Then
he added rubbing his head where it had just hit the ceiling.

What are you going to read Next?

I do'nt know.

I'm afraid I was'nt vary talkative. As I related I had been
up almost all night but it was'nt I was tired that was keeping
me from talking it was that I was Pondering on my newfound
calling as a Scholar. I was trying to think what my first act
of Scholarship should be. I realized that among other things
I was going to have to figure out what I should be a Scholar
Of. Perhaps I thought I should be an expert of Dickensology.
Become an Expert in those works that I had come to love so
much. I already had a good start having read so much of the
old boy. Then it hit me. The Entire reason I had read that whole
thing in the first place was to figure out what that blasted word

Dickensian meant. I had forgotten all about the reason that I had picked up those wonderful Books. That PHD snob had called me that name so long ago that I'd almost Forgotten the whole thing. Of course that would be my first Scholarly Act. I would delve into the Mysteries of that elusive Word. Who would have more cachet than me to figure out what that maddenizing aphorism had meant.

Man! What a Dickensian life you lead!

Indeed who better prepared than me to say what Relating of or to the Works of Charles Dickens might mean. A chill suddenly went down my spine as I faced my first challenge of Thought. I glanced up at the mountains rising before me & saw my own climb into Scholardomhood. Perhaps the way before me would be hard & filled with boulders of thought Strewn in my path but at last I would reach the top. My first step on the path up would be the Scholarizing of a single Word. No pusillanimous mendicant was I.

So it came to pass that after setting up the equipment I told Jim that I was going to climb Mt. Peele that day & that I probably would not be back until it was time to leave. He said it sounded good & went back to his own Reading. Mt. Peele is the second highest mountain in Utah. Its about 13000 feet high but that is from Sea level. Moab is about at 4000 feet & we were setting up right off of Beaver Lake which is about 10,000 feet high. So I had about 3000 more feet to go. After breaking the timber line & reaching the lovely meadows up so high even the scraggly & dwarf trees quit growing you have a mad scramble over a mass of broken & jagged boulders that seem to have been just stacked up in a big pile. Its really Strange & hard to image what kind of natural way could cause such a jumbled up rock Formation. My Sunday School teacher had once used it as proof of Noahs Ark because what could leave a stack of boulders 14000 feet high. I remember thinking that I could'nt see how Noahs Ark could have done it either but I was a good Sunday school kid & just Nodded my head. I did'nt want to seem a troublemaker. I asked one of the geologists around here once about it & he said they were called Laccoliths & that there sort of granite domes that get pushed up & worn down at the same time & something about that whole pushing & crunching makes them crack & Break & look like a pile of broken boulders. To be honest I did'nt understand it any better than the Noahs Ark story.

Well it was a hard tramp up that hill. Somehow if I climbed a real Mountain I thought it would be easier to Mount the peaks of Scholarship. I put on my thinking cap & tried real hard to think deep Thoughts. I had only 2 things to go on. First Dickensian meant that it related to the works of Charles Dickens. I knew those well. Second I had heard it used only once & that was in a Mean comment aimed at me. Since the word related to all of his works I decided that I would first look for Things all the stories sort of dealt with. Well they were usually about poor kids that had rough lives good natures & that something Good finally happened. It was'nt always kids though but even when it was someone like old man Scrooge they would start out missing something. Sometimes it was money once it was a country one other time it was a home & they would always wind up with the thing they were Missing. Now I was getting somewhere. They did'nt always get what they thought though. Take Pip all that time he was thinking that it was old Haveshem that gave him the money but Really it was the convict. Then there was David Copperfield. I wo'nt write all the paths my brain took but you can see my brain was literally on Fire & burning through the Facts like dry grass blazing up on a windy day.

I thought some more but I could not make anything derogatory out of Of or Relating to the Works of Charles Dickens. It always came out as a Happy ending. Wait. What about Sydney Carton? The guy who went to a far better place than he had ever gone before? He was hung on the Gallows. That was'nt a too happy of ending for him. Of Course it was happy for the Darnay guy & his wife. No somewhere somehow somebody was always happy or at least satisfied at the end of every story. Not happy like they wanted to be. Ah here was something. Maybe Dickensian meant that I was a good man that was'nt happy but would be made so in a Surprising way. That seemed to fit a few of the stories. But it did'nt seem to fit the only Way I had ever heard it used.

I toyed with the idea that maybe The Bob did'nt know what it meant & that maybe he was just trying to sound like a Dickens Scholar. That did'nt quite feel right either. He was an idiot but he was'nt a stupid idiot. He did have a degree in English. No I must not understand I figured. I had Reached the top but still was not a Scholar. The runt left off the teat while the other piglets suck up the sow & ain't fit but to be skewered on a stick & fed to the dog. Though I was mighty high on this mountain I was feeling mighty Low of heart.

I was deadlocked stalemated & discomfited. Nothing from Dickens seemed to fit the only way I had heard that blasted word used. I thought this way & that & nothing seemed to fit together. I was starting to run out of Gumption for climbing either of these mountains. Maybe I was'nt meant to be a Scholar after all. I sat down & looked across the Beautiful landscape below me. The mountains ended quickly & spread out in a seeming flat plain filled with cracks & gouges running this way & that. I knew they were really large canyons & as a boy I had probably explored everyone. I Sighed & thought that I was'nt going to give up that easy.

It was gorgeous up there despite feeling like a culled Piglet. A perfect kite wind was blowing & the sound of the wind meeting the top of that mountain was like some Ancient music played on really good speakers. It was so wonderful. The sun peeking through high white big clouds moving quickly across the sky as if to get away from the empty Deserts below. The Canyonlands were splashes of lines & shadows deep reds & purples all mixed together in a Magic purposeful random way. It was magniloquent & nonpareil. I thought that this is where I want to die looking at this. Just then a cloud passed the sun & the world darkened & the breeze turned chilly & I wrapped my arms around my waist & sat down low on a rock to get out of the wind. Then just as suddenly the cloud was gone the sun came out & the wind felt pleasant again. Right then I knew what the word Dickensian meant. It was clear that fast that Dickensian meant a deep bleakness & poverty & misery suffered for a purpose that will eventually turn into Light. The words came to my mind like cool water to a dry throat one in which liquid was a new sensation like a dry throat that had only known Thirst & now for the first time was getting a quenching maybe like a thirsty piglet finally getting that first drink from his Mama. Somehow the passing of the cloud had been another Sign. Another coincidence that taught me something profound. Just like in Dickens something that should never come together does! I felt a profound sense of Deepness. I was Scholarizing. And somehow I was Thinking in a way I had never Thought before. When The Bob had called me that name he had meant the first part & was giving me Hope. I remember the strange sort of faraway look he had when he said it. A sudden wave of Guilt swept over me. I had done him a wrong thinking he meant something he did'nt mean at all. I felt very Humble up there high atop with the carved up Canyonlands Valleys below. Very grateful & very in Tune with something I had never felt. I wondered if maybe I ought to go to Church Sunday. My breath was coming hard because of my exertions & the thin air did not help but my Heart was beating like a 2 barrel Block Engine from a 57 Chevy. I screamed at the top of my voice I Know what Dickensian means.

The Wind drowned out my voice & I headed back down toward Beaver Lake. The way back was fairly easy after I got back down to where the Trees started up again. On some of the steeper parts I could take a huge Sideways leap & then land some 30 feet further down the mountain than I had started. Working my way down this way I was back at the sensing station in only an hour or so after I hit the trees. Jim was scratching some notes in the same journal I had left him reading.

I said Ready to head down? I was anxious to get back down to base camp. He said Its only 2 O clock. We've got at least 2 maybe 3 Hours.

I settled down under an aspen near the Lake & started Thinking. My what hard work being a Scholar is I thought. I felt really Tired after the climb especially after being up all night. The next thing I knew was Jim kicking the bottom of my work boots & telling me to get in gear because it was time to go. Packing up did'nt take long & soon we were on our way down. After a nap I usually feel Awful. My head feels the same way my foot does when it falls asleep. Hard to move a little strange & unattached. But this time I felt Refreshed. The deep waters of Thought that I had enjoyed on the mountain returned & I started to feel pretty satisfied over my first romp in double or even Triple deep Thinking.

I was just turning my thoughts from gloating over the discovery of the meaning of Dickensian to Ricks sausage spaghetti which he would soon be whipping up. We were turning unto the driveway of the trailer we called base camp when I noticed that the place was Filled with cars & trucks. It looked like The City Market parking lot. There were government plates from 4 states Utah Colorado Wyoming & Arizona. Now here was a Mystery. Jim & I exchanged glances & hurried into the trailer. The trailer was a 5 room doublewide & the door opened to a Spacious living room. The only piece of furniture besides the lamps was a large table that nearly took up the whole place. It used to be the boardroom table for GeoTech when their office was in Grand Junction Colorado & we had Inherited it. When we walked into the room nearly 2/3s of this table was filled with mostly strangers. Rick apparently had gotten home early because he was serving up some of his famous spaghetti already. This is where he used sausage instead of hamburger like most folks make it. It was as good as anything you could get at a Fancy restaurant.

Jim I'm glad your back. Let me introduce you to some People. I almost Wet my pants. It was Mr. Roydon president of GeoTech. I had never met him before but I had seen his smiling face enough on the pamphlets that we gave out. I felt as if though I were meeting a movie star.

He said Jim is a Seismologist we hired last year to handle the operations in our Mapping project. He'll be joining us up in Denver in the next couple of weeks. He's done some pretty Impressive work down here.

Next a sequence of introductions started around the table. After Dr. Roydon said a Name someone from the table would stand up & shake Jims hand. I did'nt know that Jim was leaving in a couple of weeks.

Jim This is Dr. Nancy Massy from NASS. Bob Richfield from USDA. Dr. Betty Krum of USGS in Nevada. Carol Sandoval a statistician from USGS in Wyoming. Dr. Karen Flores from UDFG. Dr. Michael Tanner & Bob Breckenridge from the Forest Service. Dr. Steve Reyes & Russell Chang from NASA. And last but not least Dr.s Fred Jorgensen Beam Tulles & Jane Hall from BLM. And of course you know Patty & Mike from Denver.

People were leaping up & down. Reaching across the table & walking around it. Doing whatever it took to get Jims hand. Then Dr. Roydon went on about how they all had been meeting in Salt Lake and decided to drive down and see the operations work in Subsurface mapping themselves.

I'm delighted Jim said.

We've been trying to get Jim over to Denver for months now but he says he thinks better down here.

All the while I was just standing by the table staring at all the People feeling very small & unimportant. Like a wallflower at the stake Gold & Green Ball. There were no letters before my name or after my name & I was not from anywhere that could be said with just letters. Hi Brother Hyrum Thayne from M.O.A.B. It somehow did'nt sound the same. No one had motioned me to do anything so I was still standing there when Jim finally glanced over at Me.

Let me introduce Hyrum Thayne. He's one of our techs. I'd actually never been called a tech before but it sounded a little more Important than I felt.

Howdy. Howdy! How in the world howdy slipped out I could'nt guess but I was feeling sort of small again.

The talk turn from me to more things that only could be expressed in letters. GEO TRI FSU DSU on & on. Such Jabber went on all the way through dinner. I was just getting up to help Rick clear up a bit when the talk turned to things I could understand. Funny things that had happened & some such things. I decided to stay & listen when suddenly one of the stories took on a more Serious note. Dr. Krum started telling about how her sister had been hit by a drunk driver & broken her back. She went on to tell about the fight her sister had had to regain movement in her Legs & how just last week for the first time since the accident she had been able to walk a short distance. As I listened it was'nt so much the story that impressed me as much as the realization that this was a Dickensian Story. A deep suffering bleakness or misery suffered for a purpose that would one day be turned into light. This was my big chance. Here in the group of the highly educated I would demonstrate my first Scholarly Achievement. It suddenly occurred to me that this group of people were brought here for that very Purpose. A profound sense of boldness & gratitude overwhelmed me. The story had just ended & there was that pause that follows the telling of such a tale accompanied by the shaking heads & tight lips as the people all look at the person talking & say with their eyes Wow that was really Something. This was my chance. My mind raced to find a couple of morsels from my <u>Words of Power</u> book for added Emphasis. Realizing that I had to say something now or forever miss this chance I blurted out.

My what an extraordinarily perspicuous Dickensian series of Events that was. Indeed it was.

It came out much louder and stiffer than I had intended. Everyone at the table was Staring at me. Then they all started to look at each other. There was a twitter here. Then a giggle there & within seconds the whole table was Rocking with laughter. One guy was actually choking he was laughing so hard. Well naturally I joined in. I was slapping the table &

Guffawing with the best of them. My laughing too seemed to unleash them. Mr. Roydon was crying. He was cleaning his glasses & trying to gain Control of himself. The laughter started to die down & someone had to tell a joke then there was another. No one noticed as I took my plate to the kitchen. Rick was in there washing up.

Sounds like some party.

Yeah. I told a joke & it really set every body off.

Tell me.

I winked & said Too high brow. You would'nt get it.

Tell me anyway.

Ok. My what an extraordinarily perspicuous Dickensian series of events that was.

Your right. I do'nt get it.

Told you.

That night I laid there in bed & Thought. I had obviously missed the boat when it came to Scholarizing. The meaning of that Blasted word must have escaped me again. I was feeling sort of low when I heard some people in the hall talking. They were a little light headed from one too many Beers.

They both laughed as they went into another room & closed the door. I'm Sure they were laughing at me. I bit my bottom lip & after awhile or two went to sleep. The path of a Scholar was not going to be an easy one.

Letter from Dora Daphne Tanner to unknown correspondent, undated; likely late summer, 1976.

He believes me. No one believes me, but he does. The pieces are gone now—it's been six years. What did I expect? Did they blow away? They were as light as air. Did the frightened military take them away? Cart them to their secret places? We know from Vietnam they lie and lie and lie. Do they rest now in sterile labs with white-coated scientists whose slide-rules quantify minutia while human wisdom remains ignored and discarded? But he believes me.

Today we drove to the spot. He held my hand tight as we walked through gnarled and twisted sage. Here, a nest of *Pogonomyrmix* ants rose from the desert floor, vegetation stripped in a thirty-foot diameter, while trunk trails wound among scrub—little highways of meaning giving access to precious seeds. Here, a Say's phoebe flitted back and forth on what errand I could not see—occasional snatches of song leaping among the background rustle of the low brush. Here, a sagebrush lizard, there a blue belly, dry and rugged. Here, the droppings of a Paramiscus mouse. But nowhere could we find memory of the craft that had squeezed and shrunk my soul. My scorched and broken soul. We sat on a sandstone outcropping floating barely above the level of the sand. I cried. He held me but said not a word and when I looked up I saw he was weeping silently with me. What could be said? After a time, after holding me, he said simply, "I believe you." It was the only thing that could be said perhaps. But, no one, ever, ever, ever has believed me. Not my Mother, not my therapist, not the friends who once gathered to hear my poems, not the cowing crowd who come to gawk at my windows, not even my only sister, my sister who shared my life, my sister who can detect all my lies and truths, my sister who has cried, laughed, and strained with me, my sister whose divorce I grieved as if it were my own, my sister who claims to love me. My sister who says only that I need help. But he does. He does.

We went somewhere else for the picnic. Somewhere higher. In a grassy meadow. An island in the aspens. Somewhere where we could laugh. There was no laughing in the place we started. A shroud of darkness surrounds that place, even in the bright desert afternoon sunlight. But under his spell on the flanks of those enduring mountains I laughed again. It's been a long time.

He believes me.

SOURCE DOCUMENT #9:

Letter from William Babcock to Redactor. January 4, 1998.

Dear <Redactor>,

It is hard to believe that it was been two months already. Where does the time go? Since your visit, the featureless skies have offered nothing but a cold rainy drizzle that seems determined to dampen our spirits. However, despite the low drenching stratus darkening the skies, finding ourselves huddled in *Hund and Horn* talking over a dark beer, clustered around that black oak table by the hearth, still brings a warm glow. I'm convinced our time with you will install itself as one of our favorite memories. Your account of Hyrum's last days has left Edward and me talking long into the night.

You are quite astute. Yes, Edward is gay. Perhaps it would have been more awkward had either of us found enduring love. But as it is, neither of us has found *any* love except in the willing arms of the prostitutes of our student days. I suppose the conjoined twins, Chang and Eng, had always given us hope that something might develop (you may not know that in the early 19th century they each married, and between them fathered 21 children!), but it was not to be. Each of us has been in love but, alas, the object of our love has never returned our affection. For a long time I blamed Edward. I thought that with every romantic relationship I sought, Edward projected boredom and exasperation. I realized at some point that the reverse was likely true. Ah well, water under the bridge, as they say. (Edward just laughed and pointed out that perhaps the reason that we never found love was that we are circus freaks.)

Now, I suppose we must come clean. Yes, there was an inconsistency in our tale. Even now I struggle with whether to tell you this, but Edward has insisted the truth be told. Whether you reveal this is up to you. I hope you do not, but we leave that to you. The question people will ponder, I suppose, is: do we constitute one witness or two or three?

So, then, to the truth. No, we did not get this secondhand as claimed. We were there. It was not recounted to us by one of the cattle hands working the mountain. We witnessed it ourselves. It happened between Two Mile Creek and Pine Flats, high up where meadows and aspens claim the patches of terrain in equal proportion. Three-hundred-year-old Ponderosa pines grow like cathedrals in the overgrazed range and cleared forest floor. We were running late, and night had overtaken the mountain. While the moon was not quite full, it was glabrous and giving a strong light, with the aspens glowing two shades of gray, one hue reflected from the long white columnar trunks and the other from the iridescent leaves, shimmering like pale ghosts stridulating softly in the wind. The dirt road was well lit and easy to follow (not that Starry needed the illumination; I've seen him make his way back to camp even on the darkest nights).

We heard a soft moan, then a wincing cry. Starry hesitated, his ears leaping forward, assessing the fey noises. Snorting, he backed up a few steps. Marcel edged him forward, but cautiously, and then we saw it, parked off the side of the road on the edge of a meadow, first the gleam of the bumper then the rest of the white truck. The moaning grew more strident and we could see the pickup truck was not motionless, but dancing to earthy fundamental rhythms. Of course, you are thinking what we were thinking, and we thought to ride past without disturbing whatever tryst was occurring, but a sudden scream, and a man's voice yelling, "Oh Hell! What do I do! What do I do?" with such fervent pathos and despair that his cries spurred us quickly towards him. Another scream, produced in unmistakable pain, caused Starry to back up suddenly, and only some adroit reining by both Edward and me brought him under control. In the back of the truck was a scene of strangeness and horror that is hard to describe. There was Dora on her back, her legs spread wide, wearing nothing but a bloodstained tee shirt. A greenish tarp was spread on the truck bed and there stood Hyrum spinning in a small circle wringing his hands and doing a strange jig that spoke of abject confusion and fear. She was screaming. Then she suddenly stopped and gritted her teeth, ferociously holding her breath. Her face wore the same aspect of contortion that an Olympic deadlift champion grunting the final weight over his head might. Her face and neck looked as if they were about to explode. A wet mess streamed from her vagina and her back arched sending her swollen belly skyward in spasm of contraction. Hyrum suddenly looked at us and asked helplessly in a whine, "What do I do?"

Dora was suddenly screaming obscenities at all of us.

Of course, we had not a clue. We recognized she was giving birth, but I fear that our impulse was to run for some boiling water and hot towels since that was procedure in film. However, the physical presence and reality of this mess, this pain, this confusion, brokered in us a calmness and surety of action that belied our own lack of knowledge. I reached over and slapped Hyrum who was standing in the pickup such that he was easily in my reach. It had its desired effect and shocked him back into the present moment. We took control of the situation, both Edward and I giving orders that Hyrum seemed glad to obey. He got a pile of dirty laundry out of the cab to use as a pillow and helped Dora sit up against the cab in the back of the truck. She was crying, her teeth chattering, and shaking so badly it looked like she had come out of ice water. Suddenly another bad contraction gripped her whole body and she went silent except for a grunting moan that leaked from between her teeth.

Under our direction, Hyrum was holding her hand while we shouted the only thing we knew was appropriate: "Push," we said in unison.

This continued for a time, then in the middle of another fierce contraction, abruptly, in a whoosh of blood and amniotic fluid, the baby spilled onto the tarp as still as a blob of clay thrown onto a non-rotating potter's wheel. It lay there. Dora was just staring at the sky blankly. Hyrum was holding her up, but catatonic. We seemed to be the only ones who had kept our heads.

"Hyrum!" I shouted in command. "Get the baby!" He was slow to respond, but seemed to come back to himself and swiftly enough came over to the baby but seemed afraid to touch it. We again took charge.

"Quickly, hold it upside down with one hand and spank it with the other!" Edward shouted. (Our knowledge of childbirth came from TV and was all we really had to go by.)

"But..."

"Now!" Edward shouted.

Hyrum picked up the baby by the feet, holding it upside down in one hand, its umbilical cord disappearing into Dora's womb. He gave it a tentative swat on the behind.

"Harder!" I yelled. "You've got to really whack it."

He did, and just like in the movies, the baby let out a wail.

This had a strange effect on Dora. She had been sitting there panting in a state of shock, and the cry of the baby suddenly focused her completely. Her face was strangely present, as if all that existed in the world was the baby. As clichéd as it sounds, her face was one of angelic calm. Pale. At ease. And utterly and completely focused on the whimpering male child in Hyrum's arms.

"Let me have it," she commanded simply and reverently.

Hyrum handed it to her, but suddenly she pushed it back into his hands, and she spasmed again and much to our horror another baby sloshed from between her legs. Or so we thought. In retrospect, of course, it was the placenta. But something about its shape, or consistency and mass, reminded both Edward and me of Marcel. Irrationally, it seemed to us as if attached to this newborn baby was another living creature— another child of sorts.

Several things happened at that moment. Something spooked Starry and he skittered wildly back away from the truck. While we were trying to bring him under control, Dora snatched the child from Hyrum and leapt, yes leapt, over the side of the pickup and ran. I saw the placenta, which as I've explained, I thought was a child of sorts, bang against the inside wall of the pickup and then bounce behind Dora as she ran through the small meadow. She paused just long enough to reel in the placenta, and then bolted again leaping over a maze of fallen aspens and into the standing trees about hundred yards from the road. She was clutching the baby to her chest, jumping scattered logs and sprinting like a deer. The placenta, which had slipped down out of her hands again, was now bouncing horrifically on the back of her legs. Hyrum just stood there, watching her run. I was filled with horror. Starry would not settle down. He was whickering and fighting the reins. By the time we had him under control, the woman was lost in the stand. Hyrum ran after her and similarly disappeared. We started the chase shortly thereafter, but too late to find either one in the dark, despite the bright moonlight. It was to no avail. They were gone. We could not track either of them in the dark. We rode back to the truck debating what to do, when a few minutes later Hyrum came back to the truck, weeping and upset.

After conferring briefly, we rode in a sprint to our base camp and there raised the ranch manager on the wireless (yes, we really called it that). He called Search and Rescue and we rode back to the truck. Hyrum was standing in the middle of the dirt road, still weeping and stomping his feet. He said he had tried again to find her but could find nothing.

You know the rest of this sad tale. We are sorry we lied to you while you were here. This was an uncomfortable series of events, one we neither owned nor revisited. It is rare that Edward and I do not reflect and hash over such things in long dissections of this and that. But of this we never spoke. Indeed, until you brought it up again at the *Hund and Horn* we had never discussed this among ourselves. A clear case of repression. For my part, I was embarrassed on several levels: my lack of knowledge of childbirth, the panic of our horse at the most inopportune time, the fact that a murder (or kidnapping, if you believe her tale) of a baby whose birth we witnessed had taken place under my nose. Ms. Tanner never disclosed our presence at these events. When you suddenly brought it up in the midst of our conversation, you took us quite off guard, hence the depersonalization of our account and our attempt to foist it off on some unnamed work companion. Please forgive us.

Edward and I have since talked long and deeply about these strange events. Oddly, our conversation began at the

Freud museum. On display was a strange painting illustrating the unconscious with a monster—dark and ill-formed. Being a Cthulhu ourselves (as it were), the question of whether the universe contains such creatures as Ms. Tanner believed took her child is an interesting one. Hyrum's friend Rick, a Native American, believed in a creature called Yeenaaldlooshii, who roamed the deserts as a skinwalker, and could change into the form of a monster capable of killing and dining on cattle. We met a man who lived alone in the Moehau Range in New South Wales who had been chased by Yowie, the Australian equivalent of Bigfoot. Can these tales give an account of what has place in the real world? Ms. Tanner's monsters seem to Edward and me to be modern versions of ancient fears, buried deep in the psyche and part and parcel of what it means to be human. Our brain dances to rhythms of survival. Is it not better to pay attention to a possible sabertooth than to miss the real thing? Better to project into the world possible dangers that are not there than to let an actual predator escape our attention? Why else do the shadows of a coat placed carefully over a chair before bedtime, seem, in the night, to take on the sinister aspect of satyr or demon? I can remember riding Starry on moonlit nights, the shadows around us deep and menacing. He was skittish and attentive; we were all on edge, watchful, every dark place off the road a source of potential, unnamed danger. We are creatures with a long evolutionary history as prey. Did Dora see something that night? A mind traumatized with the birth of a child, exhausted, instinctual? Of course she saw aliens. What spooked Starry? Take your pick—deer, coyote, bear, squirrel, snake, partridge, any number of things. Maybe the very predator that took the baby. Alien visitors interested in child-snatching seem low on the list of best possible explanations. Abductive logic leads us quickly away from such inferences ("Clever play on words," Edward just said: think about it).

And yet. Who's to say the universe is not filled with terrors, many and varied—that there are evolved creatures that would make our deepest fears and darkest shadows seem tame indeed? However, best to stick to the things we know. I'm sure Marcel would concur had he (or she!) voice.

Again, my, and Edward's, apologies for the untruths we told. Please forgive our deception. I think, however, you will understand now our reluctance in disclosing the truth.

Sincerely,
William Babcock

REDACTOR'S NOTE:

Visit to Dora Daphne Tanner—March 8, 1998

I decided the only way to sort out some of the disparities, confusion, and uncertainty in the various narratives was to talk with Ms. Tanner myself. She had been institutionalized many years ago and currently resided in the Utah State Hospital. The cluster of white buildings strewn about the foothills of the Wasatch Range's southern arm in Provo seems typical of such institutions—neatly manicured landscapes networked with paved trails connecting the facilities. "Facilities," that's the right word.

I had previously made an appointment with Dr. Tal Bissle to interview Ms. Tanner. He was a rotund, balding man with a wry but vacant smile. His handshake was a little soft and misaligned, which seemed to broker in me a kind of suspicion about his capabilities or motives. He guided me to a chair and looked at me long enough to make me uncomfortable. Not as if he were weighing my secret thoughts, but more akin to the reasons one cannot long hold the stare of an ungulate—the fear that there is nothing behind the gaze.

When I asked about his patient, for a moment he did not seem to recognize who I was talking about. To be more charitable, I think he was a harried and distracted man who had too much on his plate, and too little time to devote to it. In our few moments of preliminary conversation, he admitted that he was a Mormon bishop and that between his duties as a psychologist at the state hospital and his Mormon Ward, to which he is essentially a pastor, he had little free time. Perhaps that explains both his blank stare and his scattered answers to my questions.

"Anyway. A sad case," he said, shaking his head slowly back and forth. "Yes. I've known our dear sweet Dora a long time. She came to us quite delusional. A ward of the court convicted of murder, but innocent by reason of insanity. My predecessor in fact testified in her defense at the trial and kept excellent notes."

He swiveled his chair toward the window, which I assumed faced toward Dora's place of residence. He placed his hands on his thighs and assumed a posture that seemed quite unnatural and stiff.

"Anyway. She believed she had been abducted by aliens."

He turned to me and said knowingly, as an aside, "Space aliens."

He resumed looking out the window. "Anyway. We put her on a regimen of antipsychotics. And while calming her somewhat, we have never felt like we've made much progress with this dear sweet sister."

He continued to stare out the window.

"Is she currently on medication?" I asked.

He turned to me with surprise, as if he'd forgotten I was there. "No. No. They didn't seem to be helping and we removed them years ago. The change in governmental support necessitated some adjustments in patients who were racking up large medical expenses, but not responding, so we took her off the meds. Anyway. She's been a model citizen since. She goes where she's told to go. Actually helps around the hospital a bit, but holds onto her notion that she was taken by aliens, impregnated, and her baby stolen. Anyway. If she had not been a ward of the court, she might be let go. She has visitors from time to time and a sister who visits occasionally. Anyway, as it is she'll be here 'til she dies."

He turned toward me again. "You would still like to meet her?"

I nodded cautiously. As I mentioned, he elicited a strange distrust. Without further comment he motioned with his large hand for me to follow and walked from the room. We crossed the courtyard to another of the white buildings. He walked in front of me, making no effort to continue our conversation. When we arrived at one of the nondescript buildings, he paused to open the door for me and we walked into the structure. We made our way past a nurse's station to a large recreation room with game tables and large Naugahyde chairs scattered about in disarray. In one corner a large projector TV sat blaring out a Family Ties rerun. Dr. Bissle motioned me over to a pillowy couch in the back of the room while he spoke to an orderly.

"She'll be here presently," he said sweetly. "I'll take my leave now. Don't expect too much. She can be chatty or not—but it will be nonsense. Good day <Redactor>."

He wandered away after chatting with the orderlies for a few minutes about a local sports team. I waited. It seemed to take a long time. The attendants kept smiling at me every time I raised an eyebrow trying to signal my impatience. Eventually, I just settled in to watch the TV. The comedies of the 80's I still find endearing. There is an innocence about them that, even as they tried to be edgy, seems quaint and refreshing. The laugh track was a stroke of genius. Generations of people have heard it again and again, but have never heard it.

Ms. Tanner finally appeared. She seemed unexpectedly old. I of course had been pouring over her letters and the writings of Hyrum. She was a young woman to me. Rationally, of course, I knew she was older, but when she approached slowly, her thick silver hair carefully styled into a ponytail, her aspect shrunken and thin, I could not get my mind around this being the bold adventurous Canyonlands poet. She was only in her fifties, yet she seemed much older. Frailer. I took a stack of paper she held in her hand and helped her into a straight-backed chair into which she lowered herself gracefully. I sat opposite her, across a small card table, and returned her papers. However, as we began to talk, I sensed an underlying vigor. As if "old person" were a role forced upon her. I suspected that if I caught her alone in her room, I might catch her dancing.

"I've come to ask you some questions," I said. "Do you understand me?"

"Of course I understand you. I've read your letter and if I didn't have something to say you would not be here."

"Thank you. May I record you?"

"Yes. Well. Of course. What would I care? My kin are mostly dead. The courts have sent me here for good. And..." Here she hesitated, "You said you believe me?"

"Yes," I said. It was not a lie—exactly.

She nodded. She then looked me in the eye and held my gaze. "You want to know the truth about the baby?"

"Yes," I said. "As I said in my letter, there are a few points I want to clear up..."

"Wait! I want to know something. You said you found Hyrum's journal in your grandfather's trailer in a box of Hyrum's things. I never knew a Mr. <Redactor's grandfather>. How did he get these things?"

I shrugged, "I'm not sure."

"And in the documents he never mentions me?" I could not tell if she were grateful or surprised.

"Not directly, but there are allusions to you that are clear."

She nodded, then refolded her hands and placed them

neatly in her lap, then looked up at me expectantly.

"I've been to the rock described in your journal. It's where you said it would be of course, but seeing it brought your story home. I want to be clear about something. You were running from them, right? Why didn't Hyrum run with you?"

She screwed her eyes up in unmistakable rage, "How could he understand what was at stake? Look, you need to understand some things. First, he was a mess. More than the nervous father, he had just helped with the delivery of our baby with that queer man with two heads shouting useless instructions at him. Hyrum was unglued. Disoriented. And I'm pretty sure about to go down in a wave of panic and confusion. There was blood everywhere, the placenta had just popped out, which he thought was another baby (and I think the two-headed cowboy was shouting for him to save it because "it was a person too")! Second, everything happened so fast. I saw the alien bastards standing on the other side of the road on the edge of the aspens, just behind where the freak was sitting on its horse. When the moon popped out from under a cloud, I saw them as clearly as I would at midday. They glided back quickly, but I screamed. Of course, I had been screaming for hours and no one paid me any attention. Hyrum had the baby, both heads of that circus creature were shouting things at him, and I had just seen the monsters. I don't know where I found the strength. I was shaking badly, as weak as the baby itself, but on seeing those things across the road, I suddenly found myself with the baby, running into the aspens. That's how scared I was. I was running in only a t-shirt, my bloody legs staggering on bare feet, sprinting fast enough that I left Hyrum and that two-headed midget on the horse in the dirt. I ran for a few hundred feet carrying the baby and the attached placenta."

She paused here looking over my head. "You know the rest."

"I'd like to hear it from you," I said.

She was silent a long time.

"I stopped at the flat-topped rock, a ways past the giant bolder with the pine sticking out of the top that you can see from the road—you know the one I mean—and laid the baby down. I passed out cold. I did not awake until I heard dogs barking. The sun was up, and the woods were filled with the sound of people yelling and calling. A man on a horse rode up and let out a yell, and he quickly wrapped me up in a blanket. I must have passed out again. I found myself swaddled in a bunch of blankets, and a kind woman in a uniform offering me a drink of water. She was a rescue worker. "Where's the baby?" I asked her. She smiled and told me that everything would be fine. She checked an IV hanging on the snag of a tree and looked uncomfortable. I passed out again, and when I woke up I was in the Moab hospital."

"When did they tell you about the baby?"

Her eyes teared up and she bit her lower lip, but carried on after a moment's pause. "Two days later when they charged me with its murder."

I nodded and instinctively took her hand. She squeezed mine tightly.

I looked at her, trying to discern if I should go on. She raised her eyes to mine and nodded. I kept her hand as I asked, "Forgive me, but"—I hesitated to be so graphic—"The umbilical cord... how close... to the child was it cut?"

She lowered her eyes suspiciously. "How would I know that?"

"I mean, of course, how much was still attached to the placenta? They found that in the bushes, right? I mean... did they estimate how close to the baby it was cut?"

"They never said," she said sharply.

I nodded. "And you never brought Hyrum into this?"

"No. No need. I know it wasn't him that killed the child. He was with the freak the whole time anyway. I was the only one alone with it. Why ruin his life too? I loved him... I still do I suppose."

"The coroner report says the cord was cut with a knife and the court transcript says the prosecutor said you used a pocket knife—"

"Look," she interrupted, pulling her hand from mine. "You read all this and I don't want to dredge it up. I was ruled incompetent to stand trial. They didn't need to convince a jury. They didn't need a 'murder' weapon. They didn't even need to find a body. They just needed a judge to sign that I was certifiably insane... and you know what? I was!" Her once small voice reached a register of seething, "My baby had been stolen by goddamn little green men from outer space. I was in an insane rage, I was in despair, and in absolute and inconsolable sorrow. What else could they call it? Put me on drugs and leave me to rot! That was all they needed to do! That's all they did do."

An orderly looked over and scowled. She looked like she might come over. We both noticed, and Dora returned to her normal voice. "Sorry. I don't need to vent at you."

I reclaimed her hand. "It's ok. I'm the one who's sorry." We were silent awhile.

"Have you tried to appeal? To find someone to represent you and reopen the case?"

She laughed, and a delightfully rich and robust laugh it was. I found myself liking this woman. She radiated depth. Her smile faded and she looked at me seriously. "If I would have recanted my story they might have. But I won't." She was looking rather tired and fatigued, and I saw her glance toward the clock.

"One more question," I said quickly. "When Hyrum went back, you said in a letter to Hyrum that he should look for the 'The Mark of the Beast.' What was—"

"The next morning when Hyrum led the rescue workers back, he saw pressed over the top of one of the two-headed man's horse's tracks a tiny footprint the size of a little child's."

I must have looked surprised because she said, "You hadn't heard that before, have you?"

I shook my head. "Where... did anyone else... ?"

"No, it was run over by a vehicle before he could draw anyone's attention to it. But he saw it and that's enough for me."

We chatted a bit more about things that do not concern this account. She was being treated well in her current situation, and expressed her contentment and acceptance of her incarceration.

Before I left, she looked me in the eye and squeezed my hand and asked, "What are you trying to do?"

"I'm not sure," was all I could truly say.

With that she handed me a manuscript.

"It's a short story," she whispered. "Maybe you will find it useful."

Hyrum's journal, hand-written manuscript.
Written between June and August, 1977.

2 weeks had passed & I had'nt done much on the path to Knowledge. The night with the bigwigs had more or less taken the wind out of the punctilious bag. Sandra had noticed that I was acting a little grouchy & contrarian & had suggested that a visit to Church would do no harm to my outlook on life. But how could I go there? I sort of felt that God was more like those PHD & government folks that were laughing at me. I sort of felt like he was playing some sort of joke on me. Was'nt it Divine direction that had led me to read that book in the first place & was'nt it inspiration from on high there on the mountain that gave me the Revelation about what the word meant? Well I could'nt go to Church quite yet if this was the kind of God that were out there. He'd had his laugh & I was'nt going to indulge him as court jester anymore than I had to.

All weekend I just sat in front of the television watching sports & having beautiful women & muscular guys tell me what to eat drink wear & drive & I was feeling sort of Low in spirits. All my friends were out of town so there was really Nothing else to do. I did'nt want to think about what had happened up there on the mountain & the television does a killer job of allowing you to sit & not have to think but I had thought myself into a Funk anyway. On the second Sunday after my rout I set in front of the TV & turned on a game. I bet I did'nt think one thought for 3 hrs & 12 minutes. I was sitting there eating Fritos & having a beer which I only drank when Sandra was'nt home & which was easy to repent of according to Brother Duncan. I looked at the clock & it was 1:01 & I looked again a second later & it was 4:13. My mind had been a blank & I had'nt Thought once in that entire period. That started me thinking about thinking & that started me thinking about thinking great Thoughts & on & on until I was Pondering about being a great Scholar once again. I realized that maybe I had been a little hasty. Perhaps one failure was not enough reason to give up on a lifes Calling. The purpose of this life was a Test anyway. Our spirits were placed on this good earth to be tried & tested to see what we were made of. Things were supposed to be hard. It seems like the closer you are to God the harder the turn things seem to take. Maybe my persecution was a trick of the Devil to set me off my real purpose in life. Perhaps the greatest Sign that I was suppose to be a Scholar was that everyone had laughed at me. My head started moving like a herd of cattle being squeezed into a loading chute to be branded. I would press on. Like the Mormon Pioneers of old I would face the elements that were thrown against me & triumph. I got in my car & stuck Breads new album in the 8-track & took a drive up the river. I came back late. Sandra was asleep so I did not wake her.

Monday morning starting the new week I loaded the truck with gusto. Today I would climb that mountain & ponder anew the great Problem of the mind that I had been destined to solve. That Mystery whose heights & breadths few dared contemplate. Today I would come to a true knowledge of what the word Dickensian meant or my name was'nt Thayne the titled bequeath to me by my noble Pioneer heritage. I remembered one of the stories that Heber J. Grant one of the prophets & presidents of the Church had told about how one night his grandpappy who had kicked the bucket some years before came & met him on a path in the spirit world. The path he said was beautiful with trees & flowers everywhere anyway the first thing his old dead grandpappy said was What have you done with my name. Well that set him to thinking. I was imagining when my grandpappy came back I'd give him an ear full about the life & trials of a Scholar & say my what Dickensian lives we all lived. Of course, my grandpappy would not likely put up with me telling him too much. One time he told my dad to do some such thing but my dad was playing with a puppy and did'nt jump right away to do the chore. So my grandpappy went into the house and grabbed his 30 30 and came back an shot the little dog in the head saying When I tell you do something you do it when I tell you to do it. When my dad tells the story he thinks it was a great Lesson. I was never sure my dad learned the right lesson. Well anyway I was excited about doing some heavy duty Thinking that morning. Suddenly a new face greeted me.

Hyrum Thayne?

Yup & you must be the new guy replacing Jim. That right? He seemed mighty young. He could'nt be more than 19 or 20 by the look of him. But there was something sort of compelling about him. Something that sort of made you to take a Liking to him right away. He had that fresh look like a pie just out of the oven before it is carved into pieces or any one snatches the edges of the Crust.

Adam. Pleased to meet you.

Adam did'nt hesitate & started loading things on the truck. He seemed to know his business & did'nt talk alot. That was good because I had set aside today for Thinking & I was'nt in the mood to be interrupted over this & that.

We got the truck loaded & in a few minutes were on our way. We were going up to a place up top of the Porcupine Ridge overlooking Castle Valley. The quickest way was to go back through Moab & take the road that runs behind the dump past the top of Nigger Bill Canyon & then onto the Ridge.

Adam had stared out the window all the way to Moab past the dump & well into the foothills. I had wanted to Think but I have to admit that Curiosity was getting the best of me. It did'nt seem like he was'nt talking because he did'nt think me worth the trouble. In fact he seemed more than friendly. But he seemed mighty Preoccupied with things.

Were you from? I could'nt stand it anymore. He looked over to me smiled & sat down in the seat like he was willing to sit & Chat awhile.

Provo. How about yourself.

Right here. Moab Utah. Lived here all my life.

I'm going to school at Brigham Young right now. My dad is a Geology professor there. I'm a dual geology philosophy major. German minor. There was a long pause & then he added. Are you a Mormon?

I nodded. He sort of breathed a sigh of relief & reached over & shook my hand. I do'nt know why Mormons shake hands so much but they do.

I'm glad. Last summer I was working at a Drilling Rig up near Evanston Wyoming. Man what a bunch of crude guys. Every night it was drinking & cards & talking about girls. I went on a Mission to Switzerland & I sort of felt like I ought to show these guys a better Way but they just laughed at me. I had a hard time. He looked out the window a minute thinking then said Well it will be good to have you here anyway. At least even if we are out numbered we can support each other. Right?

You bet. A returned Missionary that was all I needed.

This was going to be a long Summer.

Hyrum where did you go on your Mission? The question was inevitable. All young men are supposed to go on a 2 year Mission. There is no rule that says you have to but it is sort of expected.

I did'nt go. I got married instead.

I expected that All Knowing Ohhhh I see you are'nt all that committed Ohhh that has driven me crazy for years. I was surprised by his response though.

Well my dad did'nt go ether & he's a Stake President for a bunch of the BYU wards. Then he patted me on the shoulder. He seemed different from most of the Mormons here in Moab. Here among some not going on a Mission was like an admission of wife beating.

You have any Hobbies? Since we're going to be working together for at least 4 months we might as well get to know each other.

Not one of the geologist or techs I'd worked with in the last 10 years had asked me that. I just stared at him. Was this guy Serious? Did he really want to get to know me? I was skeptically surprised. It was'nt just that he was a Mormon. I'd worked with fellow Mormons before. I'd even been through a couple of BYU students. But this one was Different. I was starting to like this guy.

Well actually I'm a bit of a Scholar.

Really!? That is great! Whats your interest. I thought this was going to be a dull summer but you sound like a kindred spirit! I've often thought that Scholarship was the highest good besides of course helping our fellow man that we could do in this life.

Thats right. I agreed. Did you know that to the olden day Jews the Scholar was the most Respected person in the village?

He stared at me in Delight.

What did you study in school? What was your Major?

I was'nt ready for that question & it made me a little sad. I thought about lying but I knew if he knew anything about whatever I said I'd get nailed to the frying pan & put the cart right into the fire. But then what else could I do although I made it a mostly Truth lie.

I majored in Dickens but mostly I'm self taught. He looked puzzled & was about to say something I thought he was going to call my bluff a spade. I could'nt let this guy lose all his respect so I fest up.

I mean I'm mostly self taught like Charles Dickens.

Thats Great! Have you ever read Jude the Obscure by Hardy. Ever since I read that Book I've realized how deeply prejudicial our current system of education is.

Oh yes I often compare my self with Jude.

That book was one of the saddest books I've ever read. It just Devastated me. I see that it did'nt deter your educational pursuits though. I'm glad. It did depress me though.

Oh me too. I almost gave up being a Scholar. Have you ever read Great Expectations? That gave me some hope. I had to get the subject off of this Jude character.

Yes I loved that Book. I thought it was Dickens best.

So did I.

What a week. Every day was spent in Deep conversations about life literature philosophy religion. The only trouble was that most of the time I did'nt have a clue what he was talking about. I'd just nod my head. And say things like Wow I've never looked at things like that before & Yes I thought so-and-so too obscure to enjoy. I thought after a while he would catch on that I was completely Clueless as to what he was talking about but no so on & on he went. What a week. I thought I was going to die. Even after we got back to base camp it was all I could do to slip away with Rick for a few minutes & get a little rest from the worry of every second being discovered as a Fraud.

From the first night he insisted that since we were kindred Spirits & brothers in that sense we should have family prayer together at night. I gave in but I must admit that I felt mighty Silly kneeling down beside him while he poured out his soul to God. I wo'nt say it did'nt move me because he offered up a darned sight better prayer than Sandra did. And it was good not to hear the part about Please bless that Hyrums heart will be touched to become Active in the Church again. The second night though he said it was my turn & I panicked.

I'm no good at praying out loud. I said. Would you mind maybe saying these good night prayers. It was the first Truthful thing I had said all that day. The bequest obviously touched him a bit & he went ahead & offered up the prayers the rest of the week.

On the second week we were together I stopped at a gas station store & bought one of those Steno note-pads & a Bic pen. The whole thing Cost nearly a buck but I decided that I had better start learning some of these words he was using so I could play the part of a Scholar. I felt sort of Guilty sitting there all day nodding my head at all the right places & inside I was just wondering when he would figure out I was not quite a Scholar just yet & trying to memorize all the words he was using. On the outside the conversation was going something like this:

<Redactor's note: Even though I've been correcting a significant part of the spelling, I've made some interpretive assumptions with a more heavy hand on the next few lines to make this readable.>

Have you ever considered that Kants Categorical Imperative is really in some ways just a reframing of Christs golden rule Do unto others has you would have them do unto you?

I'm surprised that no one else has realized that Obvious connection.

On the inside the conversation was more like this

Kants Categorical Imperative-Kants Categorical Imperative-Kants Categorical Imperative-Kants Categorical Imperative & on & on. Then I'd say after every little while

Man this Diarrhea is doing me in. I'll be right back.

Then I'd run into the bushes & take out my pad & scribble down all the words I could Remember. Then come back with a Wow were going to need more toilet paper. I must have got some bad chicken somewhere. Sometimes I'd say I had a small Bladder. One time I shouted Look a coyote! & dashed into the bushes.

I suppose that I should of been more grateful for a real Scholar to have come my way to show me the way into Scholarhood. I was never one to look a gift horse in the eye as they say. But holy cow I was'nt sure I was going to be able to keep up the Pace. I sort imagined the life of a Scholar with more relaxing reflection somehow like the Scholars you see on tv sitting in their big comfy leather chair in a room of books smoking a pipe and stabbing it at who ever they were talking to whenever they were going to make a Deep comment. Or like before when I climbed the mountain & did some Deep Thinking. This was hard work. Not like real Scholarship at all.

Well by the end of the week I had compiled quite a list. Here are a few of the words:

Dye a lektik dialectic

Lazy fair laissez-faire

Inkul kate <*inculcate*>
Xesentul <*existential*>
kont <*Kant*>
cat t goryical empairitive <*categorical imperative*>
kirk a gard <*Kierkegaard*>
joys ulysis <*Joyce's* Ulysses?>
doggrowl <*doggerel*>
can deed <*Candide*>
herman ud icks <*hermeneutics*>
X a Jesus <*exegesis*>
Nars a sism <*narcissism*>
es spree de cor <*esprit de corps*>
lak konic <*laconic*>
lay miseraub <Les Misérables>
Impress a veism <*Impressionism?*>
Hey gul <*Hegel*>
bostonians <Bostonians>
plee bee an <*plebian*>
foe coo <*Foucault?*>
structuralism post struktulism <*post-structuralism*>
post-modern

Friday night I was a discouraged man. First Sandra had gone off to a Relief Society service project to help one of the Sisters families who was in the Hospital & had'nt even made me dinner. Second my <u>Dictionary</u> I got free from subscribing to <u>TV Guide</u> did'nt have but one word: Postmodern which meant after the Modern period which I had figured out pretty much on my own anyway. But I was running up dry on the words on the list of my pad. I sat on the john & flipped through the pages I had spent the week compiling. I was very Discouraged. Hanging around a real Scholar all week had made me Realize what a long road I had in front of me. My first task as a Scholar had been to figure out the meaning of one Word. I had hoped to dedicate a couple of months to the Project but now after only a week I had a list of 72 words of which 68 I still had no clue as to their meaning & most of which I had as much feel for as the word Dickensian. Did this mean I was going to have to read 68 books to just get through this weeks list? Oh brother. To top it all off I was constipated. I was not ready to give up yet however referring to Scholarship & not the bowel problem & I resolved that in the morning I would make a pilgrimage to the Library to figure out the rest of these Words. I decided to give up immediately on the Foreign sounding words like on-we <*ennui*> & that knocked my list down from 72 to 54. It was going to be a Busy weekend.

Saturday morning I woke up in sort of a bad mood I had'nt slept well & I had had an Awful dream. In my dream I was in a race like back in high school & I was suppose to take a baton from the guy in front of me but he kept running faster & faster & was Shouting words at me that had no meaning. My feet were wrapped in the red slick rock like the kind that surrounds the city of Moab & every step added some thick red Clay that was sticking to the bottom of my feet. It does'nt take a Daniel to interpret that dream. Fact is I had this dream in high school Plenty. Well I checked my feet & they were as clean as they ever are & after wiggling my toes several times I jumped out of bed. Grumpy but determined to get some Scholar work done. Sandra had wanted me to spruce up the yard a little but we Scholars do'nt have time for the trivial activities of day to day life. Ours demands Hard brainwork & Contemplation. Gardening was just not on the list.

The Library seemed cool & dark when I walked through the big glass doors. The bright desert sun had left me a bit blinded walking in to the dark but I could tell Something was out of place even before my eyes cleaned the sun out. Sister Goodson was not behind the desk. Instead of the old kindly face that had always greeted me with a Good to see you Brother Thayne the cool suspicious Stare of a stranger was glaring at me like a mother bear does a dog. She did'nt seem to fit here somehow. She seemed sort of Modern. Her hair was cut really short like one of those peter pan pixie girls. She was pretty but she was looking at me like a Hippy at Church. I did'nt belong but she had to treat me Nice.

Can I help you she forced out. I smiled & pointed at the big unabridged Dictionary on its usual stand.

Just got to look up some Words.

She waved me that direction & went back to reading her book. Her hair was way too short for a girl & it sort of Annoyed me. Like she was mixing up girlness & boyness. I was glad to leave her behind the desk because I found her somewhat unsettling to the Soul because I could'nt sort out how I ought to look at her.

I started to get a little excited though as I picked up the Dictionary & moved it over to one of the 2 couches that was placed Opposite each other in a big clear spot under some sky light windows. There was a little table in the center where on another Saturday there would have been a couple of magazines including <u>Flyfisherman</u> which Sister Goodson would of laid out especially for me. But today only some news weaklies were flopped down on the surface of the oversized coffee table which added to the feel that all was Not right. I was just starting to sit down when all of the sudden I heard someone Yelling at a little kid.

HEY! HEY! YOU HAVE TO LEAVE THAT ON ITS STAND! HEY! YES YOU! PUT THAT BACK ON THE STAND. IT IS REFERENCE ONLY.

Well I was embarrassed. She had alerted the other 2 people in the Library of my terrible irresponsibility & I was'nt quite sure what to do so I scampered over to checkout desk to Explain myself & seek a revocation of my Dignity.

I'm sorry I whispered as was fitting the Reverence I had always given this place. Sister Goodson used to let me take whatever I wanted Anywhere in the Library. I just want to look up some Words. I held out my little notebook as evidence that I was telling the Truth. By the way where is Sister Goodson? Is she sick?

First Ms. Goodson is no longer working here. Shes going on a Mission for her CHURCH. The way she emphasized Ms. And the way she spat CHURCH gave me to know that this woman had no love lost for the Mormons. There are 2 Reactions it seems among the non-Mormons in Utah. They hate us or like us. Not much in between. Adam told me that there are big fights up at the University of Utah between the folks that say although Mormons are a bit strange they deserve a bit of respect & the folks that think that we're something to tell jokes about like some sort of holdover Hillbilly pioneer. I know we are a bit Peculiar but largely thats the Lords doing. He told us to be a Peculiar people. We're just following his Direction. Anyway all this is beside the point of this story but I thought I'd better explain in case you were ever at lunch with somebody from the U of U & they started telling a Mormon joke or laughing about our Temple stuff which I never have seen so I do'nt know whats so funny & someone else is there to & interrupts them & the other person starts saying that most Mormons she knows are Good honest hard working people & they started a bit of a row you'll know what is going on.

She said There will be no more of your Latter-Day Saint Neapolitanism in this Library. If you want to look up a word do it at the Dictionary stand. Now this overstuffed UofU'n frustrated me because she had just handed me yet another word to look up & she was following the rules more strictly than the Deacons are supposed to when they pass the sacrament but I was never one to disobey orders given by those in Authority over me so I put the Dictionary back were it belonged & started to look up the words.

I have a confession to make. I cant stand up a long time. I do'nt know why but I cant. I remember once washing dishes at the Bub & Berthas River Runners Restaurant when I was in high school I had pulled up a bar stool to Sit on while I washed dishes. Seemed sort of natural to me seeing as how I had to stand there for Hours at a time. Well Bub the owner came galumphing in & burbled as he came so the famous poem goes & he was a little ticked off & said Boy you need a chair glued to your Butt. Ever since then I've been a little Sensitive about my perspicuity to sit down every chance I get but it does'nt change the fact. Bub was right. I love to sit.

I had'nt looked up 5 words when I just could'nt stand it any more. I just had to sit down. My back started aching & the bottom of my feet felt as if they had been Stood on a little too long & my knees were rocking back & forth & I found myself having a harder & Harder time concentrating on the words. Besides that I could'nt find the 5 words I was trying to look up. I walked over to the couch without the Dictionary & sat down like you would at a tumtum tree for a few minutes & thumbed through one of the magazines sitting there. I rested for about 15 minutes then got back up & started again. I tried to find 3 words this time before I had to sit down. This was not going to work. I looked over at the shallow UofU'n & her short hair sticking to the top of her head like that green thing on top of a tomato. She had all the Power. She was the Librarian. What could I do? Suddenly Dark thoughts started to take a hold of me. Murder popped into my head but that popped out again as soon as it appeared.

There were 2 Facts. One I needed to look up words. Two this was the only Dictionary in Moab big enough to hold the Scholarly words that I needed to look up. Now by some Fluke of the Universe it was going to be nigh impossible to look up my words because I was blocked by this Mormon hating conniving pixy fox with a cattle baron attitude & me with no John Wayne to come to the rescue. Desperate times called for Desperate action. Now as I've said before at this time of my life I was not very Active in the Church & when Satan has a hold of you its Amazing what strange paths he can lead you down. I decided that come hell or high water I wanted that book & I was going to check it out one way or the Other. But there were as we say in the geology office some Logistical problems. Louis Lamour books are small enough that you can get them under the back of your pants or even up your pant leg. But this was going to be a Problem. The book was as thick as a can of chili & it was easily as tall & wide as my little trucks spare tires.

The UofU'n was looking sort of nervous because I was sitting on the couch looking at her & then looking at the Dictionary then looking at her then looking at the Dictionary. I caught myself & picked up a <u>Time Magazine</u> & pretended to read it but really I was Scheming.

Its funny how we never really know what were made of until some Crisis takes our moral fiber to the point of breaking. Now I never had been what you might call a Nephi or a Lehi or even any of the great Book of Mormon Prophets but I never would have thought of my self as a thief neither. But here I was planning a Crime. Not just any Crime but a theft from a public Library. A lower act I could'nt have hardly contemplated myself doing just 5 minutes before I walked into the building. But like Judas the Evil One had planted the seed in my heart & there was no getting rid of it. Sure I could have gotten rid of the seed if I had thought of praying but I was on the outs with God. But I still never thought I would steal anything.

I analyzed the Situation from every angle. I could not walk out with that book. It was situated between the checkout desk & the door & I knew every time I walked over there the UofU'n would watch me like a Doberman pinscher guarding a dish of Alpo. I realized that in a way this was sort of a Scholarly problem. I could turn my mind to pursue a misdeed as easily as I could the great Thoughts I should be Thinking. I came up with a plan. And in that plan I discovered I am capable of Terrible things. Terrible beyond what you can Imagine.

The monster rode. Both of its gargoyle faces wide-eyed and giddy with excitement. One of them, its tongue lolling to its chin, drooling, dripping, dangling like a snake from the neck of a dark exotic dancer from Hell's shabbiest, skankyest, watering hole, clenched the leather reigns in his single greedy hand. The other: teeth set in lusty anticipation, its breath coming only from its bulbous nose, its head bobbing on the stump of a neck barely visible from behind its humped shoulder. It waved its riding crop and smacked the quarter horse's head and ears with demonic glee. The beast screamed, a loud terrified equine whinny in protest, compelling the exuberant dual freak to act as one conjoined machine in whipping the appaloosa with such ferocity that slashes appeared on the horse's hindquarters. The thing coordinated each leg to simultaneously stab razor-studded spurs into the poor beast's already bleeding flanks. They had the baby. Their masters would be pleased.

I know how the golem was made. How this double-headed demon must have been fashioned by the soulless otherworldly creatures that now controlled this hideous puppet. This is how. This is how. The freak's dark masters are a negative image of Plotinus' One. The soulless aliens must have shattered themselves like a perversion of the Kabalistic shattering of the Ein Sof. They are too empty! Too hollow to have fashioned corporality so easily in *this* universe. No. Those soulless masters had learned from me that in *this* dimension we have power that they do not, and despite their strength—the hollow power they brought coldly and passionlessly from the void—they had their vulnerabilities. But unlike the One, who contemplated herself endlessly, and whose emanations we are, they are the hole, the emptiness, the nothingness that even the One could not, cannot, sense. They are light-less. They are purpose-less. Random chaos. Without meaning. Without direction. A thingless thing that flows inward into nothingness, nonexistence, the groundlessness of all nonbeing, the dreamless void, the rent, the breaking, the tearing of what is real. Without rationality and without passion—squatting in the spaces between both. So how did they come here? How did they squeeze their way into this reality in order to take my child? How did they find place in this universe and kill its Goddess? Unman its Father? Destroy this weaving? Incinerate its growth? Dig up the anchoring root and green budding branch? They broke themselves. They mocked the One in a dark mirror shattering. And in so doing, out crawled this loveless thing, this two-headed retching from emptiness. One head for passionless rationality, the other for irrational passion. This perversion of woman. Of man. A hideous homunculus formed of fused and broken parts. Made for one purpose. To take that life born in perfection. A positive image to their dark negative. Not a yin and yang. But being and not-being. Good and Evil. Dasein and Keinsein.

The baby bounced behind them, wrapped in a sheepskin, pulled violently from its fleecy owner that morning. It still stank of blood and viscera and the baby wailed and cried and cried and cried. It cried for she that brought it into the world, but the poor precious child's mother lay bruised and bloodied beside a rock. Unconscious. The stolen innocent's father, running in circles, calling for his lover. Both lost in dissimilar ways.

The demons rode to the ship. It called them like a mother crocodile to its nestlings. They heeded. They heeded because they were framed out of those ethic-less terrors. The two-headed monster sprang from the void like Zeus from Chronos' head. But it would not supplant or kill this *patrem*. How do you kill that which has no life?

The man and the woman, the mother and the father, rode now, long after the taking. The trail more than two months cold, but the mother could feel her way after the monsters, as if the trail were fresh. As if she could see them, feel them, just ahead. As if she could intuit the red, red rock's shout, sense the story that had unfolded along this path. The ancient wind-blown sage sings her tragedy.

He, the father, followed her gladly. She had escaped. She knew they would follow, but if the baby could be retaken, all fear and doubt would be replaced with joy. How could she have murdered that which came treasured from her own body? Why did they say this? Why did they lay the blame at her feet?

And why did she think those alien beings would not have blasted up into the dark, empty places she could not follow? Why did I <*sic—Redactor's note: her use of pronouns becomes even more erratic: from she to I and back again*> not think that their angry ship would have by now blasted to a lightless universe? Why think the baby would, after weeks, be one of the spirits of this Earth, rather than gone and gone and gone? Two things. One, she could feel it. If it left this earth, I would know it. All light within me would follow it into that darkness and I would be empty here. A soulless shell. Two, the bi-headed terror was still here. H. told her that they still rode up on the mountain, searching out lost cattle, lost babies, lost minds.

They stopped at a wash and H. dug a quick hole to expose some fresh water along the cool outside bank of the gully, where hid a wet treasure, where summer rains had danced down from the La Sals and sunk deep into the sandy-bottomed torrent. The water was not so far into the sand that her cowboy could not reach it with a few swift strokes of his shovel. The horses drank deeply, sloppily. We followed their wisdom, kneeling beside the muddy hole drinking like they. Like dogs. Face down in the muddy pool.

We rested while the horses grazed nearby, our backs against the flat face of sculpted russet rock. I cried. H. held me. We made love. We rode on.

The desert brokers a quiet, a reverence, easily offended, never ignored. The wind at such times offers advice and commentary and if you listen, it will teach you unforgettable lessons of ancient sagacity and calm longing. But this she could not hear. She was a hound following a scent. She was tracking a fierce and merciless enemy—one that would give no quarter, for it knew nothing of love or maybe be-ing itself. It feared nothing until it met me. I taught it pain. I taught it that there are things that cannot be tamed by cold obsidian-like metal. That's why they took her child. It was born of something that had challenged them, confronted their emptiness, and defeated their pitiless curiosity. And she won! I beat them and crashed their ship. They would come to know such force again. Alas, why did I just not die?

She and H. rode on. The horses step step step on ancient sand. Sand torn slowly from rocks born long ago in the early Earth, torn from their mooring through this same ancient wind. Then floating down from some hoary orogeny now long gone, to a river delta as wide and deep as the Mississippi's or the Amazon's even, buried then for a million years until that sand became rock again. This rock. This red rock. This red rock exposed again to that same wind, this same rain, and then torn again anew and moved again down a river. This time the Colorado. To be piled up again in another delta, buried again for a million, or millions upon millions of years, exposed again and then basking again in the light of an older sun. Cycles within cycles. What eyes will be there then to watch this rebirth? What eyes will scan the horizon? Will the light of beauty and intelligence grace this world still? Or will the dark things have swallowed it all, negating what beauty will exist? That could exist? She wonders will the canyons still sing in the wind? Then, more hopeful she wonders, what plant will replace the sage? What scurrying thing will replace the blue-bellied lizard? Will the honey pot ants still mix their nectar and store it in their swollen bodies? What creature will descend from the coyote as evolution wanders among new and creative forms? What shape will the children of barrel cactus take, over the ions of blowing wind and drizzling rain? Will cryptogamic soil evolve to become some intelligent thing as its components specialize, differentiate, and explore new spaces in the topology of life? This she wonders. And she wonders, because she wonders what will become of her son's children. Into what creature will her own line transmogrify? What possibilities will arise? None. Unless I can find him. Unless I can take back what is mine.

She looks at her love. The face is young but not young. Concerned. Burdened and wise. Lines around the eyes just beginning. He hasn't shaved in three days. He talks about his bumblebees. He talks about them like a little boy full of passion and curiosity. Like a child in a backyard who washed out mayonnaise jar and with a lid held awkwardly, scampered among the dandelions, caught a bee and held the jar to her ear to hear the angry buzzing from this, Earth's fellow traveler. On the borrowed horse, he rocks back and forth in a motion as ancient as life itself, a force that drives us forward, ever deeper and deeper into time. A force both necessary and frightening. Is this what the creatures fear? Do they know this force is more than the sum of all the forces in their dark, flat, universe? Do they fear what we are capable of? Do they fear that by which we are driven? This force of love? Of life? Fear it they should. Fear me for I am full of its strivings, impassioned by its deep embedding in me, this child of Earth. A mother from a long line of mothers. Mothers who stretch back in time to mother apes, mother insectivores, mother reptiles, mother fish who swam with purpose, churning oceans with their thrusting fins, mothers from creatures without eyes, without limbs. Mothers coming from deep-time. From stars. No wonder these creatures fear us. We are from mothers beyond memory. And as a mother they have taken what, by the universe's most solemn and binding declaration, is mine! They will pay for entering this time. This space! They will confront forces they are unprepared to face. I will get back what is mine! My Child! My child.

Under the stars we camp. H. holds me after loving me—the second time since the birth of their child. We look out over an outcropping of Navajo sandstone at the horizon as stars climb above this ancient and calming place. The fire is low, having, like us, burned itself out in a burst of flame. Coals glow. H. tells her he is afraid. That he can't understand what's happening. He says in so many words that he is moving to new places he's never been. He's worried about me. About what they'll do when they catch me. He's afraid of the lies he's told. He is afraid of God. He is afraid of his damnation for fathering a child, for stealing, for dishonesties so deep he can't take it in. I am, she is, the only one who knows all sides of his story. I hold him and he weeps. Both of us are in trouble. He from complexities arising from his own confused darkness, me from real fiends from outside knowledge and ken. Both of us hunted and hunting. He wonders how things got so complicated. An ageless question asked by all who have wandered here for anytime at all. I do not answer for there is none to give. We watch the coals shimmering in the wind. One horse stomps and snorts. The other's ears perk up as the wind switches direction, shakes her head. Then stillness.

It is morning and they descend into a canyon. The trail steep and treacherous and leads to a small pond. H. knows this area. As a boy he says they would come this way on motorcycles and this trail leads all the way to the Colorado. Is she sure this is the right way? She is. There is no doubt now. The rocks sing the story of the abduction. The tamarisk remembers the baby's cry. The great cottonwood shutters at the memory of the barbarous things carrying such a lovely and pure vessel. A raven shouts encouragement. "This is the way. This is the way. This is the way."

And then there it is. We round a corner, wading through a deep pool lying tight between two mothering canyon walls. The horses have trouble gaining purchase as they climb out of the steep sandy bank as the stream widens on the other side of the cleft. We are wet and laughing. Yes, laughing despite our sorrows and loss. The horses see it before she does. They skitter and buck. H. is thrown as his horse bolts back into the water, and up through the narrow opening and back up the canyon. She gains control of her horse but H.'s mare keeps running, she brings her filly back around. H. is down and still. He has not moved. Then! Standing above him hover two of the creatures, their blank eyes staring down. Their cold long fingered hands reaching down. I kick the horse hard to run at them like a warrior queen, but the simple beast is unprepared to face such horrors—it screams and then bolts again back into the water. I leap from it, this time swimming to the opening of the slot canyon, and scrambling back toward the creatures. I am full of fury. H. will not wake even though she screams again and again. The woman runs down the canyon. Runs like a mountain lion. Past the body of her lover toward the ship. It sits on a small hill, formed by a stream that enters from a side canyon. The craft sits there watchful and fearless, like a vespid wasp guarding its nest. She has a jagged red rock the size of a cantaloupe in her hand. She does not know where she picked it up, but it weighs nothing in her fierce hand. She rages toward the ship. Mad with a mother's power. It is uphill to the ship, but the slope means nothing to her and she mounts it like a berserker in battle fury pulling with her all the rage that consumes her being in a fire which will burn them to ashes teaching them what it means to come between a mother and her son. She flies. The cold thing shimmers in the light of the canyon. Not like something beautiful, but like something of deep existential harm. Something of deadly intent. It is full of malice. Like a weapon. She strikes it with the force of a Goddess. There is no ring of rock on metal. Only a thud and a ping, like a hammer striking a foursquare ball. She hits it again and again and again and again and again. She screams for H. but he remains on the ground. She does not know if they have killed him. Her hands are bloody, but her mind only slightly registers her wounds. She feels nothing. Then it is gone. It did not fly away. It was just gone.

H. had a concussion. He did not wake up for two hours. Her hands were like hamburger and could not help him much. She just stared into the canyon where the ship had been. For a long time. She could no longer feel. When he awoke, he cried as he tried to bandage her hands, but he was confused. She told him what had happened. Then they were both silent until the federal marshals arrived. They tracked us here from where we left the horse trailer. I told them H. did not know who I was. I'd hired him in Moab to take me into the Canyonlands. He was silent. Sad. We had this story all worked out from the beginning. It worked without a hitch. She was returned to the white house on the hill. He went back to Moab.

She does not know where her son is. She can't feel it anymore. She fears it has left the Earth. She cries and cries and cries.

SOURCE DOCUMENT #11:

Letter from William Babcock to Redactor. June 16, 1998.

Dear <Redactor>,

As always it is delightful to get your letter. It has given us much to think about. Despite our exhaustion, today we braved the Saturday crowds on Maria-Hilferstrasse. Edward, as you'll remember from your visit, is still on his environmental kick and insists we use public transportation rather than taking a taxi, which means long walks, unrelenting delays, and nearly debilitating fatigue after the trip. It is always an ordeal. When we leave the Ubahn, and enter the crowded street (and Maria-Hilferstrasse is always crowded day or night), we are pressed from behind by the ubiquitous shoppers and the determined pedestrians who again and again try to squeeze past our slowly lurching gait, forcing the oncoming foot traffic into our "lane." Typically, those heading towards us only see us at the last second and must maneuver quickly to keep from a head-on collision with us. It is especially hard on Edward, who always seems to end up with the legs on these excursions. Yet he endures the indignities for Mother Earth. Bless him.

These environmental sensibilities of Edward emerged while running cattle up in the La Sals, where we saw the great beasts lumbering through beautiful and sensitive ecosystems that deserved better. I suppose for both of us there is a measure of guilt about watching what damage the beasts did and participating in it, but had we not spent time in the mountains, I doubt we would have learned to see such ecological connections. Boots on the ground and all that. Alas. So now we take the public conveyances, hardly a full recompense, but it makes Edward feel better.

The reason for our grand adventure was a nod toward one of our obsessions. There is an antique shop not far from the English Theater that caters to our obsession for art deco. The owner is a matronly Frau who I'm quite sure is terrified of us, but still calls us when she snags something we might enjoy. Just this week, she discovered a fascinating piece from the workshop of Karl Hagenaur likely made in the early 30s. A bronze version of us! A squat hobgoblin of sorts with duel heads sitting on rounded shoulders. It holds an iron-black spear with a bronze tip. It was a unique piece, not mentioned in any catalog, but bears the WHW stamp on the bottom. Of course we bought it. Edward wants to get an iron spear now to use whenever we are forced to brave Maria-Hilferstrasse again.

We thought to rest when we finally made it home (Edward consented to a taxi for our return), but discovered your letter and Dora's "short story" slipped under our door by the postman. We read both immediately. (Edward thought the depiction of me with my "tongue lolling out" and my "lusty gaze" were right on the mark.) You indicate that her escape from custody for a time was true. Very interesting. We were not aware of that event.

What happened to the baby? We assumed, along with others, that she had killed the poor thing, but your investigations and legwork have left me wondering. That the umbilical cord was sliced cleanly with a sharp knife and cauterized (With a match you said? How did they know that?) seems strange indeed. If it was not Dora, who did the deed? And there was, I suppose, always some doubt. I had always thought perhaps a cougar (unlikely, given the ruckus we made looking for her) or perhaps a coyote had dingoed the baby. But we had always believed with the police that she was responsible—perhaps quite mad from the events around her parturition, but Dora nonetheless always seemed the most likely culprit. You ask if she had a knife or some way to burn the umbilical cord? No. She ran nearly naked into the aspens holding only the baby. I'm sure of that. Was it Hyrum? He had time when he ran into the woods, but I am skeptical given his genuine distress over her disappearance that it was he. He was obviously quite worried about her and the child and I believe there are some things that cannot be faked. Could he have had a pocketknife? I suspect so. Even so, Hyrum was clearly in a state of anguish about Dora and the baby. My sense was, and Edward concurs, that Hyrum was genuinely excited about the baby. Neither of us thinks it could be him. Of course that leaves *us* as the perpetrator. I assure you that while we could have finagled our way off of the horse, we could not have gotten back on without help. There is a mystery here. Aliens? Space beings? I think we can reject that. However, that implies a third actor. Does it not?

Who killed the baby?

Please keep us up-to-date on whatever you find.

William Babcock

Beloved,

I feel so lost. The child is taken. I sit helpless, unknowing, unfeeling, un… what? Not unloved. While you are in the world I know that that appellation will never apply. You asked about my day? I cry endlessly. No one but you believes me. You are the only one who has ever believed me. No one but you is looking, looking for the things that took our baby.

How long did you walk the desert? Sitting alone on the ridge above the valley? I'm sure you heard the rabbit brush lilting in the wind. That's where I was taken, but who knows if they watch it. Remember my love, if they take you onto their ship, they can be defeated! I did it once. I brought them to the Earth. You can too. You must believe it. Break from their spell. Find the child. Please, Beloved, find our child.

The moon must have been new while you were out there and the stars must have blazed, revealing the Milky Way staining the sky with the denizens that mock us and who assisted the monsters that took, without conscience, our dear, dear baby. Our baby! How could it come to this? How can they have followed me so closely to know we would be there? Did they cause it to come a month early? Did they bring on the labor at that time, in that place, knowing that they could grab it with ease? No doctors. No nurses. Just you and me and that thing. That thing. Could they have been in league with the unearthly kidnappers? The thought just now occurs to me. How strange that they were there then. As if some force brought us all together at a moment fated to steal all happiness.

Beloved, you must go to the place they took it. Are the Marks of the Beast all gone? Look again. Track them. Do what you must to get them to tell you where it is. Do anything. Just get our son back.

I love you. You are the father of my child. My Cowboy. Just get it back. Please get it back.

Please.

Your Love,
Dora

Hyrum's journal, hand-written manuscript.
Written between June and August, 1977.

It came to pass that I parked the car in the rear of the Jr. High School parking lot. Sort of kiddy-corner & about a block away from the Library. It was about 3:00 am. I'd left Sandra sleeping loudly in the trailer. My heart was beating like the turning of a drilling rig & my Brain felt like bees were swarming in my poor head not to make honey but to sting and bite. I had driven All the way here without lights on. When I saw the headlights of the 2 cars that I passed I pulled over & ducked down. The Police station malingers close to the Library so as you can see I had to be very Careful and artfully Dodge the Constabulary.

I snuck through the baseball field & climbed over the fence & that put me in the alley that ran passed the State Liquor Store & some insurance shops. I was dressed all in black & wearing a black watch cap just like all the burglars did in the movies. I had even rubbed some burned cork on my face like the way old Dee Sorensen did when he played the lead in Green Pastures as a negro. On my hands were a pair of Playtex gloves that I had shoe polished black & I had bought special that day for the job. In my hand was a crowbar. I made my way without using a single street to get myself behind the Library unseen.

The back door of the city Library was Weathered & seldom used & somebody had stacked some cinder blocks up against the wall for building a storage shed or some such thing

& had'nt thought to quit stacking when they reached the door. By the time I had removed enough bricks to free the doorway it was almost 4 in the morning. Knowing it would be light very soon strengthened my Resolve & I placed the crowbar in the crack of the door. With what sounded like a train wreck the door was Wrenched from the deadbolt that was holding it in place. The door came away with such force that it violently flung wide open with a Bang. I fell back when the door opened & tripped over some cinder blocks that I had tossed behind me. The crowbar fell free & bounced among some of the other bricks that were scattered here & there. The door after bouncing off of the wall slammed closed with another Bang. I knew the gig was up & I spun like a cat & grabbed the crowbar & scampered over a wire fence that guarded some of the Citys gardening supplies. I scurried under one of the little tote trailers & waited for the Sirens to come screaming at me like Hounds & for Spotlights to be soon scouring the area like in old prison escape movies.

Nothing happened. It was actually very peaceful there under the trailer. The smell of grass clippings was strong & in a way it reminded me of being a kid & playing hide & go seek. The summer night was slightly chilled & as I peeked out from under the wagon there were 1000 stars glittering down at me. They seemed sort of oblivious to my plight & for some reason I found that very comforting. Stars are not dangerous. At least I do'nt think so. If they did'nt care maybe God did'nt neither. Maybe he saw my Need & would sort of wink at this whole episode. I remembered watching one of the Documentaries I saw on Sunday that I had started watching regularly since deciding to become a Scholar & they had talked about how Leonardo De Vinci had to dig up graves to get bodies to look at so he could draw people with their Muscles sticking out of their skin in the right places. Maybe this was like that. Maybe it was so important in the eternal scheme of things that I have this book God would overlook this little escapade. Over in the east the stars were starting to disappear in the coming dawn & I decided to Finish the job.

I stole back over the fence & checked around quickly for anyone coming but there was'nt a sound to be heard. I opened the door quietly & slipped inside. It was strangely light in the Library with one of the street lamps outside shining brightly through the Skylight. It felt very weird being in there like this. Sort of like I felt when I went into the girls bathroom in third grade. I knew it was'nt where I was supposed to be but I was pretty excited to be in such a Forbidden place. I even thought of that while I looked around me in that ghostly light surrounded by quiet books. Its funny how a place I had visited a 100 times felt so strange. Even the Air felt odd. I knew I had to hurry so I went right to the book grabbed it & started for the door. Then a thought struck me. Was I crazy? If this is the only thing missing from the Library that heathen U of U'n would be able to finger me in a second. The day before the theft Who was looking at it using it & causing a fuss about not being able to sit down with it on the couch? Me thats who. They'd know Immediately who it was.

I set down on the couch to do some Thinking. I could see that it was starting to get a little lighter & I had to act fast so I ran out the backdoor & placed the Dictionary in a safe place. Then I ran back in & started carrying out most of the reference section of the Library. There were Spanish-English Dictionaries Thesauruses books on Style & a host of other books that the Library would not let you check out because they thought that too many people would want to check them out. The fact of the matter was that I had never ever seen Anyone use a single one of these books. In 12 years of using the Library I figured that these were the most useless part of its Collection. It only took me about 5 minutes to get a stack of reference books about 3 feet in diameter & a foot or so high. Then I jumped the fence into the grounds crew storage lot & grabbed a can of Gasoline that was sitting there for the mowers. I hopped back over the fence & poured the whole thing over the books. The books were piled on a bare spot of exposed earth & far enough from the Library that I did'nt need to worry none about the fire spreading as long as the wind did'nt pick up. Suddenly it occurred to me that I did'nt have any Matches. I wondered if De Vinci had had this much trouble stealing bodies for his Artwork.

It is amazing what you can think & how fast it comes when you are in a tight Spot. At the same time I realized a way to get some fire & that I needed somehow to establish a motive for all of this. I had watched enough TV detective stories that if I just left things as they were people might not see the motive in this & might start thinking extra hard to see through my planning. I snatched my crowbar from where I had left it on the ground & ran back into the Library. It did'nt take long before I discovered what I was looking for. The hot water heater. It was Gas of course & the pilot light was giving off a calm & easy blue glow. I rolled up a piece of paper & held it up to the Pilot to make a torch. The good Lord was with me again & I began to feel more & more Adjudicated in what I was doing. There on the bottom of the water heater closet was a can of red spray paint. Motive & fire had arrived like the thought together & in the same instant. I ran back outside. About half the sky had lost its stars & a red glow was coming angrily out of the east. In a second I had sprayed Commie symbols like Hammers & Sickles all over the back wall of the Library & had thrown the torch onto the pile of books. I was thinking that the gas would have all evaporated but it went up like an explosion. I made sure there was nothing around that would allow the fire to spread to the Library & do a darned site more damage then I wanted & then I flew away with my prize. It had only taken 15 minutes from the time that I Conceived of the idea to cover my tracks & to leave the scene but it had seemed like a whole days work. I got to my car & threw the Dictionary into the back seat. It was getting sort of light but it was still dark enough I thought I would leave my headlights off. I was worried because if someone saw me in this sort of dawnish darkness driving without headlights it would have raised Suspicions. On the other hand there was no sense Advertising myself more then I needed to so I slipped away with out the headlights shining. I kept expecting to hear Sirens blaring any second once the Fire was discovered. But I heard nothing & did not meet another car all the way home. Sunday morning was coming fast & it was almost 5:30 when I pulled into my trailer court. Not a light was shining in a window & I was awful glad of that as it would of stood out something fierce me driving around that early in the morning. Especially on a Sunday.

The house was a quiet. I took the book & wrapped it in some towels & slid it under the couch. I then slipped out of my clothes & climbed back into bed with Sandra. There in the morning wrapped in a sheet with the air conditioner softly blowing her hair she reminded me of the Cheerleader I had married. Something seemed very Good with the world as I dropped off into an easy sleep.

Sandra woke me up about ten.

Hyrum I want to tell you something. Time to get up. I've been up for an hour. Come on Somethings happened. I've been on the phone all morning.

Whats happened? Its harder than I thought acting out a

part. Acting like you do'nt have a clue what shes talking about & all the while Knowing darn Well what was going on.

These are truly the last days. Hyrum I'm scared. She snuggled up to me like a little kid & I wrapped my arms around her to give her some Comfort.

Now tell me whats wrong.

Someone was tied to a stake behind the Library & all the religion books were placed around them. Then they were set on fire. Its horrible Hyrum. Were moving to Blanding. I cant stand it any more. Please Hyrum come to Church with me today.

Now Now do'nt fret. I'm sure the story is a little bit Exaggerated & that nothing more happened then a few books being burned by some kids.

No its all true. Roberta heard it from Sister Dolittle who got it from Jane whos in the Primary Presidency & she got it from Wilma whos Husband is on the volunteer fire department & he got it from Bob Miner who was there on the Scene first thing this morning when it was Discovered by the paper boy at about 7.

I have to admit I was feeling sort of a mixture of fear & Excitement that I had caused such a ruckus. It was mostly fear though.

I kept going over everything in my mind to see if there was Anything that I had forgotten. I'd heard about a burglar once that lost his wallet in the house he was burglarizing.

I went to Church that day trussed up like a Christmas Goose going a courting. Sandra was beaming like a bride as we walked through the door. She was imagining that she had Won some kind of battle but the truth was I was just too full of the jitters just to sit at home & wallow in my fear. We walked into the Foyer & were greeted by a bunch of smiles & handshakes. I was too involved with my internals to worry much about these folks pumping my hand like they were going to get water out of my mouth. Its hard coming back to the Church after you have been a way a while because Everybody makes such a big deal out of your coming back into the Fold. People beaming at you from every side. Everyone shaking your hand & saying Welcome & Good to see you again. It is enough to worry somebody silly. Bob Carson was the Elders Quorum president & one of his new councilors who I did'nt know was guiding me through the chapel to one of the pews behind where he was sitting. He had 7 kids 2 sets of twins included ages 1 to 5 & the pew more resembled an ant hive than a holy place. He started waving & whisper shouting at his kids until they were all Lined up like a row of birds on a wire. I was amazed they obeyed so well. It was'nt long however before there were a pair of eyes peering at me from the row ahead. Then another then another until I felt like I was looking at the lip of an owls nest & was being spied on by a bunch of Owlets.

I'd thought for sure that I would get a chance to get some sleep before the meeting was over but I was so Nervous I could'nt close an eye. It was when they passed the Sacrament that I was Especially worried. Now you do'nt partake of the Sacrament Unworthily. It represents a Promise to the Lord that you are willing to keep all the Covenants that you made at Baptism such as keeping the Commandments obeying the word of Wisdom doing right by your fellowman & a whole bunch of such things that are pretty darned hard & time consummating like serving in the Church. Partaking of the Sacrament also means you've been living up to what you Promised or at least your Trying to live up to them. It was pretty clear that I had been doing Nothing of the sort. And to partake of the Sacrament Unworthy was a pretty Low thing to do. Lower than the burning of a Library. Lower than about anything but killing someone. It brought Damnation to the soul they said. The trouble was if I did not partake would everybody think I'd done something wrong? Would this be an admission of guilt? But if I did partake it would be sort of like spitting in the Lords eye & trying to lie to him which was not something I was quite ready to undertake. The Deacons who though only 12 years old were passing the Sacrament were the most reverent bunch of kids I'd ever seen & seemed like a crew of student undertakers training in the art of pall bearing so Solemn and recondite were they. I remembered back when I was a Deacon we would do a fair amount of talking & giggling & carrying on like boys will but these were a Sober bunch. They were moving closer & closer with the trays of broken bread representing the body that Christ gave for our Sins & I was about to Explode. I could not partake. That was clear. I could not not partake. They gave the tray to Sandra. She took out one of the pieces of broken bread & put it to her lips. The room was quiet except for the noise of babies being carried out of the meeting crying & little kids being told to hush because this was the Sacrament. I glanced up at the Bishopric the 3 of them sitting on the stand. The bishop is the Judge in Israel & the Lord gives him a special power of Discernment. They could detect a lie like a mother bird can tell if one of her chicks has been touched & peck it dead if it was. He was'nt looking at me but I was thinking that somehow he would know what I Did in that next second.

When I look back on it it was all kind of silly. This was my first time back to Church in about 3 years & there would'nt of nobody bat an eye if I had not partaken of the Sacrament. But my mind was a fire of Confusion at that moment. I thought the whole Church was waiting to find out if I was the one that had burned the books at the Library. I felt sort of like someone who was being tried like back in the Olden days where they had to eat a scorpion. If they died they must of done the deed they were accused of. If they did'nt they must have not been guilty. If I partook I did'nt burn the books. If I did'nt I expected someone to call the cops.

I did the only thing I could have. I Pretended to take a piece of bread chew it & swallow it. It was all done very Realistically & I could tell that I had fooled Sandra at least. She had a tear in her eye & a sweet little smile all over her face.

The water was going to be Trickier. It represents the blood that Christ shed for us. It used to be wine but the prophet Joseph Smith received a Revelation that said that it mattered not what you ate or drank for the Sacrament as long as you did it unto him. One time after world war II in Germany they used potato peels because there was no bread. I always wondered why we could'nt use something a little less boring than water like Koolaid or Orange Juice or something you could at least taste. The water came in little paper cups about the size of a large thimble & after you drink the water you traditionally squash the cup & put it in a special hole in the tray. The Blessing was said & the Deacons started their round with the water. When it came me I was blessed in that one of the Cups was'nt all the way full. I raised it to my lips. I tried to pretend to drink. I mean I did'nt mean to drink for real. I had stolen a book. I knew I was'nt Worthy. I meant to just raise the cup put it to my lip & then put it back into the tray. But somehow some of the water went in. I could not just spit it out. I swallowed it. At that moment I knew I was Damned. There was no Evil I was not capable of. I was as bad a person as could be. God was after me now. I looked at Sandra & she was smiling. I was thinking of De Vinci & of becoming a Scholar. Did he sell his soul too? Verily, Verily, Did he?

SOURCE DOCUMENT #13:

Note to Hyrum Thayne from Sandra Thayne.
Undated; likely Summer 1976.

Hyrum, I'm so proud of you. Seeing you at Church has made me feel light and easy. Thank you for coming. I think these are the last days. I'm so proud of you.

Here is what we need—

Eggs

Spaghetti noodles

Tomato sauce

Breakfast cereal (you pick)

Cottage cheese

Cherry and Lime Jello

Toilet paper (you pick)

Ice Cream (get my kind this time)

Pork and Beans

Hot Dogs

Hyrum's journal, hand-written manuscript.
Written between June and August, 1977.

So weeks passed. I had hoped that after this much time things would have calmed down a bit but it seems that maybe I had gone a little Overboard with the Commie symbols painted on the walls. It was'nt just the Ruski signs I had painted to cover my tracks that had caused the Ruckus. What brung the real trouble was a scribble mark that I had sprayed when I was just starting to use the can & was trying to get a good stream flowing from the little Nozzle on the end. It looked like a G. Sandra had it from good authority that Brother Hamblin a revered old Moabite who was on the High Council had declared that the G meant that Gadianton Robbers had risen again in Moab. Now the Gadianton Robbers were a Wicked band of Mafia-like bandits that had lived in Book of Mormon times. The Book of Mormon relates how this band whose foundation was the Devil had caused nearly the entire Destruction of the Nephites. Now if your not familiar with the Book of Mormon the Nephites were usually the good guys who always tried to follow the Lords commands. The Gadianton Robbers were involved in Secret Combinations. That is Secret Oaths & Covenants of blood & murder set up to get gain & were terrifying in their cruelty & fierce defiance of all that is good. The Book of Mormon tells us that these Combinations were had from the beginning of the world when Cain killed Abel & that these Oaths have been had by every people. In fact here in Moab many of the folk believed that the whole Book of Mormon took place right Here in the Canyonlands area. A few years ago the rumor started that the ghosts of the Gadianton Robbers haunted certain of the hills around the city. It was easy to point out that most of the inactive families in the Church lived nearest to those hills. Even as Ghosts these monsters seemed to have tremendous Power over the lives of good Moabites everywhere.

Well the thought that there were Communists joining up with modern Gadianton Robbers burning the books in the Library had set the Moab Mormons aflame. I had never seen Anything like it before. Some of the wives including Sandra had started the Child Protection Society. As far as I could tell from Sandra the main purpose of the society was to sit & eat Fritos & terrify each other with stories about the Horrors that the Secret Society was waiting to inflict upon their families. Some of the stories she told even made me sleep a little less soundly at night. The bottom line was that I had accidently turned Moab into an ants nest of activity. Everybody was buying Assault rifles ammunition burglar alarms. I pity the Commies that are foolish enough to try and get into one of these folks houses.

Indeed Sandra said the world was not safe and she wanted her own Gun because she did'nt want to carry around a big man Gun and wanted a more Feminine Weapon she could carry in her purse. You are not home all day facing the prospect of Pillage or Murder or RAPE! She burst into tears & so I drove to Millers Supermarket to by a small derringer to protect Sandra from the G I had scribbled on the wall of the Library. At least it would take any suspicion off me I thought & the more I thought about continuing to cover my tracks the more I joined the rumor-mill about the Gadianton Robbers.

Actually I was having kinda a blast cause I have to admit it gave me a Powerful feeling knowing I was pulling some strings that had everyone dancing to pay the fiddler. Sunday a week after my escapade Brother Law came over to do some home teaching. I think that since I had been to Church twice in a row he was thinking he was doing some Good & was as happy as a Toad in a desert pool.

Good to be in your home Brother Thayne. Since you are the Priesthood leader in this home why do'nt you call on someone to give an opening prayer.

Brother Law I'd be honored if you would offer it.

By the time he finished the prayer I thought for sure the 1000 year Millennium would have come & gone. He went on & on & blessed about everybody in the ward & asked for blessings on the gardens he even blessed somebodys car that needed a new Radiator. The best part was when he started to ask the Lord to protect us from the evil & viciousness of the Gadianton Robbers & Communists who were afoot in the world. He asked for Special protection upon our humble trailer & asked that Sandra be protected from their Intentions while I was up on the mountain.

Sandra was teary eyed when he finished.

Brother Law Thank you so much for that lovely prayer. I need all the protection I can get while Hyrums gone. I have'nt slept well a single night since the knowledge Sacrifice at the Library.

Lately that was the new rumor that had started in the Child Protection Society. The book burning was a pagan Sacrifice of books. A Mormon was next.

Brother Thayne I do'nt think I need to remind you of the Dark Times that we are living in. The Gadianton Robbers & Environmentalists taking good jobs away from hard working folk & the people who control the TV channels down here refusing to carry General Conference from Salt Lake all go to show that we are living in the Last Days. Well Brother Thayne the massage we bring to you today is that this is all a part of a vast Scheme being brought about by the Humanist movement. Their most Diabolical teaching is that of Organic Evolution. The English say it right Evil Ution. That is the Root of the problem in our society. If people think that they are animals they start acting like animals & down & down till we ain't got nothing left but another Sodom & Gomorrah or another Pravda reading Kremlin.

Well he droned on for about another half hour about how Evolution had caused the rise of Communism & was basically responsible for All the worlds Evils. I was only sort of listening but I was able to nod at all the right places & strike a deeply concerned look on my face when it was fitting but the Truth of the matter was I just wanted a sandwich. Finally he finished & I had Sandra give the closing prayer. She at least would'nt pray till dawn. We walked them to the door & suddenly Brother Law stopped & looked me in the eye. He took a strange stance & then pointing at me said very sternly.

Brother Thayne I perceive that you will yet play a great Role in freeing us from the terror that has gripped this city. Yea I perceive that you & your Righteousness alone can save this city from this horror. He paused & looked at me & then looked down. I felt inspired to say that I cant say why. Good night Brother Thayne.

He hurried away in sort of an embarrassed way as if he had said something he could'nt help but was'nt sure what it all Meant.

Sandra was staring at me like a Cheerleader at a quarter back.

Hyrum! Did you hear that! You are the one that is going to Save this town. Oh Hyrum! She snuggled up to me & started to rub my chest.

The Lord was after me. Of course I was the only one that could free this town but why did he have to reveal it to Brother Law. Especially in front of Sandra. I had to act fast. I knew Brother Law would'nt say anything about this since it would Offend his sense of order in the Universe that I really could make a difference in the Crisis. After all I had just barely gotten Active in the Church. He would translate his own words to mean I would play a small part in a small way.

He knew the Lord could'nt have meant that I would play a Major Role. But Sandra? By midday tomorrow if there was any women in the Moab Stake that had'nt heard the Prophecy it would be because they had most likely died the night before. I had to act fast.

Sandra. I pushed her away & took on my most Mysterious voice.

I know what was meant by the words spoken tonight.

I paused to let the full weight of the statement sink in. She stared in wonder into my eyes. I suddenly wanted to kiss her but I Restrained myself.

But to act no one must know what was said tonight or my life is in Jeopardy.

Not even my mother! If you breathe a word & it must not even be spoken between us in this house again my life is forfeit.

I should'nt have added the next part but I had waxed too melodramatic like one of Mr. Bs plays from high school to exercise any Sensible control.

And Moab as a city will be swept of the Map.

Sandra started to bawl. I tried to comfort her but she was just rocking & hugging me & crying like a Newborn. I led her to the bedroom & even though it was'nt Saturday night Sandra allowed me to do the Husbandly thing.

Typed note from Sandra Thayne to Child Protection Society members. Undated; likely Fall 1976.

Dear Sisters,

Please remember to bring something to share. We are planning for about 20 Sisters at our next meeting of the Child Protection Society. Sister Sorenson will be leading a discussion on the book Prophecy, Key to the Future, by Duane S. Crowther. This will be an important meeting for those concerned about the end of times.

Your Dearest Sister,
Sandra Thayne

SOURCE DOCUMENT #15:

Single page fragment of a letter from Dora Daphne Tanner to an unknown correspondent. Undated; likely Fall 1976.

...the way the rays burned all the way to the bones. I was a sun brown girl then. Wild and willful, I would ditch school to play joyously among the ancient river alluvium frozen in stone and piled high from what must have been a Triassic, Mississippi-like delta—storing sand and debris years upon years in heaps so high and wide and deep that it would make a Canyonlands-worth of rock upon which nature could sculpt her desert landscapes. And mold for me—a fitting playground for my imagination.

You implied that we move through time. That our minds are moving from the past to the future. I think not. Have you ever noticed how no matter where you go, no matter when you are experiencing something, there you are? As if we are the one constant thing in all changes—whether spatial or temporal. There is a large cottage-sized boulder jutting out of the muddy Colorado just upriver from Moose Park on Highway 128. It might have been sloughed from the surrounding cliffs many thousands of years ago. Or maybe just fifty years ago (I've seen an old black and white photograph that shows the boulder was at least there by the 30s). A deep red-rust desert patina stains and shines on the rock's skyward facing flat side, showing which surface of the boulder once weathered in the open air when it was a share of this ancient canyon's walls. There it sits, while the water swirls by on both sides, forcing the unquestioning river to divide to either side. I think my awareness—my self—my consciousness—my what ever I am-ish-ness, is like that. I sit still, an anchored thing, as temporal changes roll past. From one perspective it looks like I am moving while the river remains still, but in truth I think that it is time itself that moves rushing past me, dividing to flow around me. Like the water and the rock, events glide past (maybe this is what Heraclitus meant?). That is why I cannot get away from myself and that travel and time never seem to provide the escape I'd hope for. You asked me why I seem...

SOURCE DOCUMENT #2, PART G:

Hyrum's journal, hand-written manuscript.
Written between June and August, 1977.

More weeks had passed & things in Moab had gotten out of control. To top it off I had made a new friend that was demanding more time. It was nice to have a new friend. However it was getting me a little Topsy Tervy with all these things going on at once. The Gadianton Robber story was spreading instead of dying down so it was good to be on the Mountain again with Adam. The cool air mixed with the fall smells & colors seemed to bring back a sense of who I was. I felt real again. Things had gotten too Haywire back down in Moab. Sandra was crying when I left and sure I was going on a secret mission to save the town. But up here every thing was real. There were rocks that were the same every time you passed. Roads that always led to the same isolated places on the Mountain. Air that you could breathe & Wind that you could feel chill you down to what was substance & bone. It let you know that there was something to you more then what everybody made you feel when you were trying to be what ever it was that they thought you were. Thats hard work. Here I could be myself Hyrum Thayne the Scholar.

Adam seemed a bit preoccupied that day. He was'nt being unfriendly but he did'nt seem to want to talk much. He was driving the truck much slower than usual & had his head about half way out the window looking this way & that. I gave up Worrying about him. It was time to start Thinking about my next Scholarly endeavor. I had a collection of words that I had gathered from Adam & from among them I felt pretty sure that there was something that would set me to the next stage of Intellectual accoutrement.

Ah Ha! I knew it! I knew it! Adam hit the brakes so hard it almost knocked me to the floor. The gray dust from the sudden stop had gathered thick about the truck & I was coughing & waving my hands trying to clear the air. When I finally got my Bearings I noticed that Adam had jumped out of the truck & was dancing up & down & running along the road cut we were passing through Yelling & Yahooing.

Look Hyrum Look at this! This is an Outcropping of Early Cretaceous Mancos Shale! I knew we could find some if we kept our eyes open. He was settling down & was squatting down looking more closely at the light colored band that crossed the road cut like frosting in a layer cake. You know this stuff is Fossiliferous & we should be able to find some Gryphaea. With that he stared digging around in the broken talus that lay in shattered pieces all the way up to the shoulder of the road. This was forced up during the last phase of the Laramide Orogeny. If we can find some shells we should be able to get a look at something that has'nt seen the light of day for over 85 million years. Sort of makes you Think does'nt it. This is the kind of Scientific talk that Adam did all the time. I started feeling like a true Scholar listening to him talk about these things. Orogenys Outcroppings Fossiliferous things & Grayphaea were some of Adams favorite things & I must say that I learned out to say these things like a pro. Half of being a Scholar is learning out to sound like one and just last Saturday I said to a friend of mine Laramide Orogeny and he was mighty impressed.

Adam pulled his Rock Hammer out from behind the

front seat of the pickup & walked over & started hammering out pieces from the strip in the roadcut. This was all fine & good but I was getting a little Antsy.

Adam this is nice & all but we've got to be up to Gold Basin in about an hour & well you've been driving pretty slow and

Oh right right sorry about that Hey on the way back to camp would you mind if maybe we stopped here for an hour or so I mean I know dinner will be Cold but we could radio and

Yeah sure. I just wanted to get going. Something he said though had set me to Thinking. If the earth was only 6000 years old then what was this the most spiritual guy I ever met talking about 85 Million year old Creatures. My Curiosity was raising itself up like a newborn lamb ready to her first suckle. And I was about that Shaky.

Adam?

Yeah. He still seemed to a bit Preoccupied but he turned toward me & raised his eyebrows. The signal he was listening.

I had to phrase this carefully. If Scholars were suppose to know how the evolution of Charles Darwin & the great age of the earth fit into the Gospel I was'nt quite ready to admit I was not the Scholar he thought I was.

How do you think Noahs ark held all those animals? I mean seems like it would have been mighty Full. I mean it seems to me that it would have been a hassle dropping off all the Kangaroos & stuff off at Australia & then floating over to Africa and

Local flood.

I stared at him for a second or two.

Local flood?

Sure. Look as you've pointed out the Ark would not have held all those animals. Not even a fraction. Besides there would have been some sign of a big flood like that. There just is'nt any there. Adam started slowing to an Annoying crawl & stuck his head out of the window as we came up on another road cut.

Adam we had really better get moving! We've got alot in front of us to cover & not alot of time left.

Oh. Right. Anyway Local flood I think pretty well explains it.

He still was'nt much in a talking mood & the way he said pretty well explains it meant That is all I want to explain it. Now he had given me something to Think about. Here was Mr. Lets Pray together every night saying he did'nt believe in Noahs Ark. Now its not that I was that firm on the idea of a flood covering up the whole earth & every animal in the world loaded up in a boat the size of a football field. But dang it it was part of Mormonism. Part of the Gospel. Part of everything I'd been taught since I was no larger than a barrel cactus. I did'nt care how much he was'nt inclined to talk he had some explaining to do. If this was'nt true than what else was'nt true. Maybe some of what my new friend was talking about had some sense about it. He was always saying that what the Mormons believed was silly & full of Mythology. But I could not argue because he was college educated & even though it was literature or something he knew lots about Science too.

Say Adam. You'll never guess what my home teacher gave me a lesson on last night. He was still staring hard at road cuts with his head half way out of the Truck like a farm dog on the way to a picnic.

mmmmm He sort of looked at me quickly poked out for one more quick look & then turned his face toward me. Whats that Hyrum?

He sounded like he had resigned himself that no matter what kind of Geologic wonders were out there he was going to have to talk to me.

Well he said that the greatest Evil in the world was the Theory of Evolution. I looked him in the eyes & smiled. I was getting good at being a Scholar. I knew that by smiling I could not go far from wrong. If Evolution was the greatest Evil on the face of the earth then Adam would know that my smile was to commend my home teacher on the great Truth he had shared with me. On the other hand if Evolution was something he believed in he would interpret my smile as that all knowing condescending smile that the initiated share with one another when they speak about the Truths Only They Know. Either way I was safe. Suddenly in the brief second as I spoke the words a Satisfaction settled over me at having thought of such a Brilliant way to approach the subject. The fruits of Scholarship were beginning to pay off.

He smiled at me & shook his head. Clearly I was one of the initiated.

Hyrum what are we going to do with these people that continue to put such a literal interpretation on the Scriptures? You know sometimes I let statements like that run off my back but sometimes it really frustrates me. You know of course that James Talmage believed in Evolution?

Really! I should'nt have acted so surprised. I expect that they taught all this stuff up at the BYU but for us in Moab hearing that one of the finest Apostles believed in Evolution was like hearing that Abe Lincoln was a member of the KKK.

Oh yeah. In fact all of the anti-evolutionary fervor came about because church leaders BH Roberts & Joseph F. Smith an Apostle who traced his descent from the Joseph Smith both wrote books. Elder Smith was extremely anti-evolutionary & Roberts was pro. Well Elder Roberts died & Joseph F. Smith got his published. Thats where this whole Debate got started & it appears that the whole thing is'nt over yet.

I was surprised. James Talmage had written <u>Jesus the Christ</u> one of the most holy Books on the life of the Savior ever written & here I was being told that he believed in Evolution. We drove a while in silence & I was tying to fit all this into my head. For a moment I forgot I was a Scholar & started asking a bunch of questions that any Scholar worth his weight in books would have known immediately. I forgot that I was one of the Learned & my curiosity got the better of me & I started delving into this faster than the water fell from the Power Dam.

So do you believe in Adam & the Garden of Eden & all the other stuff about talking snakes? I mean surely there was Adam & Eve being the first man & women & all. Everybody knows that. Right? But then of course what were the cave men & all those bones & all & the Dinosaurs & also what about all those Stories that are even in the Peril of Great Price about Adam getting Baptized? And about blessing his Posterity & all of that. You just cant throw those stories out can you? But then what about the Fossils I mean the hills are loaded with them & it seems that Noahs Ark never could explain all the bones but then what about Adam being

Adam stopped me with a laugh. I knew suddenly that my cover had been blown. I had asked some very Unscholarly things. Even though I was trying to be a Scholar all the sudden I needed to really know something. It is hard to explain but you go through life with a set of things that sort of form a bed for all the other things your head is full of to rest on. Stuff like when you get up in the morning the sun is going to be there shining down on you. That the cliffs that surround Moab were going to be red & not pea-green like the grass growing between the bricks that run the path up to your trailer. Some things get real comfy cozy in your head & you expect them to be there so much that you forget they are there. In fact they are pretty much Invisible. Its just not things that you can see & touch like the sun & the color of cliffs. Some things are apart of you that you can never see until all of the sudden something comes & wants to rearrange the whole shebang. It is like one time when I was going over to our neighbors to deliver a package that the postman had left at our place. I'd walked over there a 100 times. Knew the way like I know my own trailer. It was pitch black & the desert stars were shining in a jet black sky sparkling because they did'nt have to compete with the moon or lights from a city. All of the sudden I was falling into a hole 6 feet by 6 feet by 6 feet. It seems that the road crew had been there during the day & just left a big Hole there for some Stroller to fall into. I was alright besides being perturbed enough to throw all their equipment stacked around the area into the Hole but I thought how strange I felt when I was falling down into space. It was outside of what I'd come to expect walking in my neighborhood. It was like this Evolution business. Adam had just dug a big Hole in my homey way of looking at the way the Universe worked & I had some rearranging to do it seemed. Plus if this was wrong what else was wrong? Since taking the Sacrament unworthy & heaping up on my head Damnation I'd been thinking God had marked me one of his Forsaken. Things were unsettled enough in my life. If I was an Ape it would explain alot.

Of course I believe in Adam. Who was Adam?

The first man.

Right. Now what defines man?

I was going to say the Dictionary but quickly realized that he meant something alot deeper.

Well I suppose I do'nt know.

How are we Different from the animals?

I knew this one. It was taught from the time you were old enough to hold a Hymn Book.

We are the spirit children of God. They just have animal type Spirits. Right?

Good. Now then if Adam was the first man, then what?

He was the first person with a Spirit Child of God in him!

Right. It does'nt matter where his body came from all that matters is where his Spirit came from. Adam lived. I do'nt pretend to know what the Garden of Eden was other than it existed but I do believe that Adam lived. And is the father of Humanity just as Eve is the mother of Humanity. The difference between him & early man is that the spirit that dwelt in those creatures was not of our Spirit Race. Not one of the children of our Father in Heaven.

It was starting to make Sense. My mind was flying all the way up the Mountain to our blasting site as we climbed the mountains of Thought. My friend had told me this stuff but somehow coming from another member of the Church it sounded more possible. And scary.

Then I asked something that was laying on my mind like the weight of a boulder. If this Evolution stuff was true then maybe other things I took little stock in were true too.

So Adam Do you think that there are people on other Planets?

Most assuredly. We read in the <u>Peril of Great Price</u> that the Lord created worlds without number. There might be billions of people on other Earths. Nothing more likely I say.

I stared out the window. These were definitely new Thoughts.

What about UFOs. You know visitors from other Planets? You know that woman & her Colored husband say they was taken aboard one of those flying saucers about 10 years ago. It made the news & I saw a book in the Library about it. You think that is possible?

Adam was silent a while. Then he said I'm skeptical about that. In the Peril of Great Price the Lord says He called the first people on other planets Adam just like the first man here on Earth. I think they probably are people like us. But who knows. I'll believe in UFOs when I see one.

I said Yeah me too. But then I thought about this sort of acquaintance of mine that I met once. But who I only knew a little. It was the great poetess Dora Tanner. A bit ago I had found some of her things on the Mountain & brought them down to her. I stayed on the porch the whole time & I only met her that one time but she impressed me as a Wonderful person. The kind of person you might want to be your sister.

You know theres this lady. I only met her once but she says that she saw One in the desert & it grabbed her up & took her to there ship. What do you think about that?

You mean that crazy poet lady that lives down off Ridge Road? Yeah I heard about her. I think she is just insane. Thats what everyone says anyway. I think shes probably a poor witness. No I think if there is any Visitor from space they'll be alot like us not some bug-eyed monster. They would still be Gods children.

I did'nt know what to say because I felt like I ought to Defend this person I met that day when I was returning her things. I do'nt know her well & have only met her a couple of times in the grocery store with Sandra & lots of other people shopping but she was not Crazy. I was pretty sure about that.

Adam kept talking. My uncle thinks that the UFOs are coming from the center of Earth. He thinks its was hollowed out at Creation & that that is where the 10 Lost Tribes live.

He has some strange quotes from Admiral Byrd you know the Arctic Explorer who says he ran into the people that live there. He swears its true. Once when he was young he hitchhiked up as far North as the Great Slave Lake in Canada to look for it. He got stuck there for several years working for a mining company & never found the entrance to the Hollow Earth but he swears its there.

I do'nt think that what was her name? that Dora Lady is crazy.

Adam was a little surprised because this came out a little harsher than I meant it. I guess I'm just very protective of people who are Misunderstood.

Whos to say? Maybe something happened she cant explain & has made up the story & shes told it so many times she Believes it

I interrupted him.

Whatever it was I think she believes it was Real. Maybe thats the problem with us Scientists. Maybe we do'nt leave any room for things we do'nt understand & cant get our hands on.

I admit I was getting a little more worked up than I had a right to over this person I only met one time but I met her & I could tell she had a good Heart & would not make up stories just to cover up some other thing.

Adam could see I was starting to wear thin so changed the Subject.

Yeah I know what you mean. It is just people believe such strange things. But who knows. There is more to the world that is dreamed of in our Philosophy hey at least so says the bard.

Well I was a little put out all that morning & probably was'nt much good company. To much of this stuff was worrying me. Things improved just before lunch because we had a Surprise visitor. It was another of those strange Coincidences like the ones I've been writing about because who should be driving along the road but that poet we had been talking about that vary morning. I introduced her to Adam. Adam this is Dora Tanner. Dora this is Adam. He was mighty surprised. She said she was taking the long way to Castle Valley where she said she was meeting with some writers from up at the U of U. She pulled away & Adam said. That was Weird! We were just talking about her! I agreed. He wanted to talk more with me but I told him I felt like enjoying the Autumn air a little & I was going to go for a Hike. He was OK with that because he wanted to look a road cut just up from where the Equipment was setup. He said he would keep an eye on the sensing equipment for me & I headed up the mountain on a deer trail. I got back kind of late & Adam had loaded the truck & was getting Worried that I had gotten lost. I told him that in the La Sals I could'nt get lost if I wanted. But it got me Thinking that there was more than one way to get lost than getting lost on the mountain. Every cloud has its silver bullet.

Letter from Dora Daphne Tanner sent to her
sister Lilly Tanner Baldaia. August 11, 1976

I wish my sister were here. Would she agree or approve? Would she rail and lecture? Or would she hug me and hold me like she did long ago when we were young under the house seeking shade from the summer heat and our mother's gin rages and tearful apologies? The air was rich and earthy there and the camel crickets would watch as my sister would sketch and draw them, draw me, draw the beams holding up the floor and me among the beams as if I were necessary to the support and struts of the house. As if I were a part of that crawlspace ecosystem. And there, in those brush strokes, I found that I was necessary. That I had a place. That I completed and adorned that tiny world of cool wood and earthen floor and cricket and cement. Above, my mother and father would blunder and chew on their rages, destroying the ecosystem above us like the cows that crush the flanks of the carefully balanced mountains in which I love to hike now. Like the hulking range steers, they used up resources that pressed down the diversity of expression. Like the white-faced engulfers, they pushed away what rightfully belonged in that home, that "eco." Like the bovine devourers they ate and ate and ate up our meaning and left us depauperate eking out a niche under the house. Flourishing only in the ecotones of the margins.

What would she make of him? I wish I could teleport him there for her inspection. If she met him would she understand what he's done to capture and corrupt my heart and mind but in so doing create a thriving ecosystem in me. In my body. He'd make an interesting study for one of her paintings. How would I describe him to her? He has a subtle innocence about him that seems out of place in today's world—almost a Victorian sensibility laid on some untamable wild-west pioneer independence. He believes in things. He believes in himself. He trusts himself. He sees the world freshly, and in strange and delightful ways. He worries what God is thinking but never pays any attention to it. He loves his wife in kind and goodhearted ways, but feels no hesitation about our relationship. He's like a primitive who accepts the magic of the world, yet is drawn to bigger ideas. He reads voraciously. Can saddle a horse. Handle a four-wheel drive with adroit red-neck expertise. Would she believe that we drove up to Grand Junction to buy a modified machine gun for his wife? He changes me. He creates a new landscape incorporating but not deigning the old like the radiation of ancient fishes who first wandered onto the land, he is forming new niches, new growth, and new patterns of growth. How strange and different I've become. Me. Helping buy a machine gun.

What am I with him? I cannot guess how this list will add to my own damaged and thwarted ecosystem: I find him full of the rich kindness and conciliation that stands in sharp contrast Jed's *<Redactor: Unknown reference>* arrogance. Hyrum is affectionate, passionate, caring, independent, brave, lovely, cunning, honest, blind, confused, visionary, thoughtful, ardent, worried, gentle, god-fearing, genteel, bright, ignorant, shrewd, Mormon, handsome, puppyish, deceptive, thankful, fresh, naive, pagan, scholarly. He genuinely seems to love others and care what they feel. He is a deceiving bastard, though. It should matter. I know. I know. But… I'll let those dots linger on and on.

He says he believes me. He believes I was taken. My sister thinks me mad on some level. And I don't know if he really does, if his belief is real but it comforts and settles me. Sometimes I wonder… I cannot tell. But it is nice to hear, nevertheless I sense that he is confused, and if anything, I think he wants to believe me. He tries really, really hard to find the truth in my eyes. He looks at them long and deeply and in these searchings I think part of him is trying to puzzle out not only me, but himself, and his own mad projects. His latest is a "study" on bumblebees and I could not tell her about that; it would diminish him in her eyes and I can't do it the justice it deserves. In some ways it is a fool's errand. Maybe crazy ignorant, yet there is something blazingly quixotic but noble about it. A worthy charge at magnificent daunting windmills. Yet, in the wrong light, his attempts would cast him, as, perhaps, someone who has ignored the enlightenment and all modernity—a hickish throwback to more superstitious and naively believing eras. Could I tell him I'm a Wiccan? That I have mostly agnostic leanings? He may think I'm a "Jack Mormon," a Mormon of some kind on the outs with the Church. We don't talk about religion much, although it seems to haunt our conversation beneath the surface of things in telling ways. The proverbial elephant in the room. Still I find him with depths that Emerson would have appreciated and wandered among gladly.

The dreams? Do I tell her about those? They are still there. The light Hyrum brings into my life cannot swamp that darkness. But he does mask it. At least in part. He covers it and blankets it in distractions. Good things then can bubble up which disclose the more beautiful nature of the world. Those things that I know are there, but have had so much trouble bringing to the surface. It is not a healing. Not exactly. It does not erase, or patch, or mend, but right now it is enough, or at least it will have to do. But the planting he has provided may be the beginnings of a rich and stable and flourishing biome.

Can I tell her about Hyrum? Soon. But I will point out to her my poem "The Gift" on p. 32 of my book. I will tell her that Yes, it's about the desert landscape she did hanging in my living room. She must know I mean every word.

SOURCE DOCUMENT #17:

Letter from William Babcock to Redactor. May 5, 1998.

Dear <Redactor>,

Something rather strange has happened that we thought you should know about. Edward is frantically working on a sermon, but agrees that you should be brought into this strange affair. Where should I begin? (Edward just glanced over and said, "You know damn well where to begin!" and so it is!)

The Museum Moderner Kunst here in Wien is currently hosting an exhibition called (in translation), *Through a Glass Darkly: Visions of the Fantastic.* The exhibition features works by such artists as Ernst Fuchs, Rudof Hausner, Wolfgang Hutter and Anton Lehmden and other members of the Wien Club. But it also contains non-Austrian painters such as Vladimir Kush, Marcela Donoso, Gorge Tooker, and others painting in the magical realism vein. Edward is a patron of the museum and the art director, Ms. Streicher, and her husband, are members of Edward's congregation and often invite us to private showings, given how awkward it is to visit the museum when it is packed with jostling tourists who seem to think that we are an abstract representational piece. In fact, you will not be surprised to learn that once there was a complaint that we were ruining a patron's ability to enjoy the art, given our inherent gift to serve as a distraction. Another time we were asked by an employee to go beg elsewhere. The poor girl was sacked over it, I'm saddened to report. (Edward is demanding I get to the point.)

We were invited to a preview of this exhibition. There was

a wine and cheese tasting—a vulgar combination, I've always believed, as the two types of microorganisms seem to cause such a jagged discordance in the taste buds, although I must admit I could not pass up the *1993 Chateau Margaux* being offered. The director invited us to see some of the pieces that they had decided against showing publicly. She left us alone in one of the basement areas used for storage, accessible only through a clanking service elevator or a ladder. Our hostess left for a moment to see to the needs of her other guests. There, in this isolated oubliette, leaning against a wall, was a strikingly unsettling painting, which caused Edward to pass out cold.

The painting was large, maybe 2 m high and 3 m across. In the foreground stood two large alien figures, backs to the viewer, facing a black metallic platform. Thin and lank, the vertical creatures took up most of the height of the painting. Their heads were large and gourd shaped, stereotypical of the space aliens from popular culture; however, their naked skin was more textured in its rendering, giving them an odd sense of reality and physicality. On the table, half rising from the prone position was a woman screaming—her head thrown back, her hair black and wet, her face contorted in agony. Although her body seemed positioned erotically, orgasmicly, her scream contained no element of ecstasy—torture and panic of such purity were portrayed that we stepped back involuntarily. The creatures' torsos blocked what was being done to the woman, but it was rapacious, and her eyes shouted her hatred, pain and terror in ways few paintings have captured. Every muscle of her body was contracting and her toes were curling with a force that looked like she would clench them into fists. Edward says I'm butchering the description but the power and force of the woman twisting on the table was undeniably violent and disturbing. In contrast, the aliens seemed relaxed. Efficient.

With elbows drawn in as if they were doing the delicate work of a watchmaker, an intricate procedure out of sight, just in front of them. There was a focus about their inferred gaze, their heads and bodies turned slightly to attend the same hidden object of concern. And yet this focus did not seem to translate into intensity or hurry. The artist had captured a strange detachment in the aliens who seemed, even from the back, unconcerned about the screaming woman. The grey room is bare and stark, with oddly luminescent walls glowing softly as though they were made of a pale iridescent plastic. The table on which the woman lies is strange and otherworldly, ovoid in shape and supported by a tripod-like device just discernible between the two phantasms. A strange series of symbols is repeated along the edge of the table. I would send you a picture, but – I'll come back to that in a moment. On the wall depicted in this painting, slightly above and to the left of the table where these dark horrors are taking place, is rendered an ordinary painting, set in a rustic wooden frame of pine or apple. Oddly discordant in this extraterrestrial operating room—given the cold sterility of its surroundings—and reminiscent of something Picabia or Magritte might do.

I had just turned to examine this painting within the painting when Edward gasped, then passed out, his head falling limp beside mine. I yelled for help, but we were alone. I found a bottle of water on one of the desks, and gently splashed water on his face. He came-to slowly, and after orienting himself a bit he started screaming, "Did you see the painting! Did you see the painting!" (He says he was not screaming. He was.) I told him yes, and commented on how uncannily it reminded me of Dora's story. "Not that painting!" he yelled. "The painting within the painting!" Marcel took me over and I must admit that I almost fainted as well. The painting depicted a road winding through a mountain copse. The two-track rutted road rounded a corner in the distance. It was arched by stately, pleasant fall aspens with, seemingly, flickering yellow leaves, contrasting nicely the white of the bark of the trees flecked with the deep black scarring common to the milky trunks we know so well from our seasons in the La Sals in Utah. Heading down the road, visible only from the rear, was the back end of an Appaloosa upon which a man rode with two heads. Each adorned with a cowboy hat.

All three of us were shaking when the director returned, Marcel no less than we. Even Ms. Streicher was a little unnerved seeing the painting (she knows much of our past). She seemed apologetic, as if she thought we would imagine she had played a part in some sort of joke done in very poor taste. The artist was a living Russian painter named Pyotr Sergeyevich Shmelev. There were several of his paintings in this exhibit. She immediately sent him an email asking him when it was painted and about the story behind it. She also sent him a photo of the painting. Three days later, we received this from the painter:

Liebe Frau Streicher,

I regret but my English language is awful, but my Deutch is most wretched more. I regret to inform you have found some underwater rocks as a painting has not made by me. In my life I never saw that painting before. However as a fake not bad. It seems which on what, that I probably could have made. Style it is mine and colors. Strange is. I hope, that you inform me if you find artist. They deserve the name only below mine. He perhaps is called superb imitator.

With best regards,
Pyotr Sergeyevich

Now the director was horrified on several levels. The painting is considered very valuable, and a firestorm broke out on its authenticity with the owners (a couple from Singapore) who bought it on Maui in 1992. The director received permission to do a chemical analysis using mass spectrometry and stable isotopes at the University of Wien (which tests will likely mean more to you than it does to us) on all of the Shmelev paintings. The report came today. All of the paintings used linseed oil with an isotopic signature (don't you sound scientific, Edward just said sarcastically) common to an Obninsk paint company operating up until the collapse of the Soviet Union circa 1981-1990. Except our mystery painting. The paints from this strange work do not match any of the paints in the database. The date of the painting is likely of the same period, however. Ms. Streicher believes this implies an Indian or Chinese origin, because the database is less complete in those areas. (Edward just joked, "Or a paint from a distant galaxy." He is not very funny today.) I believe she suspects the owners themselves. I don't believe it. It must be someone familiar with, at the very least, Dora's story, and some knowledge of our presence in Moab during the same time period. I would send you a picture but there are some rumblings of lawsuits and with lawyers involved, we have been forbidden to photograph it. I apologize for the lengthy description, but I wanted to you to sense how deeply strange this painting is and how it has affected us.

What do you think of this? How widespread was Ms. Tanner's story? Was it ever published anywhere? She was quite a well-known poet, apparently. Your ideas would be most welcome. Or, as they might say at the bunk house, "Hell, even a goddamn tall-tale would do."

I hope you are well. We are feeling a little strange these days.

With deepest regards,
William Babcock.

I got home to Moab Friday night & things had gotten down right Crazy like someone had put Black Cat firecrackers in a red anthill. When I got home Sandra was meeting with the whole Relief Society Presidency from our Ward. When I walked in there was awe in their eyes & I knew Sandra had not been too good at keeping secret the role I was to play in freeing the town from the Gadianton Robber inculcated Communists. They quickly got up to go but they all looked at me with a kind of solemn Wonder.

You did'nt tell them did you? I asked.

Sandra burst into tears & said she could'nt help it. They were so worried & upset & did'nt see any hope of defeating Enemies that were so aligned with Satan. I had to tell them there was Hope. I had to let them know that there was a Righteous man who would lead us into escape from these horrible things. I did'nt tell them no specifics. I just gave them hints & Hope.

I always get rather undone when a woman cries & Sandra was blubbering like a baby so I put my arms around her & gave her some Comfort. But I myself was mighty Uncomfortable. I knew that if those bag O winds knew what the home teacher had said then it was bound to be all over the Stake in a matter of minutes. It was bad enough that everyone was so worked up but the last thing I wanted to do was to lead the charge against ghosts & Communists. Especially when they had been more or less Conjured up by me & my can of spray paint.

The next few days were not good. Sandra was always either on the phone or heading off to have planning meetings with the Child Protection Society where apparently she was starting to play a leading role. As far as I could see they had alot of meetings but really had'nt moved into any real sort of Plan. But they were starting neighborhood watches & such. Which mostly meant what it used to with everyone watching everyone elses Business.

Saturday Sandra insisted we get a better gun. The derringer I bought her was not going to cut it for a full blown Communist Gadianton Robber attack. I had hunting rifles a .22 rabbit gun & a .306 & a 30-30. I also had 4 shotguns from a 410 over-under to a 12 gauge. I had my dads old Winchester 264. I had several pistols there at the house & I kept a .22 pistol in the truck for emergencies but Sandra said Sister Flecks husband had gotten her an AR-15 modified to be fully Automatic & she said if I Loved her I would do the same. Brother Fleck knew where to get the conversion kit to make it an M16. So I drove to Grand Junction with an old & dear friend that I knew since High School to get the gun. There was not an AR-15 to be had in Moab. We went up the river road to get there. It was a beautiful drive. My friend made me stop several times just to Breathe in the air & to explore some isolated side canyons a bit. We did not get back until pretty late but Sandra was'nt mad cause I went for her. She was very happy with the gun.

Sunday after Church Sandra had headed up to another meeting. Apparently the Relief Society was having a Fireside that night & Sandra was the main speaker as one of the founding mothers of the C.P.S. The trailer was quiet. My friend had come over for a brief visit but he had to go to a reading at the local book & coffee shop so I was alone. I pulled out the Dictionary from under the couch. At least I did not have to worry about Sandra cleaning under the sofa so the book was as safe there as it would be in Fort Knox. I was struck with how big it was. It seemed so much larger & heavy here in the trailer. So out of place & well it seemed kind of Holy. Like a book from a great Church or from one of those Synagogues they talked about on the show about rabbis that changed me into a Scholar. The large gold Websters on the front seemed to be a stamp of Greatness. And the power & majesty of the word Unabridged seemed to carry something kingly & royal about it. I sat it in my lap & opened it at random. Among familiar words were words of Mystery & learning. I felt like when I was a kid at Christmas looking at the presents under the tree before my Grandfather would pass them out one at a time. I knew the presents that were mine because we had fondled them in secret hours before. I would handle them & wonder what they had inside. That was the moment of the greatest joy that little pause between knowing I had a present & opening it. I was ever impatient for my grandfather to pass me these gifts. And I had'nt felt that magic for many years. Not since I was a little tyke. But here sitting alone in the trailer sitting here with a great Dictionary on my lap I felt it again. I felt all the wonder that life can gift you. I found without even Knowing I was doing it a big smile was on my face. A grin as wide as my face would stretch. I did'nt know it was happening until I sort of looked down at my feelings & found myself smiling like a child. It was then that I remembered my grandfather & the presents. Being a Scholar was the Greatest thing I'd ever done. I could tell that.

I pulled out my notebook that had the words I'd taken down with Adam but was sad I could not find but a few of them. I think the problem was that I Spelled them after he said them but I was never sure both that I heard them right or that I wrote them down right. So in my notebook it said Xestentule. But there in the Dictionary there was'nt anything close. My soaring spirits were soon sort of slipping away as I was not doing much better than with my TV guide Dictionary. Soon I was staring out the window watching a dog sniff around our neighbors trailer. Alas I thought. Woe is me.

I was flipping through the Dictionary when suddenly I came across the word: Incandescence which said "Glow with heat." Then it hit me I was going about this all wrong! I should'nt try to find the words that Adam was flapping about. I should first find the words & then use them ON Adam. My spirits Soared again as I started finding words that I could use later. My heart was Incandescent with erudition. I would be a Scholar yet.

That evening we had Sacrament meeting & it was especially bad. Church is bad enough. First you are suppose to go for an hour & a half in the morning to priesthood. Then you go to an hour of Sunday School. Then later that day just when you are feeling like a nap you have to go to Sacrament Meeting. Its torture of a kind that would have made the dungeon masters of the Dark Ages proud. To make matters worse after Church Brother Law pulled me into the cultural hall. They had turned out all the lights to keep the teenagers from running around under the basketball hoops so it made me feel like a couple of Spies speaking salacious secrets in a secret Clandestine subterfuge.

Brother Law says Brother Thayne how goes the Work. Good Good. Brother Law. Making Good Progress.

Can you tell me what you've found?

I cannot.

Are we in Danger?

Now here I let the moment get the better of me. There is something about being in the Know when everyone else is'nt that makes you say things that are calculated to make you just a little better in the grand Scheme of things & I fear I let my weakness get the better of me.

Brother we are in Danger. I would say that maybe all of this area as far south as Monticello & maybe even Blanding are in Dangers deep & Dark.

Brother Law took a step back like he'd been pushed. What can we do? Hyrum what can we Do?

I put my hand on his shoulder & said fear not but be believing for the Lords arm will be revealed by & by. All is not lost even though I go like a lamb to the slaughter I am calm as a summer morning.

Brother Law looked at me in wonder cause I was using the words that Joseph Smith himself had used on his way to the martyrdom.

Hyrum I've built a bomb shelter just in case things go bad & I want you to know that you & Sandra are Welcome there if things go badly. My food storage is your food storage.

Blessings await you Brother Law. Blessings await you. Hopefully it will not come to that.

He nodded very Solemnly & put his hand on my shoulder & walked out of the cultural hall & left me in the dark. The prelude music was starting in the chapel for the next Wards Sacrament meeting & it sounded sad & lonely to me. I walked through the dark to the stage & sat down to Think. How did things get this Complicated? I did'nt mean to start telling stories to Brother Law. But now he Sandra & half the

Ward were running round scared & worried all cause I needed to look up some things in a Dictionary that I could'nt use & had to steal. Now not only was the Dictionary not as useful as I hoped but it was causing a Ruckus that was way beyond anything I could handle. Also I was worried about this friend of mine who was demanding more & more time. I knew I was damned but do'nt even the damned deserve some peace & Consideration?

Even the mountain did not seem to be a Place I could escape to these days. So I sat there in the dark on the stage in the cultural hall feeling plenty Sorry for myself. Such was the cost of being erudite & Scholarly I figure. Did Leonardo Di Vinci have these kinds of problems? One book at the Library says he was a homo. I do'nt believe it. I suppose they think that because he liked to draw naked men standing in circles with arms stretched out. But I think that he drew naked men because he was too embarrassed to draw naked women. Like I would feel mighty strange drawing a naked lady but I never had a moment of trouble standing around in the locker room in high school with a bunch of naked guys. So I figure people that say he was a homo just do'nt know what its like to be a guy playing sports. But all the same he had Trouble. He had to dig up bodies so he could peer inside their skins to get the muscles right in his Drawings. And so he snuck around at night with his shovel over his shoulder no doubt causing the neighbor ladies of his times Child Protection Society or whatever they called it then to wag their tongues in Undulations of cacophony.

I knew Sandra would be looking for me to go home & have some dinner & watch the Wonderful World of Disney as was our tradition on Sunday nights after Church. But I could'nt bring myself to Budge. I was quite surprised to find that my face was covered with wet tears. I did'nt even know I was bawling like a baby cutting teeth. It is funny how surprising some things can be like discovering you are crying when you did'nt even know it. Tomorrow I would be up on the mountain but right now I just wanted things to be back to Normal. I would have been glad even to be working with The Bob if things could go back to the way they were.

Note and poem from Sandra Thayne. March 31, 1977.

Dearest Hyrum,

Could you pick me some wild flowers up on the mountain like you used to do? It's been awhile and I think such beauty in the world is important in these dark times. I think Satan hates the beauties of this world which our Heavenly Father hath made. I know I have not been home as much since becoming the president of the C. P. S. but my thoughts are ever on you. I took time to compose this for you while Sister Clemens talked on the Second Coming of Jesus Christ during Sunday School this day. I wish you would have come, but I was glad you came to Sacrament:

He'll come again,
To on Earth reign
And set the world to right.
Before He does to us appear,
To save his children all quite dear,
He'll fill the world with heavenly light.
But first a darkness will descend,
And all the world it shall upend,
And give us all some fright,
But you my wonderful husband dear,
Will drive away the awful fear
That holds us all so tight.
Destroy the Robbers everyone,
And set the Communists to run,

And make the world a better sight.

It's not very good, but just a humble offering of my thought and esteem for all you are doing to save us from the evils that are upon us. You are my shining knight. My handsome prince. My everything there is. Thank you for being the righteous man I know you are.

With deep love and wet kisses,
Sandra

SOURCE DOCUMENT #19:

Letter from William Babcock to Redactor. May 20, 1998.

Dear <Redactor>,

Thank you for your letter of concern. It is always good to hear from you. You brought a little of the bright Utah sun into the gray Wien drizzle.

We did indeed find that work of art surprisingly disturbing. Your expressions of support were most welcome. I still find myself waking up at night thinking about the painting. Edward and I have visited it twice since we last wrote to you. There are some details that add to the mystery. The horse is clearly Starry. We have an old Polaroid of us astride our own "Wonder Horse." There was a pattern of black spots on our beloved Appaloosa's backside that resembles, quite strikingly in fact, the Hebrew character, aleph. We never noticed this before in all our years with Starry, but the clarity of the marking on the painting encouraged us to look at our old photos and sure enough, the marking was there. Of course, we would not have noticed the marking on the painting, were it not that the Greek letters Alpha and Omega are formed on the other side in perfect clarity on the horse in the painting. We do not have a picture of Starry from that angle, so we don't know if it was present on the real horse, but Edward insists that he would have noticed *that*. He is also deeply offended by the letters' placement on the horse's rear in that manner, much more so than I, as an atheist, am. So the mystery deepens. It is clear that the painter either has a picture of Starry, or has seen him—and he or she remembered something about that horse that we, in all our time with her, never even noticed! Or else the Hebrew character is a strange and unlikely bit of coincidence.

There have been some developments, but nothing that sheds any light on the painting's origin. The director has been valiantly trying to trace the provenance of the strange work. She contacted the gallery in Maui and they were as horrified as the museum to find out that the painting was a fake. Their records indicate that it was procured by one of their buyers in Helsinki with a lot from the Russian painter Kush. The auction house in Finland has no record of the painting whatsoever. However, the buyer for the Maui gallery does have a bill of sale from the Finnish auction house, which clearly lists the painting. They are still trying to sort out what is going on. Lawyers are now fully involved (Edward says there is now no hope that any light will ever be shed on the problem).

I hope this finds you well. When is your next visit to Wien? Are you still planning a stop on your way to Istanbul?

Best wishes,
William

Hyrum's journal, hand-written manuscript.
Written between June and August, 1977.

It seems strange to put into vocabules. But it was Sandra that set me on my path to Science. I was just getting ready to head up to the mountain after a terrible day at Church when she says to me bumble bees cant Fly.

What?

Bumble bees they cant Fly.

What do you mean they cant fly I see them fly all the time.

No Science has proved their wings is too small.

I stared at her like she did'nt know what she is talking about & all the while she wore a renitent grin.

Its cuz they have Faith. Even though their wings are too small. They have Faith they can Fly so they do.

Then verily she handed me a paper with a picture of a cartoon bumblebee on it. It was from the cosmetic distribution company thing that she had joined along with all the women in the C. P. S. Save the world & look good doing it I suppose. But it said Believe! Did you know that scientists have proven that a bumblebees wings are too small to carry her body weight as she flies from flower to flower? But she believes in herself! And no one not even someone as smart as a scientist can tell her otherwise. So next time someone says to you You cant do something. You just remember the Bumblebee and keep right on flying!

I thought on this all the way up the Mountain and kept looking at the picture on that card. I love the mountains in the Fall. The Aspen leaves are every shade of yellow under the sun & the grass which has grown tall if the deer & cows have'nt mowed it too much. Well mostly the Cows. They are everywhere on the mountain & it is hard to walk anywhere without stepping your foot into there leavings. But I love the mountains anyway despite the ever present Cows. The air is good. Cold & full of green scents. Growing & decay got a smell thats as much a part of the Mountain as is the rocks & trees sprouting on her flanks. The air & the colors & the feel of the pickup bouncing up & down & back & forth winding up the dirt road occasionally slipping on a rock jutting into the road all sort of lead one to finer & deeper Thoughts of this & that. I suppose it is the Poetry side of me coming out. I have a friend that is interested in Poetry & has been reading me some. I'm not sure I get it all. But sometimes it carries me away in nice Ways.

We had just passed the turn to Warner Lake when we came up on a patch of late blooming weeds. I asked Adam to stop & we both got out. My legs were stiff & soar & we both stretched & moved about a bit before heading over to the patch. I explained to him about bumblebees not being able to fly. He seemed surprised & expressed a bit of doubt on the matter but was willing to go along with that it might be Possible that it was the case that Science maybe was'nt where it ought to be on bumblebee flight. Sure enough there were Bombus on the flowers. Bombus I should tell you is the scientific name of Bumblebees or Humblebees as they were counted in the olden days. They are truly a Magical animal. They are covered with a diaphanous coating of black fir as fine & soft as a weasels hide. They do seem a bit Big for their wings. They skit from flower to flower making a buzzing that rates up there with a rattler shaking its tail except it is deeper & more Fuzzy sounding. Their legs dangle down with buckets of pollen & their big eyes black & shiny & dare you to find fault with their daily routine. For some Reason I have never ever been afraid of Bombus bees. They always seemed unconcerned with us people so I always let them Be. But my Scholars brain was starting to gear up to something & I says to Adam So Adam if we wanted to do some Science on these bees how would we do it? I mean like Scientists. Not just like a couple of guys watching them.

Well says he I suppose to study them we would have to do some Experiments on them. We'd have to set up a study design. Do the Experiment. Then do some Statistical analysis.

I must have looked worried because he said No no its easy. Why are you thinking of becoming a Scientist?

I owned up to it & he said Lets do it! Why not? We got lots of time. And so it is we became true Scientists.

REDACTOR'S NOTE:

Visit to Adam Pearson—March 5, 1998

Tracking down Adam proved to be a challenge. Hyrum never mentions his companion's last name and the government records from the time mention only "student help." However, the few facts listed in Hyrum's journal gave me some hints on where to search. His father was a geology professor, and by prospecting among some of the retired geology faculty at Brigham Young University, I was able to get the name of a former faculty member who had a son named Adam. I hit gold. Adam Pearson. His father had died about ten years previous. His mother seemed very suspicious of my reasons for wanting to look him up. Finally, my praise of her Hummel collection won her heart, and she provided me with the information I needed.

Adam was a management consultant with a firm in Boston. On my next trip back east, I made a point to stop to see him. He was more than accommodating and invited me to his house for dinner. He is a middle-aged man—athletic, but getting soft around the middle. He had thick, light brown hair, flecked with a bit of grey, and a big friendly smile that seemed to draw you in. His wife was small and pretty, one of those women who smile unwaveringly and bustle about endlessly, but seem uninterested in getting to know you further than she must. I'm not sure Adam told her I was coming to dinner, since she seemed a little taken-aback, but made some quick adaptations gracefully.

He was a faithful Mormon, and the house was graced by eight children aged 17 to one. We retired to his "den," which was a small closet-like affair in the basement. It housed his computer and his precious library. Most of the books seemed of an obscure Mormon variety, with titles like, *The Day of the Lord*, *The Cost of Discipleship*, and *Man: His Origin and Destiny*, but also there was a scattering of biblical commentaries, some popular scholarly books by Harold Bloom, and a number of Jewish books, including commentaries on the Talmud. High on a shelf were a collection of Lexicons, language books, and texts. A couple of well-worn copies of Lowery's translation of Kirkegaard's postscript and *Either/OR* seemed to be placed in easy reach. Lots of C.S. Lewis. On his desk was a picture of his family all in matching sweatshirts, standing in a pleasant copse, smiling broadly, everyone happy and close. Also on the desk was a picture taken while he was a Mormon missionary striking a goofy pose, he and his companion holding up their ties in the air as if they were being hung by them. It all seemed rather poignant. As if this place were a memorial to a life that had been reduced to this corner, carefully preserved, like Tiny-Tim's crutch in Scrooge's vision.

Adam, after marrying young and graduating from BYU, marched off to graduate school at Columbia with a young family of three children, for a Ph.D. in Biblical Studies. Columbia was not kind to Adam. Supporting his family required him to work most of the time. A Mormon apostle at the time, Ezra Benson (a former Secretary of Agriculture in the Eisenhower administration and later Church President), had commanded that women should stay home with their children, that couples should not delay starting large families, and that one should get an education. Adam apparently tried to keep all of these contradictory commandments at the same time, but working full time, his wife stuck in a small New York apartment all day with three small children (and one on the way after his first year there), and full-time graduate studies proved to be too much, so he took his Master's degree and bowed out of the program. While he seemed to indicate that this had been the will of the Lord and that somehow this failure had saved him from falling away from the Church, which seemed the fate, he said, of so many intellectuals and scholars, there was a bitterness and sorrow evident in his heavy face as he related these events. When asked about his current work as a consultant, he appeared uninterested in talking about it.

Like the psychologist in the Utah State Hospital, Adam also had heavy Church responsibilities. He was in a Stake Presidency, which is something like the leader of a diocese, taking care of multiple Mormon congregations. He receives no pay for his work in tending the flock. When the topic of his Church work came up, a grave weariness attended him, and I could tell this was something weighing him down. I would imagine it must be hard to be a pastor and work full time. Shades of his described graduate school experience seemed to be shaping him still.

Adam remembered Hyrum and their bee experiments quite well and spoke about those times with fondness and delight. He told me that Hyrum had an incredible sense of humor and was a clever practical joker. He said he liked to talk and was one of the most curious persons he had ever met. Always asking questions about this or that, trying to sort things out in his mind.

"He had the spirit of a philosopher with a high school dropout's education. It made for an interesting combination. He knew a lot of strange trivia, but seemed oblivious to things usually considered part of a general education," Adam mused.

I asked if I might record him and have my questions and his answers transposed. <I've cleaned up the "ums," "you knows," and pauses and restarts to read a little more smoothly> But these are largely his own words:

Me: "You were there for the bumblebee experiments were you not? What can you tell me about them?"

Adam: "Yes indeed. Hyrum came up with this funny idea that scientists claimed bumblebees could not fly. He became very interested in science and experimentation and I gave him Francis Bacon's book to read which he consumed up on the mountain in about three days."

Me: "He never mentions it in his journal."

Adam: "I'm not surprised; he read a lot. He did love to read. Anyway, he decided that the bumblebee question needed a good scientific experiment. At the time, I had just taken a statistical methods class as part of my general education requirements at BYU, and thought this would be a fun activity for him and me to do since we had lots of time. He was just delighted. I suppose I thought it was all tongue-in-cheek, and did not realize that he thought we were doing real science.

Me: "Tell me about the experiment."

Adam: "Well the experiment was designed to test how much 'Faith' Bumblebees had. I set it up with ten treatments, and with ten replications in each treatment. For each treatment, we would clip off a given percentage of the bumblebee's wing and see if it could still fly. Hyrum thought if they had a lot of faith they could fly without wings and if they had an amount in-between they ought to be able to fly until their 'Faith' ran out."

Me: "Just to clarify from the paper: were both sets of wings on each side cut, or just on one side?"

Adam laughs deeply at this: "Yes. Yes. Both sides. Hyrum

thought it would be unfair to tip them off balance in the experiment. So we cut both sides."

Me: "Did you help him write the paper?"

Adam: "Not exactly. I did the statistical analysis and gave Hyrum some scientific papers so he could see how it was done. I showed him the form with its introduction, method section, results section, and conclusion section. I showed him how to write up the results and do a bibliography, but he did the rest on his own.

Me: "Why not include you as an author?"

Adam: "Oh, I think he just did not understand authorship, multiple authors, and such things. He was just excited to be doing real science. I may have helped him here and there."

Me: "Did you know he was having an affair with Dora Tanner?"

"The Moab poet?" Adam was genuinely shocked at the news. Apparently he knew nothing.

Me: "Did he tell anyone about the paper that you know of?"

Adam: "I can't believe Hyrum would have an affair with anyone! He talked about his wife Sandra all the time. I'm quite shocked."

His wife brought in some homemade chocolate cookies and lemonade at this point, and I was glad for the interruption because Adam was clearly disturbed by the news of Hyrum's affair. The chat over cookies allowed him some distance so we could get back to the interview.

Adam: "As far as I know he kept the paper a secret. I told him about the possibility of being scooped and someone publishing our data. I know he didn't tell Sandra, because he was having trouble in Moab about something to do with communists or something, and Sandra was making a big deal about it and he didn't want her telling her friends about his becoming a scientist. I have no idea about what he told Dora. I still can't believe Hyrum would do such a thing."

Me: "How did he choose the *Newsletter of the Ecological Society of America*?"

Adam: "That was me. The Newsletter just contains letters to the editor sorts of things, news of the society, and sometimes humor. It's not peer-reviewed. Plus my father used to belong to the Ecological Society and was head of the Paleoecology section so it was lying around the house. That's how I knew about it. I thought Hyrum's paper was funny and thought they might enjoy it."

Me: "Were you surprised they published it?"

Adam: "Yes and no. It was funny. But you never know."

Me: "That was your last summer on the mountain?"

Adam: "Yeah. After that summer I went back to school and the next summer I joined my father on his sabbatical leave to Greenland. I never saw Hyrum again."

Me: "And you heard of his death—how?"

Adam: "My mom loved the stories I'd tell about Hyrum, and when the *Deseret News* in Salt Lake carried a story about the explosion that killed him, my mother clipped it and sent it to me in Greenland with a note saying how sorry she was to hear about the accident."

This was the only part of the interview relevant to Hyrum. Adam remembered the Babcock twins from the mountain and was glad to hear they were doing well. He had no details to add, but our conversation turned to Al-Ghazali and Sufi mysticism. He was a delightful conversationalist—as long as we did not stray too closely to his consulting business or his work as a Mormon stake leader.

Letter from William Babcock to Redactor. June 13, 1998.

Dear <Redactor>,

I hope you are well. There is much we would like to discuss with you. Please forgive our indulgence in giving you more of our history. You are kind to assist us with these current oddities.

Our own lives have taken another strange turn. Sunday last, after Edward's sermon on John 19:25-27, where Jesus asks John to care for his mother, Marcel carted us to the train station and parked us in front of the "Departures" table posted in the West Bahnhof. What was especially odd was that neither of us had access to the legs. This is one of the few time this has happened since our birth, and we were both quite concerned. It was clear Marcel wanted us to go somewhere, so Edward ran his finger along the column of departing trains until it rested on Melk, a small city west of us. Marcel gave a small kick, which we interpreted as indicating his interest in that destination. Suddenly, I had access to the legs again. Not knowing what to do, we surrendered to Marcel's hints, and purchased a ticket for Melk. Melk is a lovely little town nestled on a bend of the Danube about 80 km west of Vienna. There is a beautiful monastery high on a hill that maintains a working Gymnasium (in the German sense of the word) and a large library. (In fact, it is rumored that this monastery was the very place that Umberto Eco had in mind for his book, *The Name of the Rose.*) Why Marcel wanted us there we could not begin to guess. But we went.

I fear I must give you a little more of our history for these events to make sense. I've discussed it with Edward, and we have decided to share a few things about which we are normally quite quiet and reticent. I hope you will not mind a bit of our history. But you must understand something about our mother, if the events in Melk are to make any sense, so I hope that you will forgive this indulgence (and its length).

To put it briefly and bluntly, our mother was a member of the French Resistance in Lyon who used sex to seduce a German officer. We are the children of her patriotism. Our conception occurred just prior to the Allied invasion, and our father was captured shortly thereafter. He died by his own hand while in custody of the Americans. Our mother hated and loved our father. She would rarely speak about him without disdain in her voice, and yet occasionally, when she would tell us stories about her days in the Resistance (about which she was remarkably open), she seemed to lapse into an almost storybook tale that would suggest that she took great delight in our father's sense of humor, or his kind attentions to her. For example, in early spring they went on a picnic near the *Lac du Bourget*. She describes a beautiful spring day in May. The stream by which they picnicked was joyfully splashing, filling the air with that delightful sound that only running water can make. They spent the day talking. He gathered wildflowers for her, knitted her hair, and placed the fragrant blossoms carefully in the folds of her braids. He said she looked like a *Märchenprinzessin*. When she told this story her eyes teared up and she would leave the room abruptly. Usually, however, her stories were about the information she extracted from her "very stupid" lover and how that was used to feed the war efforts of the Resistance.

Both Edward and I sensed that she felt our monstrous condition was a reflection of the love and hatred she felt for our father. Somehow, her ambiguous feelings were reflected in her body's creative act. She of course never said this explicitly, but it was clear she blamed herself for our condition. She seemed to feel guilty for not destroying us when she first became aware that she was pregnant. It is hard to say with any certainty, because there were things that she would not talk about, and among those were things that might cause us pain, or disclose doubt about who we were, or our place in the world.

After the war, she met and fell in love with an American linguistics officer. He was a professor at Princeton, and despite our mother's condition (she was seven months along), they married in the US and settled into university life.

We do not know what our adoptive father's reaction was to our existence, but we never had a hint that he was disappointed or disturbed that his wife had given birth to a two-headed sideshow freak. Their marriage was to fall apart eventually (as I'll explain) while we were still quite young, but to us he was the best and most lively father imaginable. We grew to share his delight and talent for languages, and by the age of ten, besides English, we were fluent in Latin, Greek, Hebrew, French, German, and a smattering of Japanese and Sumerian. I'm not sure it was just raw talent, as it seemed to be with our father. Having someone there to practice with every day, all day, also seemed significant. Edward and I have played with language our entire lives. While learning a new language, we could become very focused on the task, spending the day bantering back and forth, challenging each other with new vocabulary, singing songs (with a penchant for the most ribald and dirty drinking songs, which we learned from our father's students), composing and reciting poetry, and such things, so that different languages became the currency of fun and games for us.

Soon after we turned twelve, our mother fell into a deep Sylvia Plath-like depression. She would lie on her bed, smoking unfiltered Camels, and staring at the ceiling. On the phonograph, she would play old French singers, like Édith Piaf. Even then, in what must have taken extraordinary effort, our mother attended to us. If we popped our heads into her room, she would call us over onto the bed. Sometimes we would sing with her some of the old war songs. I still remember lines from my favorite:

> There were three of us this morning,
> I'm the only one left this evening,
> But I must carry on,
> The limes are my prison.
> Oh, the wind, the wind is howling,
> Through the graves the wind is howling,
> Freedom soon will arrive,
> And from the shadows we'll appear.

We knew she was "sad," but it would be years before we would understand depression. Even our father seemed oblivious. It may have been he was having an affair; he was gone most of the time. Once, when we paid him an unannounced visit, we found him laughing lightly with a young woman in a way that seemed reminiscent of his interaction with our mother. The woman seemed embarrassed and rushed out quickly, her sweater buttoned wrongly. Although we were only eleven, we *had* read Ovid, and the possibility that there was more going on here than met the eye occurred to us both.

During this time, perhaps to offer her a change of

scenery (the more charitable reading, rather than getting us out of the way), our father sent our mother to visit her sister in Normandy and we accompanied her there. Although polyglot and cosmopolitan in spirit, we had travelled little outside Princeton, and our furthest journey abroad thus far had been to the Outer Banks in North Carolina. We fell in love with our mother's country; the French countryside was all we had ever dreamed it would be, with its calm and easy fields and gentle copses scattered here and there. Our mother's sister lived in a small village about 40 km from Alençon in the Communes of Orne. Our mother hired a local boy whose father had a pony and cart and put it at our disposal, granting us complete autonomy in choosing where we would go during the day. We had always enjoyed a certain amount of freedom in Princeton, but our limited mobility kept us restricted to the haunts in the neighborhoods around the university (ask us about an oft repeated encounter we had with Einstein and Gödel in which they would inquire about our day and then join us in singing a couple of German nursery rhymes as we walked with them for a block or two). But here! Oh, here we had our cart, our freedom, and all of Normandy at our disposal (or so it seemed). The boy, named Bill (his father was an American serviceman who was killed in the last days of the war), was an amicable and talkative chap who followed our orders like an army private. He acted as combination chauffeur and tour guide. Our only restriction was that, each day, we had to return for dinner that evening by eight. It was our childhood, come at last. We drove far and wide, pretending we were various pirates, elite fighters, and cowboys, with our cart becoming frigate, Sopwith Camel, or stage coach on the line from Oklahoma to Santa Fe. We visited small nearby villages, explored the ruins of forgotten fortifications, and learned to fish for wary trout from many a shady bank. We did whatever popped into our heads and went wherever we wished as long as we reached home by the appointed hour. We were never late, but that may have been more a testament to Bill's mastery (and abuse) in hurrying the pony home than to our meager ability in keeping track of time.

But I'm wandering from our tale. During this time, our mother changed entirely. She became as light-hearted, funny, and joyous as we had ever known her. She laughed often as we would recount out day's exploits over dinner. She asked many questions and seemed interested in everything we did. And most telling of all that she had entered a new place in life was her music. No more mournful nostalgic phonographs, just light and easy unaccompanied singing, which seemed to bubble up from a part of her we had never seen, as if springing from something hidden that we never suspected lay dormant there. She was genuinely and unquestionably happy.

We learned why, later. She had become a witch. A small group of Gerald Gardner's followers whose revival (and reinvention) of witchcraft was in full swing in England, had formed a satellite branch in the little village where our aunt lived. Our mother's sister had joined the group and had encouraged our mother to join them soon after her arrival. Every night in those early weeks, our mother could be found devouring the writings of these novo-witches; the titles intrigued us, and having brought nothing with us but a few books by Cicero at our father's insistence, we read the books just as soon as our mother finished one. While we found them entertaining, and they did provide fodder for some of our adventures in imagination, we were not as drawn to them as was our mother. Perhaps a little of that sense of wonder and mystery that attends such works grabbed us, but having read Apuleius' *Asinus aureus*, our sense of all things witchy had been perhaps somewhat saturated, and we found the works uninformed and derivative (and yes, we each could form such a critique by age 13!). But mother was enthralled. She could not get enough of it. At night they would meet in the small stand of woods near our aunt's farm and dance naked around a blazing fire. Yes— dare I admit it?—we did follow her once and saw them draw the protective circles with a cold small athame and call upon the Goddess for her blessing and protection. We saw them call the quarters and invoke the blessings of the powers of Air, Fire, Water, and Earth. And while the rituals were interesting, I think their nakedness was the main focus of our adolescent curiosity.

That summer, our mother also traveled with our aunt to meet Gerald Gardner, leaving us in the care of my aunt's mother-in-law. (A serious, but not unkind woman, she was very uncomfortable around the poor two-headed child. Or as she called us, "The-pair-of-you," which she used to great effect: "Will the-pair-of-you please come to dinner?"; "Where are the pair-of-you going?"; "The pair-of-you are not going anywhere until you finish the breakfast I've made for you.") After our mother returned, she seemed to blossom into an even more new and complete person. We loved having the new mother. She was more attendant and unassuming than we'd ever known her. I am quite sure that that was the happiest time of all our lives (Edward, reading over my shoulder with a big tear in his eye, just agreed).

But good things are not to last it seems, and I will have to hurry through the rest of this if our experience in Melk is to make any sense. We returned in the late fall to Princeton, one of its most delightful times, when the autumn leaves are swirling through the streets, and it's chilly enough to wake up slumbering bones. But our mother was pregnant, our father angry and embarrassed, and we were sent off to a local boarding school. The rest of the story we got from our aunt.

The child's father was one of the local witches. The baby was aborted in secret in New York. Shortly after, our mother and father divorced. Our mother returned to Princeton to be near us, and began graduate work in anthropology. For her fieldwork, she studied peasants in Portugal, and their use of amulets for protection and to coerce supernatural powers for good. But her heart was devoted to witchcraft and she began a translation of several works from the late middle ages on amulets and sigils tangentially relevant to her work in Portugal. She died suddenly of ovarian cancer in 1959. Our father was devastated and, despite the divorce, cared for her throughout her short illness. He committed suicide shortly thereafter.

Now, at last, I bring you to Melk. Upon our arrival, we went to the gorgeous library at the *Shift Melk*, a working Benedictine abbey. Not knowing what else to do, Edward asked to see some of the letters that had been written by Johannes Trithemius, whose work was tangentially relevant to some research he was doing. While we waited for the book, I got online and was browsing through the catalog of their collection, when I came across this entry:

Notes on PICATRIX, *Peggy Babcock, 1958, Presented at The International Conference on Medieval Magic, Melk Austria, 25-29.10.1955.*

I gasped. Edward, drawn to where I was looking, glanced up. I noticed he was shaking before I became aware that I was trembling as violently. How could Marcel have known this would be here? He has only access to the world through us, and yet we knew nothing of this. Had he filtered something through our conscious mind that we missed? Did he remember something that we passed over and had forgotten in an unremembered conversation with our mother? We were stunned. We immediately asked the attendant librarian for a copy of the paper.

She brought it quickly with the efficiency and aloofness that underlies all Austrian customer service. With trembling anticipation, we poured over the hand-written note. Our mother's cursive was neat and precise and seeing so much of it reminded me of the notes she had placed in our school lunches as a child. Tears were running freely down our faces and we were all shaking as we unrolled the paper (papers of such conferences are stored as scrolls at the monastery). The paper was about the creation of a homunculus, based first upon the preparation of an oracle head, as described in the 11th Century Arabic magic text, *Picatrix*. The *Picatrix* describes the preparation of an oracle head by luring a man into a sealed box, out of which only his head is allowed to protrude. The device is filled with sesame seed oil and the man is fed figs, but given no water. Incense is burned next to the head. After forty days it is ready:

> "Pulling the head out of the body, his veins will be stretched until they all separate from the first vertebra, thereby leaving the body in the oil. Subsequently, they place it on an arch on a layer of screened ashes of olive and surround it with fluffy cotton. They perfume it with a special incense of theirs, and consequently, it tells them about fluctuation of prices, the overthrow of governments, and what takes place in the world. Its eyes will remain open, and it will remind them if they miss any of their worshipping sacraments to the planets, prevent them from doing certain things, and

tell them what will happen to everyone personally. If they ask it about knowledge and art, it will be able to answer their questions."

Our mother then discusses the use of these heads through the Middle Ages, as found in other obscure Arabic works. She follows some of the talisman sigils found in *Picatrix* that wind their way through six hundred years of magic texts.

Our mother then quotes a Latin manuscript from the 16th Century, which supposedly draws on lost Arabic sources, and begins:

"In perfection, is the one, but the three in one is of greater perfection. If one seeks to bring all acts of creation together then, as Al-Ghazali writes, one must bring in the first three levels of the luminous human spirits into the light. Three heads must be brought into existence and then joined. First prepare one head from a thief who is about to be hanged. The second, from a wise man, one who has never known either a woman or a boy. The third, from an infant who has never sucked a woman's breast. See that all three are not blemished nor marred in any way."

Our mother then gives a brief outline of how to join the two adult heads by placing them in the womb of a white mare with the infant. When the mare foals, a homunculus will come forth with the body of a dwarf. One head will have the knowledge of demons and the other the knowledge of angels. The heart of the infant will control them both.

The manuscript continues:

"Then all knowledge of light and darkness will be yours. You will be able to command all beings to your will and all treasures can be found, all secrets revealed. There is nothing you cannot ask that will not be given."

Our mother ends with observations on whom the manuscript was written for, and speculates on the dark clerical underground that practiced such black magic.

Edward and I were undone. The paper was profoundly disturbing. The description seemed oddly reminiscent of our own situation. But what made it worse was in our mother's hand at the bottom she had scrawled, "Am I a mare?"

Here is what else is strange: several of the sigils our mother describes seem reminiscent of those found on the edge of the table in the strange painting that has come into our life.

We did not talk all the way back to Wien.

So what does this mean? We are both distressed and agitated, but do not know what to think or what to do. We thought we would share this strange addendum to the curious story of the painting.

Please make a point of stopping to see us on your next trip to Europe. There is much that we would like to discuss.

As always,
William

Letter from Dora Daphne Tanner to Thayne. November 1976.

Dear Hyrum,

I just watched you drive away. You looked so sure and confident behind the wheel of your truck. I wanted to tell you this while you were here. You deserve to hear what I have to say face-to-face, but written words are the pressed sandstone from which I'm carved (how well you know this) and I cannot say well with rusty voice what fingers may more easily tell. I tried. All through dinner I tried to let it emerge amid your laughter and delight over the bumblebees and the coffee. Over the chickpea humus and tortillas, I almost blurted it out, but your laugh arrested my tongue, and your lovely eyes entangled my own. And your smile. Your smile was so infectious that I found my own mouth mirroring yours, and I could not find a way to lay this before you. Over the rhubarb pie, it almost burst out of me like an explosion, but the whipped cream above your lip made me giggle, and the moment passed. But you must know. So I will write the words. Try them on for size on this paper. I made this parchment from the birch bark we collected near Warner Lake. The ink is from France. I'll let these words pass from there into your mind, and see what comes of it:

Hyrum we have made something new in the universe. The question we must decide is, do we give this thing expression? I say we, but it is I who will decide. Sorry, Hyrum. It is yours too, but it will feed off my life essence, so I will decide, but I need your advice and counsel. You are a wise and valued prophet (even if you can't protect me from the Gadianton Robbers (I'm smiling)). Not every idea that comes into my head deserves or has right to utterance.

You would not be keen on me flitting through words, hiding what I mean in imagery and poetry, I think. So I will speak directly. Hyrum, I'm pregnant. It is yours. It is mine. It is an expression of both our bodies, but it is from mine that it will find purchase on this planet. And so I seek your strength and wisdom to decide if this sprouting seed should become a chapter in the pages of the world, or will end up an idea whose time has not yet come, but you must know that since you have told me time and time again that you will not leave Sandra, I realize that I will be on my own for much longer than the moment that we have come together. I'm being wordy and confused in this "announcement," but I want to get it out and give it to you before I chicken out and do something without your ever knowing. And you deserve better than that. Hyrum, I love you. Please come to me after you get this. I need you.

Your beloved,
Dora

Hyrum's journal, hand-written manuscript.
Written between June and August, 1977.

They were days never to be forgotten those Unforgettable days. Yea, the flowers were blooming gloriously & the bees were about their duty like home teachers on the last day of the month. And there was Adam & I with real clipboards from the Millers Supermarket loaded with graph paper just like real Scientists. We used Mechanical pencils. Not the cheap clear plastic ones either with thick leads where you can see the screw lines winding up the barrel but real expensive ones from Grand Junction with .5 HB leads that break so easy you had to be Careful not to press very hard. The guy at the store said that these kinds of leads were very popular with students & Adam seemed Impressed when I showed him. I paid $6.95 for the pencil & it made me feel good to know that I was not skimping on the Science. The most important bit of equipment Adam bought up at the BYU. Real Science scissors. Little ones. Sharp as a razor & no longer than my thumb. The medal from which they were made was black like the barrel of my Ruger Blackhawk .41 mag. Adam also bought a Probe which was like a real thin medal thing made for pushing down the wings of bugs when you were studying them. Adam had some idea that we had to Replicate everything & assign what he called the Treatments to make this real Science. I took him at his word because his dad is a real scientist but I had to capture more bees than I ever would of guessed we would have needed.

Replicating is what Adam said made the difference between Science & just goofing around. So we Replicated.

The bees were as Easy as toast to capture seeing as how bumblebees or Bombus I mean are big & slow. I had a mayonnaise jar & I could pretty much capture one at will seeing as how many there were flying hither & yon. I'd just spy one on a flower & put the jar over & cap the experimental unit (which is a technical scientific word meaning the Unit on which one will do the Experiment in our case Bombuses). Now the hardest part was wrestling one so that you could hold it without being Stung but we soon enough had this problem licked because if you gave the jar a good shaking & then when the Bombus was stunned you just poured it out onto the tree stump you could just hold it down on the wood between your thumb & fingers. Now our experiment was on this wise. We aimed to figure out how much Faith these bees had. As Sandra had said real Scientists had figured out that if you look at the size of the wings & the size of bumblebees there is no way that they should be able to fly. Its like a helicopter trying to fly with its back tail prop on top & nothing else it wont get into the air. So Scientists speculate that they must fly by the kind of Faith that the Brother of Jared showed in the <u>Book of Mormon</u> when he got the stones to glow for the submarines & give Light while they blew on the wind to America. So we aimed to elucidate & illuminate exactly how much Faith they had by cutting off their wings in incremental increments of increasing size & thereby forcing them to Doubt their ability to fly. So it took both of us. Me holding the Bombus down & Adam holding the wing still with a wing-holding-down Probe & then scissoring off the right amount for the Experiment. This was more work than you would guess from me writing this. The little creatures were mighty wry for all their round clumsiness & about half the time they Squirmed their way to freedom. I have to own up that if they got too loose I would let them go. I got Stung a couple of times & it was enough to warn me that I should not be too Stubborn in letting them go if they were Bound & determine to get away. So after Adam had snipped off a piece of each wing we would see what Happened. Now here is the first bit of Science that we learned & I'll be willing to bet that you do'nt know from looking at them but Bombuses have a total of 4 wings! It is true. Adam did'nt know this either & so we had to adjust our protocols which is a word of power way of saying the rules we were following for our Experiment. After he had clipped the right wings according what we had written down on the clipboard we would watch what Happened. It turns out that Bombuses can have 50% of their wings cut before they start to Doubt they can fly. After that they just sort of buzzed around on the stump like spinning tops zigging this way & that over the top surface of the stump. When you chopped off too much of the wings they just crawled around. They did'nt seem to notice much that their wings were gone because they just skittered about on the ground as if that was Normal & it was pretty clear they did'nt know what they were missing which was their wings. So we wrote that down as our first Scientific finding. Bees after they have 75% of their wings chopped off no longer Believe they can fly.

On the last day of our Experiment we were surprised to find none other than the beautiful poet Dora Tanner driving by for no reason & stopping to talk to us just be friendly & have a chat. At first she was not too happy about what we were doing. She said we were torturing creatures of the Earth but we showed her how they did'nt seem to mind the torture so we asked if it was really torture if they did not seem to notice?

We won her over & she became interested in what we were doing. She seemed to like the idea that bees might have Faith. Someone said she was atheist but I do'nt believe it. She is too kind a person to be an atheist. But sometimes I think that may not be such a bad idea. I feel God sometimes looking down at me with his face all screwed up in anger. He knows what I am doing. Or what I've done when I took that Sacrament. He is Not happy. I do'nt know if there is forgiveness for that sort of thing. So maybe if I was an atheist I would'nt have these feelings of Doom. Anyway she joined us & became a really expert Bombus holder & made us wish she had joined us long ago because the work would have gone much faster with her than without her. She was laughing the whole time & kept making fun of us about the bees having Faith. But despite her being a great poet & a big tease she does not know much about Science so all her good natured fun-poking failed to dissuade us from our Task.

But by the end of the day we had a clipboard full of Data. We were happy. Dora left & feeling good I told Adam that I wanted to stay & enjoy nature & that I would hitch-hike back to Moab since it was coming up on the weekend there were lots of people coming & going in the La Sals & that someone would bring me home. He was worried of course but finally left me alone to enjoy the pleasures of Nature. We were Scientists at last which is a Good feeling.

SOURCE DOCUMENT #22:

Moab LDS 4th Ward newsletter. August 29, 1976.

MESSAGES

Bishop's Reminder: We will all be going to the Stake Farm to help with picking peaches on Wednesday evening. We expect every able-bodied man, woman and child to be there. After, we will be having a picnic at the Lion's Park on the Colorado. If you didn't pick peaches you are still welcome to the party. Bring one of your inactive neighbors and receive an extra portion of the Lord's Blessings.

High Priest Group Leader: Remember to do your home teaching by the 15th of this month so we are sure to have it done by the 30th!

Elder's Quorum: Remember to do your home teaching and come and help Thomas Thrip move to his new trailer on Saturday. His wife will be making pancakes and I hear there'll be a rasher of bacon for those that get there early.

Boy Scouts: This Saturday we will be removing Widow Cummings's stump and planting flowers. There will be no horsing around because Brother Hamming will be using dynamite to blow it out. Also bring your .22s and we will go shooting behind the dump afterwards to work on the Rifle Merit Badge.

Youth: Tuesday night at Mutual we will be practicing for the Gold and Green Ball floor show. Sis. Demster will be showing us the waltz we will be doing to Moody Blues "Nights in White Satin." Come one and all!

Relief Society: Sunday after Sacrament meeting Sister Thayne will be leading us in a special fireside on how to handle the end of times events that are happening here in Moab. She has recently been elected as the President of the Child Protection Society and her presentation will tell about how to best keep our families safe in these dark times.

Be true and faithful in all things, for behold I come quickly.

SOURCE DOCUMENT #2, PART K:

Hyrum's journal, hand-written manuscript.
Written between June and August, 1977.

Things had gone down Hill in Moab. Indeed Sandra was leading an effort to try & scare the willies out of everyone in the city. Rumors were flying left & right & all of them ended in the destruction of the town by the Communists joining forces with the Ghosts of the Gadianton Robbers. I was feeling mighty good about my Science efforts on the Mountain & was excited to tell everyone about my discoveries on the faith of Bombuses but no one wanted to know anything about it. All they wanted to talk about was End of time things. Now I probably should have known better but come Sunday Sandra wanted me to talk on Things seeing how I was suppose to Save the day & all. I figured that I could'nt get out of it or people would get Suspicious of me & I would get found out. I was getting more & more worried about getting caught so I decided to move the Dictionary that was under the couch in my trailer. Trouble was it was so dang Big. I found an old leather briefcase at the rummage store but it was'nt quite thick enough. So I took out a hunting knife & cut the spine down the middle & made 2 books out of the one. One with words running from A to M & the other from N to Z or pretty much anyways cause I got a few Ms in the N side. I took the A through Ms to the storage area in the basement of Star Hall which was never locked & had a whole bunch of old props & Sets for Plays. But when I came for the second half Sandra was home so I quick stuffed the second half in the briefcase & was stuffing it under the couch when she walked in. I was not fast enough & she asked What are you Doing? I says to her I cant tell you.

She was getting more & more Impressed when I acted all Mysterious.

Whats that your putting under the couch?

Now I should have just said Old Papers or something but I said

Ancient Records.

Her eyes got wide & she could hardly speak but she says What kind of Ancient Records? Like Joseph Smiths Gold Plates?

Now things got the better of me.

No. They are a copy of records of the Appearance of the Gadianton Robbers back in 1887 when Ralph Hawks drove them from Moab way back when. This is not the first time it has Happened. They have lived in this area since <u>Book of Mormon</u> times.

Oh Hyrum!

Yes it was Ralph Hawks that figured out how to drive them away. Then of course there was not the Communists to join up with so they joined up with the Navahos to take upon them corporeal bodies. But Hawks figured out how to undo their Power & wrote down the instructions & buried them up near the Hole in the Rock place that that guy dug south of town and built the tourist Museum thing.

Hyrum!

Yup. Fact is the guy that dug those Holes trying to build him a house in the rock was trying to find these Papers & thats why he kept Digging. Cause these Papers tell not only how to undo the Power of the Gadianton Robbers but how to Call upon them. There are people in the world that would kill me to have these Papers.

Hyrum. Please. What do we do?

There are Witches and Sorcerers in the world that want these. They are looking for them right now. Do not open that suitcase. There are Dangers you do not understand.

Upon this last Sandra was all undone. She burst into tears & held on to me like there was going to be no tomorrow. She was just weeping & crying & moaning & muttering about this being the Last Days & the End of the world.

Clearly I had Overdone it. Where this stuff comes from I have no idea. I did'nt plan on making up a Story like this but it just came out. Now I bet you can guess what happened over the course of the week. Sunday I helped Sandra with her Fireside. I was mostly supposed to just read the Scriptures about the Gadianton Robbers. But I got a bit carried away & got everybody worked up about how these were an Ancient band who knew the secrets of Master Mayhem. But after reading these Scriptures I read something from a book I found at the Library. It was in a book called <u>Scenes of Terror</u>. It had stuff like Edger Allan Poes the Raven which of course everybodys heard. But then it had a bit from something called the Magic Shooter by an opera guy named Carl Maria von Weber. I had never before heard of it but it was good stuff. So I started by reading the sections of the <u>Book of Mormon </u>where the evil Gadianton Robbers are introduced—

And now behold, those murderers and plunderers were a band who had been formed by Kishkumen and Gadianton. And now it had come to pass that there were many, even among the Nephites, of Gadianton's band. But behold, they were more numerous among the more wicked part of the Lamanites. And they were called Gadianton's robbers and murderers.

And it was they who did murder the chief judge Cezoram, and his son, while in the judgment-seat; and behold, they were not found.

And now it came to pass that when the Lamanites found that there were robbers among them they were exceedingly sorrowful; and they did use every means in their power to destroy them off the face of the earth.

But behold, Satan did stir up the hearts of the more part of the Nephites, insomuch that they did unite with those bands of robbers, and did enter into their covenants and their oaths, that they would protect and preserve one another in whatsoever difficult circumstances they should be placed, that they should not suffer for their murders, and their plunderings, and their stealings.

And it came to pass that they did have their signs, yea, their secret signs, and their secret words; and this that they might distinguish a brother who had entered into the covenant, that whatsoever wickedness his brother should do he should not be injured by his brother, nor by those who did belong to his band, who had taken this covenant.

And thus they might murder, and plunder, and steal, and commit whoredoms and all manner of wickedness, contrary to the laws of their country and also the laws of their God.

And whosoever of those who belonged to their band should reveal unto the world of their wickedness and their abominations, should be tried, not according to the laws of their country, but according to the laws of their wickedness, which had been given by Gadianton and Kishkumen.

Now behold, it is these secret oaths and covenants which Alma commanded his son should not go forth unto the world, lest they should be a means of bringing down the people unto destruction.

Now behold, those secret oaths and covenants did not come forth unto Gadianton from the records which were delivered unto Helaman; but behold, they were put into the heart of Gadianton by that same being who did entice our first parents to partake of the forbidden fruit—

Yea, that same being who did plot with Cain, that if he would murder his brother Abel it should not be known unto the world. And he did plot with Cain and his followers from that time forth.

And also it is that same being who put it into the hearts of the people to build a tower sufficiently high that they might get to heaven. And it was that same being who led on the people who came from that tower into this land; who spread the works of darkness and abominations over all the face of the land, until he dragged the people down to an entire destruction, and to an everlasting hell.

Yea, it is that same being who put it into the heart of Gadianton to still carry on the work of darkness, and of secret murder; and he has brought it forth from the beginning of man even down to this time.

And behold, it is he who is the author of all sin. And behold, he doth carry on his works of darkness and secret murder, and doth hand down their plots, and their oaths, and their covenants, and their plans of awful wickedness, from generation to generation according as he can get hold upon the hearts of the children of men.

Then I read this from the Magic Shooter which I told everyone was from an Ancient manuscript that was had among the ancient Nephites after I had changed it up a bit but pretty much just left it as is except I changed the names. I said that a righteous Lamanite had been hiding in bushes & recorded this whole thing. So I said.

This was given by a Nephite to try & raise the spirit of
Cain from the dead

Moonmilk fell on weeds!

Uhui!

Spiders web is dewed with blood!

Uhui!

Ere the evening falls again –

Uhui!

Will the gentle bride be slain!

Uhui!

E're the next descent of night,

Will the sacrifice be done!

Uhui! Uhui!

Gadianton

*Rips his hunting knife out, plunges it into the skull, raises the
knife with the skull, turns round three times & calls out*

Cain! Cain! Appear!

By the wizards cranium,

Cain! Cain! Appear!

Then I went on reading as Cain was Raised and his
Secrets gotten, with me on the fly changing the words of the
opera into the Scariest and most Frightening text imaginable
all run together with the Book of Mormon. This opera was
just what I needed. Luckily no one had ever heard of this and
so everyone thought it was right out of the Ancient records. I
ended with this. And then the righteous Lamanite who was
recording this writes that he could stand no more & fled the
scene. Now I must say I did this with terribly good Effect. I
had done a bit of acting in high school in fact playing opposite
Brimly Nuddles Enry Iggins in My Fair Lady as his good
friend Colonel Hugh Pickering the very one who made the
wager with Dr. Higgins about Liza Dolittle. Each part in

my reading I told in a Different voice. As Gadianton I was so scary with my sinister gravelly voice that a couple of the sisters covered their faces as I read. It was utter Silence when I finished. One man was openly crying & saying Its the end sure. Not alone did some of the women weep. Indeed my eyes were moved to wetness. I was staring off into space after for Dramatic effect. I gathered myself together & motioned for Sandra to take the floor.

It turned out to be a terrible Mistake and much of what followed can be laid at her feet. Because I had said this much Sandra figured it was OK to tell about the Brief Case & Ralph Hawks in the second half of the talk. My O My. The combination of all this set the town ablaze. In fact it was like fire hoses spraying a burning house with a stream of Gasoline.

Why did I do this? I'm not sure. Sometimes I just get caught up in things in ways that make no sense. I would have been much happier talking about bumblebees & their Faith. Or talking about Evolution like me & Adam did nowadays. But even though that is what I wanted to do that is not what I did do. Instead I dig a deeper & deeper Hole about these Gadianton Robbers. The very thing I want to be done with. The very thing I want to fix I Break even more. Why I do this I do not know. I seem my worst Enemy mostly. A real Enemy could not do worse I think. But it was not a sudden error like it was a Temptation that I gave into in a moment of Weakness. No I had looked up stuff in the Library & taken the time to change it & make it a good Story. All the while thinking that I would not use it but then when it came time I stood right up & played the part I'd been planning for & denying I was ever going to do. I guess you cant Plan a sin & then not do it. I have wondered if it was part of what changed in me when I drank that bit of Sacrament water. I Drank Damnation to my soul. That is sure.

Well it was all out of my mouth no matter where my inclination to do crazy things came from. I was suppose to Save the town. I had Ancient manuscripts to do so & the Powers of good & Evil were lining up for a final Battle. Damn I complicated things. Also this week I got news from a friend that was both wonderful & Terrible. I am as confused as an Ant plucked from his line of friends marching to a Picnic & then dropped a mile away on tarry pavement. I do'nt know what to do anymore. Also I found out something strange about my Friend. Something he never told me but sort of means Strange things. He is some kind of Warlock. Or was a Warlock. A male witch or something who is male & a witch is because my friend is a man. I do'nt know why she did'nt tell me. It seems Strange & important because I thought he was an atheist or agnostic or something more neutral like a person gone Inactive. My whole world is getting Stranger & Stranger.

Letter from Dora Daphne Tanner to spirit guide.
February 8, 1977.

Faewolf, last session you blessed me. You blessed the child. You laid your hands on my belly and sang songs from another time, a time when feminine Earth was maiden, mother, and crone, when women walked in power and wonder and were wild and untamed. Your hands were warm and healing. I felt the blessing enter my tight skin and melt and endow the baby with that warmth, with that healing, with that power. You begged, you pled, you cajoled the Goddess to come, to come into my life, to make herself known. I cannot say if she did. I cannot say if she has taken away the darkness that has seeded, planted, and watered a shoot of black terror within me, but when I got home, I penned this. I penned this for you. I penned this thinking about your escape from that place that so long held you captive. About those things you opened to me. I am grateful. This is my gift to you:

"Once, long ago, lived a poor woodcutter's daughter. She was beautiful, but hated by her stepmother who made her life miserable and worked her from long before dawn until late at night. The unfortunate girl was made to sleep on a palisade under a pile of rags used by the woodcutter to clean his tools, and every night she cried until sleep came and offered her merciful peace. Now in that same country lived a King kind and wise. Every day he would come to the parapet of his magnificent castle and give instructions to the people on how to live, serve, and be happy. All who followed the kind King found their lives blessed by the fairies of the land who helped all those who loved the King. The King did not talk of the Queen, but when asked, said that the Queen fared well, and that she was about the circumspect duties of a Queen. However, the town's people longed to see the Queen, for it was well known that while there was no man that had ever beheld the Queen in living memory, she was the most fair and comely woman who had ever lived. One day the folk of village came together and begged the King to let them see the Queen. This made the King angry for he had declared that no one could speak of the Queen and that she was only to remain in her subjects' memories and was never to be talked about. So the King sent his knights, who, with a great show of kindness and chivalry, slew the wicked people who asked him to bring forth the Queen. And so never again was the Queen spoken about, but always she was present in the memory of the people as the King had said was proper and right. Now meanwhile, back in the forest, the woodcutter's daughter one day was beaten by her stepmother so severely that she thought her life was forfeit, and so when the night came she fled into the forest. She ran under the dark and fearsome trees without thought of her danger. So great was her fear of her stepmother that she gave no thought of the evils of the forest and thought only of escaping the cruelty of her father's house. At long last, she came to a clearing and was surprised to find women dancing in a happy circle under the moon. In the center was a woman of great power and beauty such as the girl had never before imagined. As she approached, the dancing stopped and the Lady beckoned her to come forward. She came and bowed and noticed that the Lady wore a crown of iron around her head that gleamed in the moonlight like a diamond. The Lady beckoned her to speak and she told her wherefore her bruises and cuts had come. Then the Lady stretched forth her hand and with a single touch healed the girl of all her ills. As she did, the woodcutter's daughter recognized in her heart that this was the Queen of all the land which no man in living memory had seen nor heard. And then the Lady said to the girl, Come now and dance in my circle. Raise your voices such that even the moon can hear your cries of joy. For the day is given to the good King and he reigns in the light of day while I am hid way in high towers where no man may approach. But in the circle, under the moon, all my daughters and those sons who wish so may be healed. And ever after the woodcutter's daughter danced in the Queen's circle where neither stepmother, nor King's knights, nor harm of beast nor demon could come. The girl lived happily ever after. So mote it be."

But here is the irony, my dear witch. Here is the strange thing that I cannot wrap even the beginning of a thought around. Why does this contradiction and paradox scream so loudly at whatever core may lie at the center of this becoming, this being? Why does his gift to me seem so full of light? Why when I know he is betrayer, adulterer, liar, snake-oil salesman, con-artist, untruth teller, schemer, deceiver, cheater, scammer, and bastard, why Faewolf, why does he bring such delight? Why, when I know he is a Mormon? When I know that he believes, at some deep deep level, all their lies and harms? And why, dear priestess, why do I know he loves me more than anyone, ever, ever has? Why, when I feel his arms around me (forgive my lapses into Harlequin imagery) do I feel at once whole and holy? I know in theory with my rational soul, with my Aristotelian core, that he betrays all that you and I have ever stood for. But I ask you. I ask it with all my heart. I ask it in simplicity. Could it not be that even our transcendental mother Sarah Margaret, our hero, our Lady, our beloved, died happy in the Italian's arms? Could it be that at the moment of shipwreck, when the Fire Island waves lapped at the boat, she had no regrets? Thoreau never found her papers on that cold sandy shore. He looked and did not find a page. But I think he would have found this, if he had just looked a little harder. If he had just looked a bit more carefully, perhaps sandwiched in the root-mass of a large drift-stump, it would have been there, sea soaked and faded, but nevertheless, legible in her neat hand:

"Ossoli and Angelo have to be written in somewhere"

So it is. I know in the end he will abandon me. I know that I will spend nights upon nights alone. There will be diapers to change. Tuition to manage. Yes. Yes. I know all this. As you say. Homework to help with. Late nights trying to break a fever. I will weave a thousand spells cursing and blessing his name. Of that I'm sure. But right now. In this place, at this time, I am happy to place my heart in the one light place it has ever been. Forgive me. I betray everything I know. Even so I say it too: *So mote it be.*

SOURCE DOCUMENT #24:

Paper by Hyrum Thayne published in
the Bulletin of the Ecological Society of America
and letter from editor of same. March 1977.

Fideistic Bombus: **An Erudite Didactic Treatment of How Much They do Believe**

Hyrum L. Thayne Esq., PhD

ABSTRACT

This is a scientific study that answers the interrogative of how much faith does a Bombus have? We chopped off the wings of Bombuses with proper scientific surgical steel scissors according to experimental treatments and protocols. We found they didn't have faith to fly after 20% of their wings were sacrificed off.

INTRODUCTION

Bumblebees are accurately called in Latin <u>Bombus</u> which is underlined to signify that this name is the right appellation for this animal in scientific studies (Webster). Now, just like helicopters Bumbuses use their wings to fly. However, Science has proven that there is not enough wing to fly with their rotunded bodies. So scientists know they fly by having faith. They believe they can fly because they never knew their wings were not enormous enough to do so. So we undertook to find the point where they started to doubt enough that their efforts where thwarted and they no longer believed they can fly.

(Table 1)

Science Treatments	Amount we chopped
1	20% 1 pair of wings
2	20% 2 pair of wings
3	50% 1 pair of wings
4	50% 2 pair of wings
5	75% 1 pair of wings
6	75% 2 pair of wings
7	100% 1 pair of wings
8	100% 2 pair of wings
9	0% 1 pair of wings
10	0% 1 pair of wings

METHODS

We chopped off wings in the following amounts

Now we also replicated with 20 bees in each one of these numbered categories. We captured the bees with Kraft Mayonnaise jars and cut the wings with surgical steel scissors on a large aspen stump about knee high and held down the wings with probes from Brigham Young University Home of the Cougars.

RESULTS

The Bombuses that had 20% of their wings cuts flew a bit, so still had faith (p < 0.001). Bombuses without their back wings flew a little screwywampus but still had faith to fly mostly (p < 0.001). Bombuses otherwise just buzzed around on the stump flopping this way and that and so seemed compromised as to faith (p < 0.001). Bombuses without wings just walked around and so had no faith if they had any at all that they could fly (p < 0.001). Bombuses with all their wings flew properly but seemed a little confused when let out the mayonnaise jar due to their being shook up a bit to settle them down ($p < 0.001$).

CONCLUSION

Bombuses can have a little faith when their wings are clipped a bit. But all in all they cannot stand too much before their faith starts to waver. Let this be a lesson that a little Faith goes a long ways.

Gary Felton, Ph.D.
Editor
Bulletin of the Ecological Society of America
Iowa State University
Department of Biology
Ames, Iowa 50011

Jan. 6, 1977
Hyrum Thayne
24 Navajo Dr.
Moab, UT 84532

Dear Dr. Thayne:

Your letter was delightful and we will definitely publish it in the next bulletin (out in a couple of weeks if we are lucky). It had us all in stitches. I just wanted to pass on the well wishes of Stan Lieberman (who is at this moment leaning over my shoulder). He recalls fond memories of you from Colorado State. He said to tell you that he married that student that you introduced him to in Costa Rica back in '66 when you were there studying the parasitic hymenoptera of leaf miners. He says he owes you one (I'm not sure if that's good or bad)! He wanted to pass on that it's delightful to see you've kept your sense of humor. It sounds like your retirement in Utah is going well and you are keeping busy.

Warmest Regards,

Gary

Letter fragment from William Babcock, the third numbered page
<The rest were lost due to my own negligence>. September 1998.

decided. He is just sitting here listening to Liszt's *Totendanz*
with his eyes closed. If he knew, I'm not sure what he would do.

So we will come to Moab then. The trip will likely be our
last, we have grown too old and worn to make such trips, but
this one seems necessary, I am afraid. If Marcel is behind the
madness, or they are in conspiratorial communication then I
will just have to go along for the ride.

My worries are many and stress is high. A haze seems
to gather around me in strange and unsettling ways. The
painting, your revelation of the use of Weber's libretto from
Der Freischütz in Hyrum's deception, our discovery of the
notes from our mother on *Picatrix*, the Wiccan background of
Ms. Tanner and our mother, all seem confusingly linked albeit
obviously coincidental. These, plus the possible murder of a
baby, have all unsettled us. Perhaps this is what has unhinged
Edward so. Poor Edward, he doesn't seem to be aware of how
deeply psychotic he seems to me, who knows him so well. His
dearest friend and brother! How my heart aches. I'm glad I
will never have to live without him. He speaks only in Hebrew
now. And seems angry when I answer in anything but that
language. He never communicates with others when we go
out, or for that matter even to our butler, Hermann. But he
refuses to be examined by anyone, and he rightly points out
that any pharmaceuticals that might be administered would

have an unknown, and possibly risky, effect on Marcel. It is a strange mix of rationality, exhibited in his concern for Marcel, and an obsession with our returning to the La Sals.

We have purchased the painting. Please, again, do not mention the escape in a public letter. More strange news is not what he needs right now. I'm glad I intercepted your email.

I will have our travel agent send you copies of our itinerary. I look forward to seeing you in Salt Lake. Thank you again for indulging in Edward's mad whim. I don't know if he will speak to you except in Hebrew, but were he in his right mind, he would send his most warm regards.

Best wishes,
William

It is Sunday Morning of a unseasonably cool Spring
Moab day. Hells Bells things have become as confused as a
Mouse in a clothes dryer. Indeed I find myself in Trouble in
ways deep & proficient. Well anyway it came to Pass that
somehow the Editor of the <u>Times Independent</u> got a hold
of the fact that I had a Scientific publication coming out in
the <u>Bulletin of the Ecological Society of America</u> & decided
to do a front page story of the local boy who done Good. So
I told my Story to Marcy Green who I knew in high school
& who I may have even kissed once & who wrote up a fine
piece about my Bombus story. Sandra bought up about every
copy in the City & I think may have gone door to door just
in case anybody did'nt see it. On the front was a fine picture
of us sitting at the Kitchen table with a Mayonnaise jar &
some dead bumble bees scattered about the table for good
measure. In the picture I'm pointing out the jar with my
finger & Sandra is looking at me with eyes lit up like the
coals of a wind graced campfire. Its all fine & good but now
I've had nothing but Trouble. Brother Law came over again
& now that I've revealed I've got secret Manuscripts & am
a famous bumblebee Scholar he is all bowing & scraping his
knees to find out what I'm going to do to save the Town.
What Hope is there? He says. What can we Plan for when
the World is fraught with such Dangers? Hyrum. He says.

You are the only one smart enough to Save us. What are you going to Do?

He looked as sad & unhappy & Worried as ever I'd seen a man. He was ringing his hands this way & that & the old Felt cowboy hat he was wearing looked like it was about to be twisted into a rope. I says back to him I have located their lair so get the brethren together we will act on it soon. I figured that would give me a couple of months to sort things out & maybe even let this thing die a natural death but it looked like it was not to be. He galvanized every one & he declared himself my Deputy & took it upon himself to set up a meeting every week to discuss how best they could assist me in the Destruction of the Gadianton Robbers.

Well if it is to be then it is to be. The work has dried up like it does every fall when the Passes start to fill with snow. So I was in my usual winter layoff starting about this time but I was kept busy enough. I got invited to the Rotary Club to talk about my bumblebee work. I was invited by the Daughters of Utah Pioneers to talk about the Last Days & the upcoming attack by the Gadianton Robbers & Commies at which time I took it upon myself to read the ancient Manuscript I had found. So more & more I was becoming a first rate Scholar. I picked up a book out of the Library called The First 2000 Years by Cleon Skousen so I was able to learn all about Cain who was the author of the secret Combinations that were the Heart & Soul of the Gadianton Robbers ways of making oaths and covenants. So my Reputation was growing by leaps & bounds. To the non-Mormons I am a self-made Scientist & to a Sizeable chunk of the Mormons I was a figure right out of the old days. In fact after a Fireside I was giving for the Second Ward an old codger came up & asked if I was the one Mighty & Strong that had been spoken about in the Doctrine

& Covenants. I did'nt know what he was talking about so I looked it up & sure enough there it was. It says this in section 85 verse 7

> And it shall come to pass that I the Lord God, will send one mighty & strong, holding the scepter of power in his hand, clothed with light for a covering, whose mouth shall utter words, eternal words; while his bowels shall be a fountain of truth, to set in order the house of God, & to arrange by lot the inheritances of the saints whose names are found, & the names of their fathers, & of their children, enrolled in the book of the law of God.

I stood there holding the scriptures the old guy had handed me & after reading it I said to him I Cannot deny it. Holy Cow where did that come from? I do'nt know. But he just nodded & ambled out of the Chapel. Well the next day Sandra was existentially ecstatic. Someone had slipped $2000 dollars Cash under the crack of our trailers kitchen door with a note saying that there was one dollar representing each of the stripling warriors from the Book of Alma. The letter was addressed to One Mighty & Strong. Well that was not the end of it. Apparently someone told the way of it & for the next 2 weeks we got envelope after envelope of Money all of it based upon the 2000 Stripling Warriors. Most of it was 2000 pennies however the big one was a full 10000 dollars with a note saying
Dear Brother Thayne. I hope when I stand before the great bar of the Most High that you will stand forth & speak on my behalf that I did give you $5 dollars for each the warriors.
We were rich! Sandra wanted to buy a car with it but I asked her how that would look so she agreed to just buy a new

living room set with a new color TV & new component Stereo system with a Pioneer receiver turntable & Bose speakers. I've never heard Jethro Tull or Led Zeppelin sound like this. But all of this mess is weighing on my Conscience like a bear on a rug. But even so having been spoiled with good sounds I felt in necessary to outfit the car with a new 8 track and some new speakers. Moody Blues sounded like they were in the back seat playing a personal Concert for me I kept expecting dry ice smoke to come crawling from back there and lasers to start dancing on the ceiling like it was a real stage. I knew that the Lord was actually somehow cursing me seeing how there were no Gadianton Robbers & people were just giving me money for Nothing. I knew he had to be pretty upset about things so I was feeling a little spooked with his angry Eye looking down at me.

I also bought at this time with some of the money hardback editions all of the books that Dora Tanner a local Poetess & author had written. You'll remember she helped us a bit on the Bombus Experiments so I thought I should read some of her work since she is a local Scholar of sorts & I am to. So I bought all 5 of her Poetry books & her book <u>Desert Canyon Dreams</u> which is a book of her writings that just came out & is mostly a book about her Thoughts & it is'nt poetry so far as I can tell but I'm not a very good judge I'm afraid.

Well they wanted me & Sandra to sit in Chuck Murrys convertible or Dr. Tindials Model T in the Easter Day parade & made me the Grand Marshall & Master of Ceremonies. Sandra was existentially ecstatic & had bought herself a new Spring dress with matching hat & gloves. It cost over $100 dollars all told for something she'd wear only once.

SOURCE DOCUMENT #26:

*Letter from Dora Daphne Tanner to Lilly Tanner Baldaia.
April 13, 1977.*

Dear Lilly,

I expected many things from you, but not this. Surprise? Yes. Disappointment? Yes. Anger? Quite possibly. Disapproval? Almost certainly. But Joy? Excitement? Offers of help and support? Not at all. What's happened to you, dear sister? There was a time when I could predict your reaction with mathematical precision. We are all changing.

The skin of my belly seems to have stretched tight, way beyond the point where I would have guessed it would have popped like a balloon. But I find as it expands, my horizons grow in proportion. Life seems new and fresh and I'm seeing the colors of the world in both more vibrant shades and more subtle hues. I've also detected a new kind of music humming in the air that slides through me and into me, its melody enchanting and redeeming. It is more than the addition of just a new instrumentation on the universe's stage—it is a new variation. No, a new kind of variation. Not a restatement of well-worn themes. It seems a new orchestration for a whole new symphony, complete with new tones and new chords never heard before. I know something springs in me from a new dimension that connects me to wild and untamed harmonies and resonating vibrations out of the throbbing heart of the universe.

You asked about "the other woman." I care nothing about her. She seems irrelevant to me. I've seen her three times. The first was in the parking lot of Walker's Drug. I was in the bank and saw her and Hyrum drive up. They got out of the car, and I was struck by how ordinary they seemed together. He opened the door for her, and she maneuvered out from behind the wheel. She is blond and overweight but she carries it well and tends to that classic renaissance beauty one sees in paintings from the 16th century. Her eyes are spectacular—large and haunting. They walked into the store without saying anything to each other.

The second time, I ran into her in Miller's Super Market. We passed each other in the aisle lined with pasta. Of course she did not give me a glance, although I could not take my eyes off of her.

The third time was strange and worrisome—well, potentially worrisome for Hyrum, anyway. It was at the Easter Jeep-Safari Parade. Hyrum, for some absurd reason, was elected the Grand Marshal. He was riding with Sandra (that's the other woman's name). She waving like the grand princess on her way to the ball from the back seat of a sputtering Model T. Hyrum seemed to be eating it up, too. I have to admit, I was caught up in the excitement. As their car passed me, from the crowd I caught Hyrum's eye and yelled, "It kicked." And pointed to my belly. Hyrum's hand reached out reflexively as if to place his hand on it from the distance. Then I looked up. Sandra was staring at his hand, and then she looked up directly at me. I think she saw the whole exchange. I don't have words for the anger and hatred that attended that gaze. It was a rage like none I've ever experienced. Like a fury's from a Greek saga, as if she saw through us in an instant. Then it was gone. She was back to smiling and waving. Hyrum never saw anything, and in retrospect I cant help but think I imagined it—my guilty conscience (and yes, I do have moments of guilt about this affair) reconstructing her harmless gaze into a vision of wrath and recognition. As I say, it seemed only present for an instant and then it was gone. She never glanced my way again.

But there they are. My three encounters with my paramour's wife.

Your words were so kind about my poor new book. I'm scared to death what the critics are going to do with it. I did hear from my agent that the poetry reviewer for the *New York Review of Books* is going to do a review soon. It's got me shaking. She absolutely destroyed Ted Hughes' last book, and she rarely says anything positive about anyone. I wish she wasn't the one whose review will probably lead the pack. This could go very, very badly, and I'm scared.

Yes, "Miner's Basin" was for you. It's as true now as it was then, when "her skirts clattered around her skinned knees."

I love you. Your support has been the greatest gift I've ever received (well except maybe the one that has inverted my bellybutton). Give everyone my love. And yes, do tell them about their new cousin.

Love,
Dora

Babcock twins' personal journal. October 2, 1998.
Transcribed from a recorded cassette tape.

We've turned onto I-70 and are passing Green River on the left. It seems like we are coming to an end—an archetypal terminus that brokers final things. Edward sits with his eyes closed. His mouth is moving and I can make out his raspy whispers because his voice vibrates in ways that pass to me through skin and bone. It is the Shema Yisrael: "Hear O Israel, the Lord is our God, the LORD is one." He has repeated it in Hebrew since we left Austria. <Redactor> picked us up in Salt Lake on Sunday, and we rested for three days before driving down here. We visited the Mormon Temple visitor's center and heard the Mormon Tabernacle Choir sing magnificently. Such acoustics rival any opera house in Wien. Edward seems to notice nothing. But his eyes keep opening. He's noticed the Bookcliffs rising to the north, an imposing wall of eroded gullies carved in the copper blue greens of this barren land.

<Edward's Voice> Look! The La Sals! <The sound of weeping>

* * *

We are passing the Moab airport. It's so much bigger than I remember. When we turned off I-70 and onto Highway 191, I read the sign: "Moab 39 miles." Edward's head snapped up. His mouth stopped moving and his eyes cleared and a smile opened his face. He said in English, "Look, the La Sals." And there they were, rising blue like gods to the southeast. Not the shabby desert gods of Western monotheism. True gods. Gods of might and power emerging from the canyons and washes to dominate and subdue. Edward is smiling. I am bawling. Tears are running down my face. <Redactor> is rattling on about something. The radio out of Grand Junction is playing a song from someone named Martina McBride; it seems out of place in the face of such power as stands before us. But the La Sals are calling us, reaching out and demanding our worship. <Redactor>, <Redactor>! Could you turn the radio off? Thank you. I hear Edward try to start the Shema but it is as if the lesser Hebrew god too must fall to his knees before these montane gods: "Peale, Tukuhnikivatz, Waas, Mann rule here!" the desert cries. Thunderclouds are forming to the south. Even they seem afraid to approach these deities. Edward's eyes seem wide and sparkling. We are starting our descent through the narrow canyon that announces our arrival to Moab. Edward's gaze has turned inward, and the Shema begins again. High mothering walls bathe us in shadow. Red rock talus litters the hillside slopes that rise up on either side of us until they meet the sheer rocky cliffs between which we now fall.

* * *

We are in the Apache Hotel on the east end of town. I'm anxious to press on and get into the mountains. My hopes are that Edward might find healing since his brief exclamations in the face of the La Sals. But <Redactor> is right, it is late. After supper, <Redactor> takes us on a tour. We visit Dora's old house on 4th South, then Hyrum's. The trailer park where Hyrum lived is still a trailer park, but his is, of course, long gone. We've prepared for bed. I find myself so filled with joy and sorrow at the same time, as if an end is coming, as if we are entering a culmination of something. We are drowning in finality. Edward has nodded off and I hear his breathing, soft next to me, a very familiar and comforting sound. I find it bringing tears to my eyes. He does not seem to notice I am recording this. Edward? Edward? No. He does not hear me. The intake and release of his breath in sleep seems more earthy and attuned to natural rhythms than the Shema he's muttered for the last few weeks. He seems more like my Edward, and it is easy for me to imagine that he is back to normal and it is the man I've known all my life beside me. Even though he is asleep, Marcel has not given me the legs. That is odd, of course. Not unheard of, but rare enough for me to be concerned, and be touched by a taint of fear that Marcel is not right, either. Did the madness of one slide over to the other? If one is healed, will the other follow? I had a bit of hope today when we saw the La Sals, and I can't help but let a little optimism bubble to the surface that he is still there somewhere, that maybe when we get up into the La Sals tomorrow, he will awake and come to himself. I was thinking, as I watched him, of Nietzsche and his descent into madness. Perhaps our brains can only handle so much genius, and if it burns too hot, it gets used up. Maybe the genius squeezes and constricts the sane until it just goes away. Edward, I know, believes in God. I'm smiling as I think of this. He's told me many times that "believe in God" is not the right way to phrase it. He does not believe in God he claims, but he knows God. It did not come through a rational reading of Barth or Tillich, he told me. He was not convinced by Kierkegaard that he ought to make a leap of faith, or that he had to embrace a rational absurdity with the passion of the infinite. He said, "God came to me. Not as a person, or a vision, or some manifestation of the senses." Rather, he explained, he became aware of His presence—an "other" that he has formed a relationship with. A presence he has befriended in a mutual exchange of being-there-for-each-other. That is what I've never understood. I've been with him my whole life. How can I have missed out on their close relationship? Did God for some reason choose him and leave me out—like Jacob and Esau? So must it be. But he claims that that is why atheists will never understand the so-called "belief in God," because it is not a belief. It is a relationship. "God is there for me," he says. "Just like you are." I've never made sense of his words. I asked him how he didn't know that it was just Marcel he was aware of? How could he be sure that it was not some cluster of nerves in his own brain, a god module as they call it now, and he laughed and said that he could not explain the phenomenal experience of God any more than he could explain the experience of smelling a rose or the feel of a cool rag on an overheated forehead. I understood this intellectually. "Why don't I feel God?" I once asked him. He did not answer for a long time and then said simply, "I don't know." I can't help but wonder if his being touched by God was the beginning of his madness. His experience with God came shortly after our return to Vienna, and although it has been there for many, many years, I can't help but wonder if his "experience" with God has just been a part of the long slow descent into madness, one in which this "God" of his has crept forward inch by inch until it grabbed his whole mind. Richard Dawkins says that religion is a virus, and I think there must be some truth to that. I cannot help but see Edward's embracing God as a slowly growing malady that has moved from an inconvenience to a life-threatening illness. I must go to bed. Tomorrow we will visit our old haunts. So many memories. I wish I could pray.

SOURCE DOCUMENT #28:

Letter from Dora Daphne Tanner to spirit guide.
May 2, 1977.

Faewolf, I've done something terrible.

I disgraced myself with dark outrage. On a ledge above the mouth of Moonflower Canyon. You know the place, downriver on the south bank—the canyon with the pool at the terminus where we have done a ritual or two and where the wind makes a low moaning when coming up the Colorado from the north? I was not going to miss this. I am greedy for experience. I knew he was coming to this place. He told me the plan. I betrayed it.

I got there early and parked on the gravel road a little further down from the canyon, at the place where the canyon opens and the Colorado flows past a small wetland. Birds gather there to twitter and call in their crystal voices. I've heard the trill-pause-trill of blue grosbeaks playing among the sedges, and the chatter-whistle of the sunny chats flitting invisibly in green tamarisk that tangles the water's edge, and twice I have seen a great blue heron rise reluctantly and glide downriver to a less- busy feeding ground than my presence allows.

Nearby, hiding in a sandstone chimney crack, there is an old Anasazi ladder (so they say—who knows) that winds its way up a narrow slot—merely a series of notched logs rather than the geometric rungs that make a Western ladder. But the hand- and footholds designed into those natural posts take you, with some grunting effort, to the rim of the canyon. Despite my enormous belly, I pushed and pulled my way to the top—you know how I like to climb and scamper among the red rocks. It is second nature to me, just as climbing trees was when I was a little girl, when I would sway with the wind as the high branches tossed back and forth and I would pretend I was a witch on an untamed broom. Portends of becoming. Foreshadowings.

The morning was cool enough that I wrapped my body in a thick rusty-brown alpaca wool blanket I'd carried from the pickup. Looking down like an unbaptized rusalka from a tree, I watched shadows press and define the canyon into existence. There. There, to the right, on the edge of my visual horizon, I could just make out a scattered mist dancing on the surface of the calm brown water which rests in the small shaded pool nestled at the end of the canyon. I wonder how many generations of water skippers I have watched skate there on otherwise still water, sending tiny ripples that eventually spread to cover its entire surface? Many. Many, I think. The pond was barely discernable from my perch. The sun was climbing and I could tell it would soon heat up, but for the time being, the chill felt friendly. Inviting. I shared a ledge with a twisted *Artemisia* that did not seem to resent the company. Grasses hugged the wall, but the ledge was mostly bare dirt except for the cryptogamic soil sheltering under the shade of the nearby sagebrush. I sat with my back against the wall, my bare feet just reaching the edge, which dropped about 75 feet into the canyon. I waited. I ran my hands over my belly and sang songs to my baby, who seemed as content and peaceful as the morning. We both listened to a black phoebe warning others that he had staked a claim on that tiny patch of bushy woodland.

I had not seen Hyrum for a week because my college roommate, Yalemtsehay from Ethiopia, had been visiting.

She is a wild and brave woman who has settled in Salt Lake to finish law school. She must have found me anxious and distracted during her visit because she sang songs to me as if I were a child. At my request, she gave me Bob Marley dreadlocks. (She actually met him once. She was from Awasa and had met Haile Selassie when she was a little girl and so Marley, when he heard she was there, actually wanted to meet her after a concert. Now, however, she has a nearly shaved head for convenience, and has given up her Rastafarian life.) She sang as she molded my hair. My dreadlocks, I fear, made me look more like a mop than a Regae queen. I wondered what he would say when he saw them.

I must have dozed, because I heard the slamming of car doors as a distant thunder. I jolted awake with that sudden panic that hits when you've fallen asleep too near a cliff's edge.

I could hear talking long before I caught a glimpse of them, marching single-file through the tamarisk on a well-trodden path that followed the creek bed to a large and ancient cottonwood which stood like a monument right below where I was watching. The canyon seemed to balk at their presence. Their crunching, shouting, grunting, blathering on and on and on, the way they broke sticks in the violence of their approach, unsettled and angered me. They caused unholy echoes to slam back and forth among the red rock walls. They came in their Sunday best. Their uniform. Their white shirts and ties, their skirts, smocks, and hair-dos. Hyrum was there, but looking like a god in his white shirt, bolo tie cinched with a large tiger-eye set in Navajo silver, a corduroy coat, red checked bell-bottoms, and platform shoes. His sideburns made him look like a prophet of some disco-based mythos. His hair was long and still wet from the shower. He could turn me on from the distance. He was followed by a crowd of men and women all looking odd and ill-placed, trying to negotiate the sandy path through the twisted vegetation in Sunday school attire and hard-soled shoes. They looked comical, but menacingly so, like a parade sent from a strange, orderly hell to entrain and restrict heaven's natural freeform.

They came to the edge of the pool carefully and gingerly, trying not to soil their finery. A large-bellied man with a shiny, slippery crimson face took a position of power in front of the group. His bolo tie, unlike Hyrum's, looked like an excuse rather than an adornment. He was stern and serious, and his voice deep and thickly inflected with that rural Moab accent that we find so creepily inbred in Southern Utah—an ill-formed sound. He looked around, and all eyes were locked toward him.

Hear the sound and cadence of his voice: "My good Brothers and Sisters, we are gathered here to rid our town of an infestation of dire evil. The ghosts of the Gadianton Robbers and communists have set upon us with a vengeance. I've had it impressed upon my mind, by the Holy Spirit of God, that there stands one among us who has the power of the priesthood strong in him and who can wither these evil spirits, root and branch. Brother Thayne. The time is now yours."

Hyrum seemed strangely present, as if a power really was emanating from him. A fire burned from his countenance, a visible glow of animal magnetism. He gazed slowly over the gathering, looking them in the eyes as if he were weighing their worthiness to be present. My little shyster. Man, was he good. He intoned clearly and with a commanding voice. He exuded power as he spoke: "My Brothers and Sisters. I am humbled to be an instrument in the hand of almighty God this morning. I am humbled that I can stand here and help this town be rid of its plague and trial. But God has given me the means and power to see it through. Brother Donner, would you give us an opening prayer and then I will remove these ghosts that haunt us, and the commies who have joined them."

This Brother Donner rose up and offered a prayer. The wind was gusting so I could only pick out pieces of it, but I did hear a bit: "Our kind and gracious... yea... your children are gathered here today to offer thanks for the blessings that we have enjoyed as the citizens of Moab and of this great nation, even the United States of America... and as members of thy Holy Church. We thank thee... living prophets, yea even... thank thee at this time, especially for Brother Thayne this morning whose worthiness permits this meeting. Now Father... we have also been attacked on every side by spirits of him who fell from your presence. Yea even the Father of Lies, our mortal enemy, who seeks thy power... Father, his followers of ancient days have returned even now and... and set their sights on our wives, our... These so-called Gadianton Robbers have risen up in these the last days to destroy our peace and happiness... communists... Stalin himself... come humbly in the spirit of fasting and prayer... relief from this oppression from the enemy of our soul and his minions... humbly pray... Amen."

The last word was repeated by those gathered below. The bowed heads raised and everyone opened their eyes. There was a feeling of calm. Of holiness?

I suddenly found myself raging. Mad and teary eyed. There was something so sincere about this prayer. Something so deeply rooted in these people and their land that my sense of their silliness melted away. They seemed wholesome to me. People of the land. Salt of the Earth. They were all in tears. Except Sandra, Hyrum's wife. She seemed subdued, but not in the same way. She was looking at Hyrum narrowly as if sizing up his worthiness. There was something strange about it. The times I'd met her before, she seemed to look at Hyrum with wonder and appreciation. Perhaps she was beginning to see him differently. The thought could not be helped, but a feeling of schadenfreude jumped up from me. Maybe she would leave him?

I was furious at Hyrum. He was playing these people like dupes. Like fools, simpletons. Treating them as if they were idiot children who deserved to be mistreated and jeered at. Taking the things they held most sacred and using them and playing with them and mocking all that they stood for. I was starting to feel an untamable rage. He was a lying son of a bitch. He smiled kindly and slowly raised his hand and bent his arm in a square, and intoned solemnly, so softly I could not make out the words from my blind, something about "Jesus Christ," "Priesthood," and stuff like "root and branch," and "command you depart." Clearly, he was casting out demons.

Suddenly I found myself in a roiling fury. He was really being a jerkwad. Cad. Charlatan. Fake. A man without qualities. I wasn't going to let him get away with it! Cast out demons? Not today. I jumped to my feet. I gave an unholy trilling scream. I looked down at faces reflecting abject terror. I can imagine what they saw—a frightening and dreadful spirit with wild hair sprouting everywhere from my recent dreadlocks. Wrapped in my alpaca blanket, stretching it out like a cape. Then, in the voice of a demon, harsh, otherworldly, imitating the husky raspy yell of the possessed in *The Exorcist* I screamed:

"Weeee will never go! You have no power. We will hunt you down. You and your children. For generations and generations we will prey upon you like the beasts you are. WE ARE THE GADIANTON ROBBERS! We will destroy you."

I then dropped down out of sight on the ledge and moved against the cliff face to where they could not see me. I felt horrible at what I'd just done. Hyrum's poor face registered recognition, then hurt, then fear. Everyone else: terror. Except Sandra's. She seemed blank and cold as she stared up at me. I heard them running away. I could hear the branches breaking, the echoes of their panicked retreat. The sound of cars starting, engines revving in the distance, tires squealing as they fled the scene. I peeked over the edge and they were all gone. The canyon quieted. Emptied of its supplicants, prayers, and rituals, it again seemed to have entered that holy and tranquil state of nature where sacredness can always be discerned in the spaces left behind. Flitting birds again began to sing, led by the descending notes of a wren's piping. The wind played among the tamarisk and rippled the surface of the pool below. All was restored to peace. Hyrum was gone too. I felt like shit.

Faewolf, sometimes I wish you were Jesus and could redeem me properly. I may have forever ruined any relationship with my child's father.

Hyrum's journal, hand-written manuscript.
Written between June and August, 1977.

The life of a Scholar continues to be harder & Harder. I had a big fight with my good friend the one I mentioned who has been having a bit of trouble. He did me a bad turn & I was quite upset about it cause it Messes things up royally. I do'nt know what he was Thinking & he should not even have been there anyway & I do'nt know. Well past is past & we made up & everything is squared away between us. That is except for the Mess he left for me to clean up.

I'm afraid the Gadianton rigmarole is still going & if anything gotten worse. I went up the canyon to offer a prayer with the Bishop & some of the people of the Ward & it ended with everyone thinking they saw a malicious & Dangerous spirit high up on the ridge. I think it was a teenager playing a prank & tried to explain that to the others. Tried to bring a little Rationality & Science in their lives but they all insisted it was the ghost of a real Gadianton Robber. As a result the rumor mill is going crazy. Sister Dallon claims that they have come into the house at night & tried to have their way with her. She declares with great Solemnity & Fervent Locutions that the end is soon upon us. Brother Law is insisting to everyone that I am still the one Mighty & Strong & Money keeps pouring in from all over the place making me fairly shine with Guilt. To top it off Sandra has become even more moody & sour. She is constantly Snapping at me & looking at me in ways that would curdle fresh milk.. I think she is punishing me for not letting her buy a car. Verily, she is seeking revenge in all kinds of ways that seem unusual for her. First she took my .22 rabbit gun & which I've had since I was 9 & ran over it with the car & said it was an accident. Out back we keep a 55 gallon drum in which we burn some of our garbage so we do'nt have to hull it to the Dump & I discovered she had burned some of my books most of them the new Poetry ones. I yelled at her about it but she just sat there like a wart on a Witchs nose & would say nothing to me except that I deserved Everything I got. Then she said that there was no way I was the One Mighty & Strong that was prophesized about in the Doctrine & Covenants & that I should give back all the money I got. This is a strange thing to say because no one is enjoying the Money more than Sandra. I mean shes been spending to beat the band. The second we find another check in the mail or something slipped under the trailer door she jumps in the car & runs for the store & Buys something. I've been telling her that she is suppose to give me the Money for fighting the Gadianton Robbers but she is like a Deaf woman when it comes to my Husbandly admonitions. I tried to tell her that she ought to follow the leadership of the Priesthood & do what I say but she just looked at me with cold angry eyes & got up & drove away. I have half a mind just to buy her a car & put all this nonsense behind us but of course that would be giving into her whims & that would just set up a Situation that none of us could live with. I can tell you that this weekend I'm going on a Coyote hunt & I will be glad to get out of this house & get on the Mountain again. My good friend is going with me. He has a condition & it will be a Rougher hunt for him than usual because of this medical thing. He is a brave soul. I'm not sure he ought to go but this thing will be over in a month or so says the doctor so I guess

she knows best. I'd better go get my .306 out of the closet &
hide it before Sandra accidently runs over it too & the hunt is
Spoiled. I must say my chest has been feeling a little tight these
days & I feel like things are Rushing along too Fast & Furious
& my conscience weighs upon me thick & Dirty. What can I
do though? Its not like I brought all this on myself. Could I
help that little slip of water out of the Sacrament cup? It was
accidental. Does'nt that count for nothing? Now things are a
Mess. I just wanted to be a Scholar & come to understand the
world like a Rabbi of old & all of the sudden I find that I am
mixed up in all kinds of Things.

SOURCE DOCUMENT #29:

Poem from Dora Daphne Tanner's book, Red Rock Runs Through My Veins *(1979), written approximately February 1977.*

You articulate things badly,
you mess with my words and confuse
even the wind-carved rock, wherein I, I
have resisted
such complexities for eons.
You have taken soft buzzing harmonies
delicate themes and stamped out
discordant tones that rage against
soft flowering simplicities.
And in me? In me? In me?
This is the strange thing, a gift
has branched out new and unexpected,
from such noise as you have banged out
like a drum.
A throbbing tom-tom-tom
that has become—what?
How can such a melodious strain arise? In me?
From you?
You are beautiful beyond description,
you are wise—careful, cold, and cunning.
Could this
Song of ours be as dangerous as you,
as gorgeous as you?
You pollinated not just a pistil,

but a theme, a wave front
that gathers from the discord, from the
complexity, nuance, direction, meaning,
And quiet song.
We are entangled in thick complexities,
full of sweetness and sting,
like a hive of honeybees—
No—
like Bumblebees
with wings uncut.

Telegram from Lilly Tanner Baldaia to Dora Daphne Tanner.
June 12th, 1977.

Dearest Dora STOP

I have contacted a criminal lawyer with
more experience than Yalemtsehay STOP

He will contact you shortly and we are
paying for this STOP

We will post bail or whatever it takes to
help STOP

Please do not worry STOP

We believe you are innocent STOP

We love you and all our thoughts and
prayers are with you STOP

Love your Sister Lilly STOP

SOURCE DOCUMENT #31:

Poem by Sandra Thayne. Written July, 1977.
Given to <Redactor> October, 1998.

<According to Sandra the poem was untitled and unfinished.
Never given to Hyrum.>

I look back and wonder when,
You turned from me your Celestial frien'.
I stood by you through thick and thin,
I mended your socks from the rusty bin.
Spaghetti was your favorite dish,
And I even cleaned your catch of fish.
I look at you and wonder why,
The Lord chose you then you stoop to lie.

News reports covering the death of Hyrum Thayne.

From the *Deseret News* Sunday, August 21, 1977
Explosion at Church Picnic Ends in Tragedy

MOAB – Tragedy struck yesterday when a mine explosion killed a man attending an LDS Church party near Moab, Utah. Killed was Moab resident Hyrum Thayne. Injured and still in critical condition is high school history teacher David Hamblin, who is expected to survive. No other injuries were reported, and the LDS missionaries serving in Moab were not in attendance. According to witnesses, Thayne was recreating a scene from *The Book of Mormon* when his pyrotechnics exploded prematurely.

"It's just lucky no children were killed," said Deputy Sheriff Caleb Donaldson. "I try and warn people to be very careful with illegal fireworks and year after year we have tragedies like this."

Search and rescue responded as quickly as possible after a 911 call was placed by someone attending the gathering. However, because of the isolation and inaccessibility of where the accident occurred, it was several hours before teams could get to the location high on the Moab Rim. While the Grand County Search and Rescue is credited with saving Hamblin's life, the shaft was too deep to explore thoroughly, and Thayne's body has not yet been recovered.

Seth Garcia from Grand County Search and Rescue was

one of the first on the scene. "Something went wrong, but what that is I don't think we will ever know. The rope dropping into the hole had been severed by the explosion about fifteen feet down from the lip of the edge. Thayne was below that—about twenty-five feet from the edge—based on the length of the rope that remained. When the explosion went off, he likely plummeted thousands of feet to the bottom. But there is something strange in all this. The explosion occurred between Thayne and the edge. It seems odd that he would have laid the charges so close to the edge and then continued down. But the blast marks are pretty clear."

Thayne, a member of the Moab 4th Ward, is survived by his wife Sandra. He is remembered as a first-rate scholar of bumblebee folklore.

From the *Salt Lake Tribune* Tuesday, August 23, 1977
Moab Man Killed in Explosion

MOAB – In a set of circumstances that can only be called bizarre, one man is dead and another man remains in critical but stable condition in Moab's Allen Memorial Hospital after trying to blow up an alleged nest of KGB agents hiding in a cave outside of Moab, Utah.

"We are having trouble constructing the story," says Police Chief Douglas Wills, "but apparently, a rather sizable group of people believed that communists were infesting the Moab Rim. Hyrum Thayne, a local man known for his scientific work up on the mountain, apparently convinced people that he had the means to rid the town of these agents of the Soviet government and was attempting to take the law into his own hands. In trying to blow up their 'nest' in Endless Cave, something went wrong. The dynamite he was using was illegal and appears to have gone off accidently. We have located the person who provided the explosives and charges are pending."

Witnesses say Thayne had climbed into the cave to set off the charge while a group of people stood outside praying and singing hymns. Thayne is survived by his wife, Sandra Thayne.

From the *Times Independent* Thursday, August 25, 1977
The Death of Hyrum Thayne
By Editor-in-Chief Frank Franklin

The community is still reeling after the death of Hyrum Thayne last Saturday. He was one of Moab's beloved citizens. You will recall that Thayne lead the Easter Parade down Main Street this year in recognition of his fine work in bumblebee ecology, which he conducted up in the La Sals where he worked during the summer. Many were calling him "The Scholar of Moab."

What happened? The facts are still jumbled, but we at the *Times* have pressed both of our reporters into service to get the story. It begins in June of last year when the City Library was broken into and much of the reference section burned (*Times Independent* story June 24, 1976). Hyrum came to believe that the spirits of old *Book of Mormon* robbers possessed local communists and that KGB agents were attempting to undermine free education in the United States in the promotion of socialist agendas.

Thayne identified Endless Cave as the location of the band that had burglarized the library and was going to try and "blow them to kingdom come," as Jeb Marcus, local mechanic, reported. The band was also believed by several of Thayne's associates to be linked to the occult, and in particular, ghosts from a group of robbers mentioned in *The Book of Mormon*.

Lily B., who asked not be identified, reported that she had experienced the ghosts with Thayne and several others: "Yeah, I was there. We all went up to Moonflower Canyon to use the priesthood against these evil apparitions. It was our bishop, his councilors, their wives, and a bunch of the auxiliary organization leaders. Well, the bishop said a prayer and Hyrum started the exercise of his priesthood and all of the sudden, one of them robbers appeared up on a cliff where nobody, but nobody, could get to without a rope. And there weren't no rope neither. It was a girl robber, and as far as we knew we hadn't ever even heard of a girl robber so it made it all the more scary and frightening. She started holler'n some robber gibberish what none of us could understand. And then she flew into the air like superman. I kid you not she just pointed her fist into the air and up up and away she flew. I saw it with my own eyes. O, I was screaming bloody murder. So was everyone. Even some of the Priesthood brethren was yellen to beat the band. I never seen such pandemonium."

Saturday, a group gathered at the Swanny City Park. Thayne addressed them, said one man who wishes to remain anonymous. "He said that Satan desires to sift us as wheat, but that the Gadianton Band would have no power over us. He asked us to screw up our courage and to walk forward in faith." After Thayne's speech, a group of about fifty men, women, and some children hiked up to Endless Cave to see the communists rooted out.

Robert Grisle, our police reporter, hiked up to the cave to get the lay of the land. He reports that the hike was a long one and "I was surprised so many had travelled so far." The entrance to the cave sits right on the corner where the Moab Valley and the Colorado River connect on the southwest side of the river. A hole, a crack really, disappears into the base of the canyon wall and goes straight back into the ancient sandstone. It is pitch black inside, and even with a good flashlight one can never see a formal roof—the height of the crack heading upward is indiscernible because it seems to disappear among the folds of the rock. This cave continues on for about 300 feet and then comes to a sudden drop, ostensibly all the way down to the Colorado River. "If you drop a stone, you can hear it bouncing downward as it hits on small ledges, the sound fading away until there is silence, leaving the impression that it became too distant to hear, rather than reaching the bottom. Endless cave is well-named," Grisle declares.

The witnesses we interviewed said that when the people had assembled at the mouth of the cave, a couple of men pulled out some climbing rope knotted about every foot. Another man was bundling sticks of dynamite with masking tape. He then drilled a hole in the side of one of the sticks with the leather punch of his Swiss army knife, and pushed a blasting cap into the cavity, which he then attached to a green fuse.

Thayne then gave the following speech (pieced together from three accounts). Those listening felt they were hearing the voice of a prophet. Many remained firm in the conviction that, "Hyrum's name will be remembered as a leader in the Latter Days." The speech was reconstructed as follows:

"My good brothers and sisters. You know why we are here. The Gadianton Robbers have inculcated and surreptitiously vindicated all we hold dear. Having arisen from the dust, they have killed and ruled with blood and terror on this God's green Earth. I do not know why I have been chosen to bring these monsters to destruction. But be assured their reign is over. They are trapped in yonder cave and you are here to witness their destruction. It is through hard trials that I have found out their secret lair and know that they are trapped within. They are hid in a room carved like the Hole in the Rock House. They are hiding about thirty feet down from the edge of where the hole starts. I will climb down and toss in the TNT and that will be that. They will never return again. Without those commie bodies the ghosts will flee these lands. So I have been promised by an angel of the Lord."

Dallon Brandon, in his late 70's, was asked if he believed in these Gadianton Robbers. "It ain't a matter of believe or none, sir. It's a fact. Yes, sir, I've seen stuff that would chill you to the bone. I seen these ghosts and they ain't nothing to be taken of no account. I seen them walk in the night and they've got fierce eyes and I promise you that if it wasn't for the power of the priesthood, I would not be standing here today. The Lord raised up Hyrum sure to do those Robbers right."

But something went terribly wrong. Witnesses say that some time after Thayne and Hamblin entered the cave, there was a huge explosion. The bang was deafening. Then stillness for what seemed like a long time, as the people stood gathered in huddled silence. Suddenly there was powerful outrushing of air from the cave, followed by a cloud of white dust. Pandemonium broke out. Sandra, Thayne's wife, screamed. Parents grabbed children, who were starting to raise a chorus of fearful crying. Dust continued to pour from the cave, and people ran back and forth, up and down, in a panicked, unorganized mass.

Bob McKesson reports that the Bishop of the Moab Latter-day Saint Fourth Ward called over one of the young men and whispered in his ear whereupon the boy bolted like a racehorse. "I learned later from this young man, Billy Jenson, that the bishop had whispered, "Don't panic anyone, but you go get Search and Rescue. Now!"

It was about three hours after the explosion before Search

and Rescue could receive the news of the accident and get up to its location. Dick Werkman, a volunteer fireman from Moab, led a team into the cave. "We found Dave Hamblin trying to crawl from the hole. He was in shock and severely disoriented. Blood was coming from both of his ears and his hands were bloody, apparently from trying to crawl out. No sign of Thayne, but a rope secured by a large boulder dangled over the side. I pulled it up and found nothing but a frayed end about fifteen feet down from the edge." Hyrum Thayne was apparently gone forever.

Dave Hamblin, Thayne's companion in the cave, suffered a broken leg, a pierced lung from a couple of his broken ribs, and a slight concussion. He is still recovering in the Moab hospital. He helped us reconstruct what happened in the cave. They entered the cave and secured the rope to a large boulder near the drop. Thayne seemed nervous and took a long time heading over the side. The dynamite was in a bag draped around his neck, with about fifteen feet of safety fuse hanging out. This length was expected to have about a fifteen-minute burn, which should have been enough time to light the fuse with a lighter, toss the explosives into the room of robbers, and get back up the rope. Hamblin was standing guard at the top, and the plan was that after Thayne climbed to safety they were going to stay and push down any communists that tried to climb up the rope after Thayne.

He said Thayne seemed to have trouble climbing down the rope and kept shouting up to him to make sure they were still there.

"I'm lighting the fuse," Thayne said. Then, "Pull me up. Pull me up."

Hamblin said he was back by the boulder where the rope was tied, making sure it held, when the dynamite exploded.

Hamblin had no ideas on how the dynamite might have been set off, but suspects the possessed communists might have had something to do with it.

It is a tragic tale all around and as the facts unfold, *The Times Independent* will continue to cover this story until we have all the details. Our condolences go to the Thayne family and their friends and associates.

SOURCE DOCUMENT #33:

*Hyrum Thayne's eulogy, delivered by Marne Law,
September 3, 1977. Transcribed from tape recording by Sandra
Thayne, January 1980. Given to <Redactor> October, 1998.*

It is my honor this day to stand before you and offer up a few words about our beloved brother Hyrum Thayne. He is gone now but will not be forgotten. My Brothers and Sisters, we were in great danger and the good Lord provided us with a great man to rid this valley of an infestation like unto nothing we have ever seen. Like something from the Book of Mormon itself. That such a man did arise speaks truly that we are at last in the days spoken of by all the prophets since the beginning of the world.

I look down and see Sister Thayne and think of the blessed memory of our great champion. Her cheeks are streaked with sorrow now but there will come a day where those tears will be dried and you will stand by his side through the eternities as his Queen and Priestess. We weep now, but by and by, we will rejoice.

What can we say of dear Brother Thayne? He was born at this time and at this place to do the work he was called upon to do. Of this we know beyond a shadow of a doubt. He is the finest blood this town has ever produced.

He was raised up in the last days to rid the world of the Gadianton Robbers. With the support of his lovely helpmate who has headed the Child Protection Society for these many months, and who mourns in silence here on the front row, he has sacrificed his life that we might be free. Greater love has no man than he that lays his life down for his friends. Sandra has told me things that make it clear that for Hyrum the veil was thin. She has told us things that would set your hair standing up on end. He has seen visions and had visitors from on high. He conversed with angels on a regular basis and Sandra caught him talking in the bathroom with a light glowing from the inside such that showed that he was conversing with angels as bright as the noonday sun. He was a spiritual giant of epic proportions.

Who else could have taken on so directly the wicked One's purposes in the world? He took on the Gadianton Robbers and the communists who gave them power. He offered his own life to root them from their nest there in Endless Cave. May his memory ever be bright. He discovered that they were holed up with a small band of Soviet Communists who were KGB agents sent by Brezhnev himself to seek out the secrets of the Gadianton Robbers to align themselves with secret combinations which they hope to use to bring down the government of this the United States and to spy on the good people of Moab. And Hyrum ended their reign. He stopped their designs upon this fair land. And we have him to thank. His courage will not soon be forgotten.

I apologize for losing control. I cannot seem to contain my emotions this day.

To go on, those that went to high school with Hyrum know that even then he was as smart as a whip. Who knew that in addition to his great faith, he would become one of the preeminent scientists of our age? It is wondrous to contemplate that he would show the world of so-called atheist scientists, evolutionists, godless socialists, and communists that faith existed in the world, yea even among the most humble of creatures. Yea, even the lowly bumblebee. I saw them in the garden this morning about their work. It reminded me that in this life we are here only for a short time. Hyrum's time has passed, but we will meet him again in a better place, a place without fear or dread. In which place Hyrum will surely stand with all his contributions to the world made bare and his countenance will shine down upon us once again. Then we will all be led with him into the highest kingdom, yea, even the Celestial Kingdom and into the Lord's presence with these words: "Well done, thou good and faithful servant. Thou hast been faithful over a few things, and I will make thee ruler over many things. Enter thou into the joy of thy Lord."

I humbly leave you with these things in the name of our Lord, even Jesus Christ. In the Name of Jesus Christ. Amen.

From Dora Daphne Tanner's file in the Utah State Hospital, Provo, UT. September 14, 1978.

I sit here alone. The walls are bright, an off-white that dulls and dampens emotion. The door is secure. A small window that captures a modicum of natural light sits high with just enough area to provide evidence that there is another world outside my captivity. The greenish window glass in the door is embedded with a kind of chicken wire, giving a sense of permanence and authority. On the wall opposite is a mirror, a window meant only to be gazed through in one direction. From out to in. I sit here alone. I sit here alone. I sit here alone in the world. The remnants of an uneaten breakfast sit untouched on a tray on a small chrome gurney beside my bed. They think I am violent. I am violent. When emptied of all humanity, what else could I be? The sterility of the room reminds me of the ship and the others who took me long ago. The efficiency. The uniformity of sharp lines cuts through any aesthetic sense like an athame. The room is full of implements, not tools. Apparatuses, not gear. Equipment, not craft. Hyrum is dead. I am (and vast thought has gone into finding this word), forsaken. Forsaken. It fits so perfectly, so snuggly that I've made it a blanket that I've wrapped myself in. Forsaken. Who has forsaken me? God, Goddess, Hyrum, Mother, Father, Sis, government, the universe, law, city, ethics, community, nature, meaning, hope, the sun, the moon, the stars, the sound of crickets, the blue of sky, the touch of a lover, the feel of the wind, belief, doubt, light, the pleasures of my skin, the taste of his mouth, the smell of the morning, my eyes, the slow feel of spring water on my tongue, my child, my ch—

Let that dash stretch like a line into eternity, a parallel line that has lost its partner and goes on and on as lines do, forever running without accompaniment into the blankness of forever. That's what it means to be forsaken, to lose all hope that there is anything but emptiness forever. There will never be an intersection with another line, only endless running on and on. If they would let me I would fall into nothing, disappear in an empty heartless void and who would miss me? Who would mourn my brief appearance here on the edge of this dangerous galaxy fraught with terror? Who would notice that I have left this blasted and fallen world? A world filled with nothing but meaningless abject sorrow.

My child? In what dimension do you dwell? Do they warm you there? Do they feed you? Do they clothe you in blue pajamas with little attached feet? Who changes your diapers? Who comes to your cries? Who lifts you and holds you warm and safe? Who presses you to her breast? Who sings to you lullabies, softly and longingly in the night? Who tells you stories? Who presses lips to your round belly and blows with loud farty trumpeting to draw out your giggling and laughter? Whose finger do you clutch and bring to your mouth? What face elicits your first smile? Who rubs your gums when your teeth are cutting hard through your tender mouth? Who drinks in your smell with deep purposeful breaths? Who touches the soft hair of your tender head and rubs softly, creating supple swirls among your locks? Who holds your feet and squeezes so softly, rubbing the soles with her thumb? Who pats your back until a careful burp bubbles up and signals satisfaction? Who bounces you up and down when you cry and cry? Who listens by the door to make sure you are breathing? Who covers you with blankets whether you need the extra warmth or not? Who loves you? Who loves you? Who loves you? But mark this well, little one. I will find you. I will hunt this universe until you are found even if I must do this in death. My spirit will scour every realm that this pale existence haunts, and I will rage! I will burn like a white-hot star until those that have taken you feel this pain! This sorrow! This terror. If they have a civilization in their black existence I will raze it in my fury. And I will find you and take you home. There is not a god that will stop me. A monster-god showed his face when you came into existence and were taken out of it. I will find that monster-god and if he does not help find you I will become a god myself, like the Mormons say we will, and I will raze existence itself and I will crack that god wide open and out of the slaying I will build a better universe than this. How hard could it be to make some improvement on this wreck! AND NO MOTHER WILL EVER, EVER, EVER BE TORN FROM HER CHILD. I SWEAR IT. I WILL DAMN THIS MONSTER GOD IN HIS OWN HELL AND MAKE A BETTER PLACE THAN THIS HORROR!

And no one will ever, ever, ever be forsaken like this.

Hyrum's journal, hand-written manuscript.
Written August 1977 (This is Hyrum's last entry and
seems to have been made a few weeks after the longer
document was finished. A different pen was used).

So I'm going to end this. Verily, I have been Sadder than I've ever been. It is time to end the Gadianton Robbers once & for all. So I hope this works. I know at least that no ghost will appear to contradict me. The ghost is gone. It will be dramatic & hopefully all the Fireworks will convince folks that the power has gone forth into the world & the Gadianton Robbers have departed Hence & I can live with some measure of peace & continue my Scholarly pursuits. Sandra seems back to normal at least. She has seemed so mad & angry the last few weeks but lately she has seemed back to her old Self. She has taken to visiting her mother almost every day & I'm glad I'm not being dragged there. Sandras mother is as goody-good of a Mormon as you can find. She sees things one way & one way only & if its not written in the Scriptures then she does not believe it. I cant abide going over to her house because she starts in on me almost at once. She has a mutty little yappy dog that always nips at my heels & who she treats like a child. Ooo Bobo this and Ooo Bobo that. And she is always whispering to it & cuddling it so I avoid that place like a Elephant does a mouse. But Sandra has not seemed right up till this week. I think having all that money finally got to her & she had what they call a Nervous breakdown. Toward the end there she was a Terror. Not speaking to me & Storming around the house. I'm glad to see that she has Settled down. She is at her mothers now. Its times like this I believe that Heavenly Father might be watching me. Seeing what I do & Waiting for just the right moment to let the other hammer fall.

So it is settled. Most of the Ward is going to meet at the Park for a barbeque & then we are going up to Endless Cave to put an end to this Nonsensicalness and Fuss. Things have been so hard lately it is hard to believe that this hunk of my Trouble is about to be Over. And there are troubles you cannot imagine. I can scarcely take them in any more. I feel like a squirrel in the back of a Camper shell covered pickup being bounced along a rutty dirt road with too little to get my claws into and no control over the fourwheeling roughness of the ride.

I'm not the only one I suppose. Yea a young beautiful Poet in our midst took it upon herself to lose her baby after it was had up on the mountain. Some are saying that she killed it herself in Cold blood after having birthed it. I happen to know 2 of the Cowboys who was on hand for the blessed event & they agree there ain't no way she did it. Now you may say that this does'nt have anything to do with my confessions & in that you would be right but it seems to me that verily it is a matter of Truth. You see while there ain't no Gadianton Robbers there are things in the world that are hard to believe & some say if you cant See things with your own eyes then those things are not. So here is the poser you might say. Dora tells a story about how she was taken one night by strange Creatures from outer Space. She tells it & I over heard her telling it to a friend at the Sundowner Restaurant or I would not know these things myself in a way that you know she is speaking the Truth. I think if people would look into my eyes a little harder & not try &

just hear what they want to believe like there are Gadianton Robbers about they would see right through me to the Scholar underneath & know that I was making up the Whole Mess. But that night in the Restaurant when I overheard her tell her friend about these Creatures I could see her eyes shining with Truth & honesty & there was no doubt in my mind that the things she was saying were 100% True & blue. Somethings you just know. I have read some of her Poetry. Now most of it does not make much sense to me & it does not rhyme but that is the new way of things & so you cant judge a Poem by how well it rhymes. So something Strange happened & if it happened Once who is to say that it might not happen again? Now I know this sounds far fetched & almost like my Sanity has slipped a notch down its cog but it could be that something bad like this happened to her again. Anyway I hope they find the baby. I started even praying for it even though I'm pretty sure Heavenly Father has it in for me. I feel bad for this great Poet although she do'nt mean anything in particular to me. They have locked her away. I think on this baby all the time though. It was a baby boy. Think it would have grown up to be a Fine boy. I think it would have been the kind of boy who would have played down on the Creek & caught Pollywogs like I did. I think it would have grown up to be a good boy. Maybe a Scientist Like me. I cant help but think about this Boy all the time. I do'nt know why. I just wonder about him. About who he was. And who he might have been. I think he was a Special boy.

Anyway after the Gadianton Robbers are rid of I plan to settle down into a life of Scholarship. My studies of the Bees brought me a load of Joy & I aim to do more. I need Joy. I am tired of watering my Pillow at Night. Maybe not Science with Bombus this next time but there are Ants up on the mountain everywhere & it may be that there are questions that still confuse Scientists & that my studies could Clear up once & for all. There is much Science to be done. I'm just the man to do it but I'll have to burn that bridge when I come to it.

SOURCE DOCUMENT #35:

William Babcock's personal journal. October 1998.

Our good friend <Redactor> has been very patient. We are unusually tired and stayed in our hotel to rest while <Redactor> busied himself with some errands that needed running. I'm looking in the large hotel mirror. I see Edward's eyes are closed. His mouth is moving slightly and there is a glowing softness about his face. A grace that bespeaks peace. I look at my own reflection. My brow is lined. When did I get so old? But even given the wrinkles, the frowns of worry seem to stretch it in new ways. Marcel has yet to grant me access to our legs. I've decided to record the events that led to Edward's madness. Perhaps in writing it I will recall things that might help me bring him back.

It was late on a Tuesday morning. The weather had turned delightfully warm, almost 15 C, and Edward and I decided to take a walk in the Mozart Park and stop at our favorite antiquarian bookshop. It was near the museums and if we felt up to it, we thought we would take a peek at an Egyptian exhibition from Berlin that was making the rounds through Europe.

The bookshop was inexplicably closed, so we wandered down the street staring dreamily into the windows. We bought an ice cream cone and laughed deliciously when not only one of us dropped his cone, but we both did (Edward dropped his first and I got in several good licks before mine tumbled to the pavement). There was a clothier that displayed a beautiful

Austrian hat that Edward had often expressed some interest in. The day was so beautiful; we could not seem to keep from indulging every whim that presented itself, and we not only purchased the hat for Edward, but on a lark we bought a matching pair. We would normally have bought different hats, but these seemed so perfect, and complemented our coat so well, we could not resist. It may have been my last happy moment.

We stepped out into the mid-summer sun and each took a deep breath and commented on the fineness of the air and the almost spring-like feel to the weather. We strolled a bit and took the Straussenbahn around the Ring just for fun. We ended up in the Jewish quarter near Swedenplotz and decided, since we had not had any luck visiting our favorite bookstore, we would poke around in one that specializes in Jewish antiquarian books. We were just browsing the stacks when Edward noticed a large Quatro in Yiddish called, *The Reuven Tsetsov Illustrations and His Mystical School.* I asked Edward if he had ever heard of it. He said he had not and asked the storekeeper to carry it over to a table and gave us a pair of white cotton gloves with which to handle the book. The volume was dated 1878. It was filled with glorious woodcuts, intricate and exceptionally realistic. Each was a scene from the Zohar with its Aramaic text printed below. The woodcuts were as richly detailed as Dore's, but with an otherworldly quality that seemed quite modern and reminiscent of the Wien Club. But then we turned a page and we both gasped. I laughed out loud. There on the page was a portrait head that can only be described as a classic post-Betty-and-Barney-Hill alien, its large eyes staring at us. The text beneath in Aramaic said,

"The king will rejoice in Elohim. When supernal Power is aroused to embrace Him beneath His head, drawing Him close in joy, so that all will be one, then the king will rejoice, the joy of a stream issuing through a single secret, hidden channel, flowing into him. Two who are one, and so the world is consummated in existence."

On the page opposite was a typical alchemical drawing of the marriage of the King and Queen. It was completely inappropriate to the text of the Zohar. The King and Queen were not joined as seen typically in these kinds of esoteric drawings—with the body of a man and a woman (including their clothing) split down the middle. This drawing had two heads emerging from a single body, like ours, dressed in a Medieval page's costume. Just below his chest was a radiant spark scattering rays of bright light in all directions. Two heads and a star glowing like the sun about where Marcel would be. I smiled and said something flippant about how everyone was drawing us these days. But Edward was silent, almost breathless as he looked at the picture. Marcel passed the legs to Edward at that moment (I have not had them back since). Of course, I thought nothing of it at the time. I looked at the picture a little more closely, and in Hebrew (not Aramaic like the rest of the Zohar) was written *The Marriage of Serpent*. Underneath that title was this text from the Zohar:

> "So the mystery of the word is written: Now the serpent was slyer than any creature of the field that YHVH Elohim had made—mystery of the evil serpent descending from above, skimming the surface of bitter waters, seducing below till they fall into his nets. This serpent is death of the world, penetrating a person's blind gut. He is on the left, while another, of life, is on the right, both accompanying each human, as they have established."

I joked with Edward, "Why is the evil serpent on the left. Evil and 'left'? How does that make me feel?"

Edward did not answer.

The pictures were strange. Of course, in other alchemical works this picture should have been the marriage of the King and Queen. The marriage of the serpent really makes no sense either from the Zohar or from standard alchemical texts. And the illustration made no sense. I was blathering on about the Devil's using the snake in the Garden of Eden and trying to speculate on Kabbalah and the biblical text, but Edward was clearly not listening. Edward closed the book, and called the man over and inquired how much he was asking. The man looked at Edward, and quoted an outrageous price of 140,000 schillings. I was certain it was not worth half that, but Edward nodded, and, over my protests, handed the man our Mestro Card. Edward instructed the man to deliver it to our apartment which, as you can imagine, he was glad to do. That night Edward started speaking only in Hebrew.

I've gone over the events again and again, trying to pull some meaning from what happened. Edward and Marcel seemed to have entered into some sort of conspiracy that has left me out. Of course, my taste for Hebrew mysticism is limited and my reading of Aramaic abysmal, but I've since been pouring over the Zohar and the Tsetsov illustrations looking for what Edward saw. My eyes are watering as I write; I find nothing except the vague allusions to two becoming one and the left-right versions of the serpent, and the odd coincidence of illustrations that seem to play with themes from our life. But coincidences are just that. I've always paid less attention to them than Edward has. When we filter through the randomness of life, like clams looking for nuggets of significance, we are bound to come across such parcels of meaning and circumstance that attract our gaze and command our attention. Yet, what of them? To embrace them all is to wander from mirage to mirage in a world created by irrational constructions of existence's noise. And maybe madness brokers no rationality. It may be that there will be no explanation that will offer itself to disclose the reasons for Edward's departure from the world of cause and effect. We stand in relationship closer than any human beings really ought to. I've been there for *all* his experiences. We started with the same phenotypical brain at birth, genetically identical heads; we've had identical experiences, identical nature and nurture, yet here we are—he gay, me straight; he religious, me an unbeliever; he mad, me clinging to rationality by a thread. Can the universe depend so thoroughly on who is on the right and who is on the left? Is it all chaos, and hung precariously on such tiny breaks in symmetry? I look out our window and there are red rocks forming the canyons, broken and scarred by such tiny deviations in rain and wind—compounded and summing eons of such differences. And here am I. My brother mad. A mind that is completely "other" having sided with him…. Ah Marcel. What are you? I have often wondered. Since Marcel experiences both of us inwardly, is he a more complete person? An entity of wholeness, combined of our two consciousnesses? Maybe he does not see us as separate entities. Neurologists these days say that the average human mind is composed of many others, all competing and experiencing some phenomenological reality. But the self that I experience from all these competing "persons" is one complete thing, one consciousness. One consciousness. Me. Maybe Marcel is like that? Maybe he is the higher consciousness formed from our separate contributions, like the two hemispheres of a single brain. I am but one piece of his/her more comprehensive whole, providing input to his integrated self. He sees with both Edward's and my eyes, hears with both of our sets of ears. It maybe that the way that the feeling and control of the legs is parceled out is an unconscious act of something much other and loftier than I can comprehend. I remember once riding trail on a warm early autumn day near Warner Lake. The fall aspens stretched up the slopes of the La Sals in a patchwork of soft yellows and greens rising until they met the dark igneous incursions of the higher mountains. The landscape seemed filled with a wonderous complexity and charged with the meaning that emerges only when one is situated in nature's full and subtle tranquility. We were listening to the clop, clop, clop of Starry's hoof beats, attending to the motion of her body rather than the inner chatter of our own thoughts, when suddenly, quite unexpectedly, I seemed to flow into Edward and Marcel in a strange and expansive way. The feeling lasted only for a moment and has ever been indescribable, but Edward felt it as well, as if we apprehended each other and Marcel for just an instant. I have been reluctant to think on this event as meaning something—perhaps we were all doing something no more mystical than simultaneously falling asleep—but even so, something happened and maybe this kind of coming together is something closer to what God is (if there be such a thing). Maybe God is just the integration of millions of such consciousnesses? Marcel is just a smaller version of God. A divine entity with only two such consciousnesses, far from God's integration of billions to be sure, but infinitely higher than a single consciousness. Who can say?

It's later in the day. Edward is asleep. <Redactor> asked if I would like to visit Sandra. She lives in a small home not far from here (and of course "anywhere" in Moab is not far from here by Vienna standards). I told him no. I did not want to disturb Edward and I have no real interest anymore in the quest to piece together the story of Hyrum. I think back on the coincidences, the paintings, the books, the chance meetings— they all look to me like the daily horoscopes from *Heute Austria* in which you draw on whatever relevancies matter to you and that bear on the text, then pick and choose meaning into a Rorschach test of your own devising and embrace whatever you find there. Edward is Mad. What else matters anymore?

REDACTOR'S NOTE:

Interview with Sandra, Oct. 1998

I visited with Sandra at the home she purchased in Moab with the insurance money she received after Hyrum's death. It's a small adobe home built on 2nd east in the 1920's. She keeps a lovely garden with a clematis trellis gracing the entryway, which leads to a small yard overgrown with lilacs. Two cottonwoods sprout from either side of a walkway that leads to her porch. Their roots have twisted and cracked the cement, making it buckle here and collapse there, creating a bit of uneven pacing and a tripping hazard. She met me at the screen door and invited me in. The furniture was worn and the house had an odd unidentifiable odor—neither pleasant nor unpleasant. Time seems to have made her simple. She tends to wander a bit in conversation, but to convey the meat of the interview, I only need report a fraction of what was actually a very long conversation.

We chatted about her garden. I told her I was there to ask some questions about her life with Hyrum. Her face lit up like a child's at Christmas.

"My first husband! He was a delight! A learned man. There is a statue of him near the ward house!" Then, unlike the previous sentences, which were spoken with a sense of almost reverence and remembered praise, the last was spoken flatly, without emotion. "He saved the town from the Gadianton Robbers."

"Sandra. Did you believe there were Gadianton Robbers?"

"Of course! We all saw what they did. I led the Child Protection Society for a time to keep those monsters at bay. They killed that bitch's child."

This surprised me. The word "bitch" seemed so uncharacteristic of Sandra during our conversation to this point.

"I think she was accused of killing her child. Not the Gadianton Robbers."

She gave a sharp sound like, "Phifft" and continued. "She went loony after that, or maybe she always was, but she didn't kill that child. It was the Robbers. She was out cold when that child was murdered."

"They never found a body. Some people believe it may have been a wild animal."

She shook her head. "It was Robbers. Or them what was under their control, as was abundantly happening back then. And Hyrum put an end to them sure. He died a martyr saving us from their like."

I spoke my last question carefully and nonchalantly: "Sandra, where do you suppose they buried the child?"

She just looked away and shrugged. "How would I know?"

REDACTOR'S EPILOGUE

These are the notes that end this tale.

I pick up Dora at the Best Western on the south end of town. She's been there at my expense since she escaped from the State Hospital two months ago. She contacted me and asked for help. I could not resist. Her sister had died shortly before, and in her mourning, Dora decided enough was enough and mustered the conviction that it was time to go. While attending a children's play being staged at Brigham Young University especially for the patients, she bolted. She hid in an unlocked study room in the Harold B. Lee Library, spending the night quietly lying on the rugged floor until the next day. She stole two unattended backpacks lying on a table, along with a jacket hanging from one of the chairs. The students were away searching the stacks, or maybe even gone to lunch (she said BYU students are astonishingly trusting, and there were a number of unattended packs to choose from). She found $343 in cash among the goods she'd stolen, and she hopped a Greyhound to Moab from the Provo bus station.

I gave her my materials and she read through them all, including my exchanges with the Babcock twins. When she was finished, she called me on the phone and asked me to come over to her hotel room.

"We need to go up there," she said firmly.

"To the mountain. To the place…?"

"Yes. To the place. We all need to be there. Can you arrange for that freak to come?"

"Dora. They had nothing to do with it."

"I know," she sighed. "I know. I've always known. The medicine. My abduction by monsters. I blamed everyone. But someone took my baby. They were there. Hyrum was there. I was there. Who else could have taken it? We need to go back up there. All of us."

"Why?"

"I don't know. Please. Can you get the twins here? Please. My life has been stolen from me. Please help an old woman close things."

So it was arranged. She insisted they bring the painting. She thought it was a part of the story. It had to be. Meanwhile, I fly from Grand Junction, Colorado, to Milwaukee to pick up a box of things Dora's sister had left to her: mostly personal remembrances of their mother and childhood. I then fly to Salt Lake and pick up William and Edward. Edward, sadly, seems to have slipped further off the deep end. He babbles in Hebrew, his eyes fixed to the horizon. How good it is to see them. Despite the burdens William carries, he is as friendly and affable as ever, although he cannot mask the sorrow in his eyes each time he gazes toward Edward. I have grown close to these men and find myself infused with gratitude for their friendship and willingness to travel so far under such fragility of body and mind, and for such tenuous reasons. William, I suspect, has come not at Dora's request, but in some hope that there is something in returning to their old haunts that may shake Edward's mooring loose from the dark world he has entered.

William and Edward seem to have aged a decade in the months since I last saw them. Their eyes sag somewhat, and their skin appears more blotched with age spots, this despite a soft translucence. They seem frail and move much more slowly than I remember. Still, they manage. That is something. We drive south, in quiet conversation about the strange things that have happened. William seems more sad and anxious than I ever remember him.

Back in Moab, Dora has set the agenda. She does not want to meet the twins until we go up on the mountain, but she wants to see the painting. William has decided not to bring it back to Vienna. He will donate it to the Museum of Moab (whose curators, when told about its mysterious origins, made it clear that they were eager to have it, especially since it tied together such fascinating Moab personalities and events: the abduction of baby-killing poet Dora Daphne Tanner and the fabled cowboying Siamese twins). I take Dora to see it.

Since her escape, she has seemed more vibrant and alive than the old woman shuffling through the halls of the State Hospital. But as we enter the museum she seems small and vulnerable and clutches my arm. She has read its description in William's letter, but she is not prepared for its reality. Its size and presence frighten even me, and as the director uncovers it in the back room, we both gasp. Dora's eyes are wide with terror and she is trembling, but she does not flinch away. She looks at it closely. She examines the aliens and the table for some time, looks at the picture of the twins hanging on the wall, and then turns away.

"That's enough," she says.

The next day we will drive up to the La Sals, to the place she gave birth so many years ago.

I first pick up the twins at the Apache Hotel. Edward is unchanged and still muttering. William seems nervous and expectant. At the Holiday Inn, Dora comes out. The greetings are awkward. Last time they met was on the mountain the night Dora gave birth. William tries to sound warm and greets her like an old friend, but there is stiffness and restraint in his voice. I wonder if he is remembering her short story in which she depicts him as a monster in league with the aliens. It's not clear that Dora does not think that. Dora is cautious and withholds her hand from his, extended in greeting, but she bows awkwardly, not formally, and with a small grace that seems to extend a scrap of friendship, despite her obvious attempt to keep some distance. She looks at William, then at Edward, and says, "I'm sorry about your brother. <Redactor> told me."

William nods. "Thank you."

I suggest we get in the truck. Dora climbs into the rear seat of the extended-cab pickup that I've rented and I help the twins into the front seat.

As I climb into the driver's side, William says, "I had feeling in the legs for that. I think Marcel wants this trip too."

I nod. I do not know what to say.

We've decided to take the long way and drive down the river road, up Castle Valley and onto the Loop Road. It will take us most of the day to get to the site of Dora's parturition, but all of us want to spend some time up in the mountains, renewing our acquaintance with the young laccoliths.

As we climb through the scrub oak, Waas rises steeply to the west. Just after we pass Webb Hollow, a couple of young jet-black steers block our path. I honk, but they don't budge. "Damn things," Dora says crossly. I look over at William, and he is smiling. Even so, a sadness graces his eyes that the grin masks poorly. He asks me to roll down the window. I do, and he lets out a wild (and loud), "Yee Aaaa Yeah Whoop Yeah!" The cow gives a kick and lumbers into the scrub oak. Edward does not seem to have noticed, but I glance back in the mirror, and Dora has not been able to suppress a smile. I roll up the window.

I try to keep up the chatter, but after a while give up and allow us to fall into the rhythms of Edward's repetition of the Shema. Somehow, as we drive though the gambel oaks of the eastern slopes, the chant does not sound out of place. The gravel road kicks up white dust in our wake. As we make our way past the Brumley Ridge, the aspens are golden and stand with quiet dignity. They seem to demand an acknowledgement that we are ephemeral, momentary things, passing like a breeze, a moment's breath, and then gone. As we make our way through the Geyser Pass, with Haystack Mountain on our left and Mount Mellerthin on our right, we cross a cattle gate. There is a loud bang, and the flap, flap, flap of a blown tire. The steering goes slushy, forcing me over. I walk back to the cattle guard and discover a piece of rebar poking up between the slats. It probably bounced from the back of someone's pickup. It has torn a monstrous hole in the tire.

The twins and Dora pile out of the vehicle and sit down on a blanket that I've spread off the road in the shade of a small aspen grove. They do not chat. It takes me much longer to change the tire than it should have. The mounting bracket of the brace holding the spare under the truck bed is bent, and I have to hammer at it with a rock to straighten it out enough to twist it off with the tire iron. William, bless his heart, keeps calling over to see if there is anything he can do.

I bring them some water and turkey sandwiches that I picked up at Subway before we left the city. William cuts theirs with a small pocketknife while Edward holds the sandwich steady on a plastic plate placed flat on the ground. Edward does not stop his chant, but orchestrates this maneuver mechanically and with ease. He pauses to eat small pieces of the sandwich. What is this madness that allows him to continue the complex coordination that it takes to manage both William's and his own basic needs, and yet seems to have removed him from other aspects of the world?

Dora watches them, carefully. William does not seem to notice, but suddenly he looks up and says, "We did not take your baby."

Tears well up in Dora's eyes, but she says nothing.

William scoots closer (I wonder if he has control of their legs?). He puts his hand on her arm, and says, "We are not in league with aliens either."

"You think I'm crazy," she says quietly, and then adds, "I don't know anything anymore… but no, you're not with them. No one of flesh and blood could be."

William, still holding onto her arm, asks, perhaps a little too professorially, "Dora, why could it not have been a coyote or a cougar?"

She pulls her arm away. "You don't know them," she says flatly, "I do. The umbilical cord was cut clean!"

"Dora, which is more likely: some Moab coroner mistook the nature of the cut, or that aliens came and took your baby? Go with the probabilities." William seems especially weary. "Go with the probabilities."

Suddenly, she reaches for her handbag and shuffles around for something. I have a horrified flash that she is reaching for a handgun, but she simply pulls out a photograph, somewhat yellowed, the corners stained less, as if it had been pulled from an old-style photo album mount.

"Here," she says. "This was in the box my sister sent. What do your probabilities do with this?"

William looks at the photo and gasps, his hand shaking. He looks at Dora, then looks at the photo, then looks at Dora. "How?… Where?" His lips are trembling. He looks at me, his eyes wild with surprise, and shakily hands me the photograph.

It is clearly the photo used to construct the painting within the painting William brought from Vienna: the twins, on Starry, riding down an aspen-lined road.

"Dora, did you take this?" I ask.

"I suppose I did. I don't remember it. Probably when I was helping Hyrum with his bumblebee studies."

"But the painting? How..." William is till shaking. Edward continues his muttering, Hebrew coming continuously from his lips.

"My sister must have done it. How it ended up in Europe, I can't guess... maybe she painted it while she was living in Kuwait back when her Portuguese husband worked for an oil company—I don't know—but you can see some of the symbols from an amulet her grandmother-in-law wore around the table in the painting. But she knew my story. I must have sent her this photo for some reason. Of course, she could not have shown me the painting—it would be too painful for me." She pauses, then adds, "My sister didn't believe me. She thought I was sick." She trails off... "I cannot imagine why she painted this."

William takes the photograph from me and waves it in front of Edward. "Edward! Edward! See, there is a rational explanation! It's not supernatural! Look! Look! Come back. Come back. Please, Edward. The symbols on the table from the Picatrix! They are from Moorish magic! Her husband was Portuguese. It all makes sense. Edward! Edward!"

William tries holding it at different distances from Edward's face, but he stares straight ahead, obviously not seeing the painting, nor does he pause. William keeps trying, keeps begging, but nothing happens.

Dora says, "How strange the painting comes to you, then winds up in Moab. Circles within circles. I take a photo not far from here on the mountain. I send it to my sister. Who turns it into a painting. That shows up in Vienna. That ends up in your hands—the subject of the photo. Who comes back to Moab, with my sister's painting. That leads us to sitting here, with the photo in your hands." She looks at William and smiles with assurance. "How can you say that it is not supernatural? Not magical? There is something big here. Something unfolding."

William looks at her with tears welling up in his eyes. He covers them with his hand; his mouth is a straight line, lips pinched. Finally, he says, "Coincidences happen. We live in Vienna, the art capital of Europe. We are intimately involved in the art world. It is no surprise that a painting mistaken—or forged, it would appear—to be a Shmelev should wind up there. It is no surprise that we should see it, since we saw much of the art that makes its way to Wien. It is no surprise we would be affected by it because it involves our history. Our own filter of importance brings it out of its obscurity and to the attention of those attending to our history, like <Redactor>. <Redactor> has been gathering pieces of the story into a coherent whole. That those pieces should reintegrate under his direction is neither surprising, nor evidence of divine—or alien—intervention." He is still shaking. "My own brother gave in to the temptation of mistaking perfectly understandable flows of events as coincidental improbabilities suggesting divine intervention. I will not."

Dora scowls, "Very tidy. Thousands of coincidences just happen ..."

"Yes, Dora, an act of memory and attention, not of teleology."

"What about finding your own mother's work in Melk? You ascribe everything you cannot understand to chance. The photo makes its way around the world in a painting and then reappears in the mountains where it was taken. You are missing the power of emergence! You try to tick-tock this into a reduction that does not fit or make any sense. You cannot fit it together without grotesque twistings. How can all of this just be coincidence? This is the story of life on earth: simple things turn into complex things. Evolution. Things emerge. Life is emergence.... You are just like them. The monsters. Trying to reduce the world in order to manufacture a nihilism in its living heart. Trying to create a void of your own making. There is more there than that. All this means something. It has to."

William looks at Dora, frowns, and says coldly, "It means nothing. Cause and effect. We are a broken stick, a bit of debris cast on the tide. We move to currents that we cannot understand, but they 'mean' nothing."

Dora almost growls, "I'm glad that works for you. I'm still missing a son. He means something."

A raven caws above our heads. Dora looks toward it and then back at William. No one speaks for a few minutes, until William turns to me and says, "It's late. Perhaps you should finish the tire. I would not like my brother and me to have to spend the night on the mountain."

I finish the tire and we climb back into the pickup and drive forward. Luck is not with us, and we take a wrong turn, near Dark Canyon Lake, that requires us to backtrack. By the time we reach the turnoff to our destination, the sun is below the horizon and only the tops of the mountains have not entered into the Earth shadow. I ask William if we should head back down. He looks tired. I'm worried about him. Edward continues his chant, but it has sunk to barely a whisper—perhaps the most disturbing sign of the triad's weariness.

He looks at me a long time before answering, "No, go on. Let's get this over with. You can drive in the dark and we can sleep when we get back on the gravel."

"Are you sure?"

"Go on. Wir sind nur sehr müde."

I can sense just how worn out they are. I pull onto the dirt road for the last three miles, before we get to the main road that runs to Buckeye Reservoir, which will take us past the site of these infamous events. It is rough terrain, and although I drive slowly and carefully, trying to reduce the jostling, William is forced to hold on to the side handle with his active hand, reaching over from the left across Edward. Dora remains silent, but seems alert—animated and expectant.

It is fully dark now, and the high-beams light up the two-rut dirt road that meanders through the thick white-barked trees on either side. Insects fly up before the truck like ashes from a fire, causing a constant snow of haphazard motion. A deer, a small three-point buck, leaps onto the road. It runs ahead of us a short distance before it makes a four-legged leap into the trees and snowberry on the side. In a couple of places, the road runs so close to small aspens, they scrape the side of the truck.

"I don't think the road was this bad when we were here," William says anxiously.

"It wasn't," Dora agreed. "This has gone to Hell since our day."

"It used to be a short cut between Dark Canyon and Canopy Gap, I think," William replies.

"Yeah. Probably unnecessary since they graded most of the road."

We have to cross a small gully that cuts deeply across the road, and everyone holds their breath as we dip sharply to the left. I hold on to William's arm to keep him from falling into me. He doesn't seem to mind. One-handed, I steer us out of the streamlet cleft and back onto the road. I am disappointed the short conversation does not resume as we continue on.

We hit better road and meander north again. At last, I pull off onto a small meadow of grass, forbs, and sagebrush that runs gently down a small slope to a stand of aspens. A large boulder, the size of a small cottage, rests on the edge of the meadow. A twisted ponderosa pine grows right out of the top of the rock. "We are here," I proclaim unnecessarily. Everyone knows where we are.

Dora is wide-eyed and panting, her mouth open, obviously in the throes of something like a panic attack. I jump out of the cab and help her out of the back. I instinctively put my arms around her and she pushes me away.

"Take me there," she breathes.

"Are you OK?" I ask, grasping her by the shoulders.

She seems to realize for the first time since leaving the truck that I am there with her.

"What?"

"Are you OK?"

"Yes." She relaxes a bit.

The twins climb out of the other door and with surprising swiftness clamber over to our side. Both of their faces are ashen white, and they are staring at the ground. Edward has quit talking and is breathing hard. Both of their hands are shaking badly.

William speaks first. "Why are we here, Dora?" He sounds exhausted. His voice is flat.

She does not answer him, but is staring into the trees.

Finally, she speaks. "I can't feel him."

"Who, Dora?" William's voice seems very hard. "Who, Dora? Who? A coyote ate your baby. Get used to the idea."

She spins around and violently slaps Edward on the face,

and Edward, for the first time since he arrived, registers an emotion—surprise. His eyes widen and he focuses on Dora for just a second, then loudly begins repeating the Shema once again. I step quickly between the twins and Dora and gently grab Dora's upraised hand which was prepared to strike the other face.

William laughs sadly. "You can't even kill the right messenger."

Dora, looks at first enraged, then horrified, then bursts into tears.

"Let's all settle down?" I say, rather pathetically. I am feeling agitated at the turn things have taken. We were supposed to have been here hours ago, before sunset. This was supposed to bring some sort of healing. This was supposed to be a meaningful moment that brought truth and peace to a complex story, which had only produced tragedy. I thought this would somehow undo all that. Whatever I had determined to shape with this had melted into chaos. Dora is bawling hysterically. William, who noticed the flash of attention that emerged for a moment in Edward, is softly saying over and over again, "Edward. Can you hear me? Edward. Edward, listen. Listen, can you hear me? Can you hear my voice? Edward, come back to me."

There is an old aspen log paralleling the road about ten yards into the meadow. I lead the twins over and set them down. Their combined voices, Edward's in a guttural Hebrew, and William's calling to his lost brother, form a strange duet.

It is fully dark and the sky is awash with that magic found only in the wide basins secreted in the La Sals. Stars so fill the sky that I am sure no one on Earth has ever seen a sky so clear, so black, and so rich with light. I pause for a moment to look up, and feel both immeasurably small and immeasurably important in the same instant. I look back at the twins. Edward is still weakly repeating the Hebrew phrase, and William is now looking at the ground, silent.

At that moment, the meadow explodes in bright, unearthly, orange light. The entire basin becomes alive and as visible as if in a bright full moon. Shadows leap away, and the entire backside of the La Sals is dazzlingly disclosed. Above us, a glowing orb lights up the sky. I can see the detailed landscape patterns that the aspens shape on the flanks of mountains alight in the radiant glow.

"An exploding meteor!" I shout in delight.

Several things happen at once.

Dora screams. She is pointing toward the tree line at the edge of the meadow downhill from us. She bellows in an unearthly screech-whine, "The bastards! The bastards! They're back!"

There is something there. As the light fades back into the darkness of night, something white and indistinct moves swiftly into the aspens. Dora looks at me in terror, her eyes flaming like the meteor. I look back toward the trees and whatever it was is gone. I look at William and his eyes are locked onto the place as well, a look of confusion contorting his face.

Suddenly, Edward's head lolls forward, and in that motion I know he is dead. It's hard to explain, but it does not even cross my mind that he has just passed out or gone to sleep. He is dead. The next few moments are pandemonium. William screams, "Edward!"

Dora growls in a low voice, "You are not getting away this time." Then she bellows, "Give me back my son!" and takes off toward the aspens. I am unglued. I start after her, then halfway to the tree line, I turn and run back to Edward, then to the truck again. I'm not sure why, but I want something. I run back to Edward, then back down the hill after Dora. Hearing William calling me, I turn around and run back up to him and Edward.

I bend down and support them. They seem to be falling forward.

"I haven't long," William says, smiling oddly, almost mischievously. He holds onto my arm, but his grip is weak.

"I'll get you down the mountain and come back for Dora." I move to lift his light body.

He laughs, "Shush. Please be quiet."

Apparently, I was talking. I stop.

"I haven't long," he repeats, "and I need you to listen."

He is breathing very oddly. Edward's hand is limp at his side and his head, completely unsupported, is bouncing oddly and loosely with William's labored breath.

"Marcel has become present to me. It's important you tell them he was not mad. Do you get that? He was not mad."

I nod. "Yes. I understand." I don't.

He glances at Edward, and laughs again. "He's suffered a stroke and half his brain has just died."

"I understand," I say, but I am confused. Is he talking about Edward or Marcel?

William is breathing hard, with more difficulty, as if he is forcing himself to breathe by sheer force of will.

"Hear, O Israel. The Lord is One."

Then, like Edward, he shifts to Hebrew. But his eyes are bright, and he is looking at me earnestly and alive—unlike his brother's previous blank and absent stare.

"I wish I believed," he says simply.

He stops talking and his eyes look past me at the sky. I follow his gaze. The Milky Way is still burning magnificently and stretches across the now fully black sky, like something alive and watching. It is oddly quiet, even in light of William's gasping breath.

"Scatter our ashes up here. OK?"

"I will."

His eyes are moist, bright and intent. He's staring at the night sky. Then his eyes rest on me, and with soft concern he whispers, breathy, but clear, "Don't worry. I've not existed longer than I've existed. It's far more my natural state, I would say." He smiles.

He looks back at the tree line where Dora has disappeared and smiles up at me, "Sie hatte aber recht.. . ."

He is gone.

I pick them up, carry them gently to the truck, and lay them on the seat bed in the back cab of the truck. I clumsily buckle them in, trying to wrap one shoulder strap around their legs and another around their torso in such a way that Edward's head won't fall between the seats. My eyes are a blur, and I am crying frantically. When I think the body is secure, I remember Dora, but the rest of the night is a fog. I have no flashlight, so I pull the truck around to shine the headlights into the aspens below. I leave the truck engine running and take off into the trees calling her name. I run through the woods calling, navigating though the aspens by the truck's lights. I search until dawn. Calling, listening, calling again. Listening to the silence. Listening to only the insects calling in return. Listening to the wind in the leaves.

I did not find her. The truck was out of gas and the twins were growing stiff by dawn. Weeping, I ran toward Buckeye.

A family in a jeep found me and drove me down to Paradox, Colorado.

A search was mounted for Dora by Moab's, Monticello's, and Paradox's search and rescue teams on horseback, foot, and four-wheelers. A local tracker's hounds were brought in. They gave up long before I did. I stayed about two weeks on the mountain, looking, walking the small streams into which she might have fallen, checking any debris under which she might have crawled. Everybody kept saying we ought to find her.

We never did.

Neither the twins nor Dora had living relatives. The twins had an excellent solicitor, and their estate was well in order when I called with the sad news they were gone. In his will, William established a Chair in Marcel's name in the Department of Cognitive Studies at the University of Vienna. Edward left almost everything to support his congregation and a few museum projects. Apparently, they did not anticipate coming back to Vienna.

In late autumn, I carried Edward, William, and Marcel's ashes to the mountain and honored their last behest. The golden leaves of the aspens had mostly already fallen, and the tall white trees were nearly bare, with a few flitting yellow stragglers bravely hanging on before the winter winds pulled them from their mooring. The sun was high and clear in a cloudless sky, and the air was cool, almost brisk, playing with becoming cold. I hiked to a small meadow high up on the flanks deep in Wixom land, along a trail that is part of one of the Cooperate Wildlife Management Units set up to allow wealthy hunters to take big mule deer bucks. Old man Wixsom, still alive but waning, gladly granted me permission to enter his private lands. He also gave me the gate keys to do so. I sketched for him the final years of the Babcock twins, whom he recalled with delight as "That two-headed cowboy." At the end of the story, he wiped his eyes and said simply, "Go do your duty, son. And may God bless their souls. It will feel good having their …company when I do the same in a few years."

A serendipitous wind gathered and rattled the bare aspen branches as I tossed the ashes into the air. The sudden breeze felt like a blessing on their lives—an acknowledgment from the mountain that they belonged and were accepted. A homecoming. The grey cloud lifted from the simple clay urn and seemed to whorl for just a moment before taking flight into the dark and wild forest they loved. I wept a little, but found myself grinning from ear to ear.

So ends the tale of Hyrum Thayne, Scholar of Moab, as much as I've been able to construct. The lives he touched were many, including my own. I have wondered much what William's last words meant. What was Dora right about? Or was he referring to Marcel, whom the twins seemed to feminize from time to time? I think he meant Dora. But even so, "She was right, you know…" seems odd. Was she right about coincidence? Fate? Aliens?

Everything and nothing, I suppose. A mystery. As is life.

I end with this poem I found in Dora's hotel room, sketched in the back of a popular book on modern cosmology that I found on her nightstand:

SOURCE DOCUMENT #36:

Poem, Both Hyrums, *By Dora Daphne Tanner,*
from Desert Loves, *published posthumously, 2002.*

You have both become part of the landscape
bubbling up for a moment among the sage
and sedge, finding voice, then disappearing
like the cactus wren's song—sounding clear and
strong, for a moment, singing boldly its momentary emergence,
followed by the silence voiced by a plateau canyon wind.
I can no longer piece together more than
confusion. My memories dance, leap randomly,
and I cannot frame them properly anymore.
Who were you, Hyrum? Did I ever know you?
And you, little Hyrum. My stolen treasure.
I knew you only for a moment,
but in that instant? Love, meaning,
exultation, rending, anguish, blood, bond, fracturing,
healing, binding, filling, atonement, reaching,
consciousness, goddess, emptying, clarity, forgiveness,
abandonment, holiness. Yes, especially that, I touched
the sacred. Holiness.
How odd you flowered out of disgrace, lies, passion, lust,
ignorance, fear, desire, belief, love, wetness, delight, hatred,
bliss, anger, confusion, profanity, yearning, laughter,
contentment, animality, drive. Yes, especially that: I touched
the push and straining of fate. Elan Vital.

I list words. But they fail. I could write an infinity
of such, and still they would fall away inadequate.
The wind continues to carve and define
this dry land. I hope both of your
scattered elements will enter into other beings,
other stones. Other stories.
Perhaps we will be together again, our elements,
joined in a Bur buttercup, the three of us merging,
situated on the edge of a spring.
And reuniting there,
we will grow as one toward the sun,
a star whose death is as inevitable as
our own. Yet forever lives in this moment.
With us.

NOTES

Translations from the Zohar are from *The Zohar: Pritzker Edition*. 2004. Translation and Commentary by Daniel C. Matt. Stanford University Press, Stanford, CA. p. 173 & pp. 288-289.

Translations from *The Picatrix*, from Ghayat Al-Hakim. 2000. *Picatrix: The Goal of the Wise*. Translated from the Arabic by Hashem Atallah Ouroboros Press. 2002. Seattle. p. 158.

Quotes from *Book of Mormon*: Helaman 6:18-30 1952 The Church of Jesus Christ of Latter-day Saints, Salt Lake City, Utah.

Text from Carl Maria von Weber's Magic Shooter From: http://www.opera-guide.ch/opera. php?uilang=de&id=419#libretto Accessed, May 14, 2011.

STEVEN L. PECK

Steven L. Peck is an evolutionary ecologist, poet and writer, and graduate of Moab's Grand County High. His scientific work has appeared in such places as *American Naturalist, Newsweek, Evolution, Trends in Ecology and Evolution, Biological Theory, Agriculture and Human Values,* and *Biology & Philosophy.* He has won numerous awards for his fiction, poetry, and essays, which have appeared in *Bellowing Ark, Dialogue, Irreantum, Pedestal Magazine, Red Rock Review, Glyphs III, Tales of the Talisman, Victorian Violet Press, Warp and Weave, The Wilderness Interface Zone,* and many other places. He lives in Pleasant Grove, Utah.

ACKNOWLEDGEMENTS

While I'm certain they don't remember me, the staff at the Phil Cafe in Vienna served some delicious breakfasts and did not seem to mind while I sat at my table and wrote for hours at a time.

I would like to thank Torrey House Press and the new friends I've made there for their help and support in moving this work forward and making its publication a reality. I'm grateful to Mark Bailey for finding and championing this work. I'm especially grateful to my editor, Kirsten Allen, whose suggestions and insights have made this book significantly better than it would have been if I were left on my own.

This work would be impossible without help from friends: In particular, all my friends at BCC, especially Mark Brown, Sam Brown, John Fowles, Kristine Haglund, Ronan Head, Brad Kramer, and Marintha Miles, who helped me get some of the cultural artifacts right. Steve and Jaylyn Hawks read multiple drafts from the very beginning of this novel's formation, and their suggestions and input were essential in making this work much, much better than it would have been. Mostly, I would like to thank my wife, Lori Peck, without whose help and patience this creation would have been impossible. All the mistakes are, and will continue to be, mine.

PUBLISHER'S MESSAGE

What I want to speak for is not so much the wilderness uses, valuable as those are, but the wilderness idea, which is a resource in itself. Being an intangible and spiritual resource, it will seem mystical to the practical minded—but then anything that cannot be moved by a bulldozer is likely to seem mystical to them.

— Wallace Stegner, *Wilderness Letter*

At Torrey House Press, we seek to increase awareness of and appreciation for the land, history, people, economy, and cultures of the Colorado Plateau and the American West through the power of pen. In particular we hope to help create an increased understanding of the value of natural landscape through the eyes and experiences of sympathetic characters in enlightening, entertaining stories. This begs the question then, what is the value of wilderness?

In his *Wilderness Letter* to Congress in 1960, Wallace Stegner said, "Without any remaining wilderness we are committed wholly, without chance for even momentary reflection and rest, to a headlong drive into our technological termite-life, the Brave New World of a completely man-controlled environment. We need wilderness preserved—as much of it as is still left, and as many kinds—because it was the challenge against which our character as a people was formed. The reminder and the reassurance that it is still there is good for our spiritual health even if we never once in ten years set foot in it. It is good for us when we are young, because of the incomparable sanity it can bring briefly, as vacation and rest, into our insane lives. It is important to us when we are old simply because it is there—important, that is, simply as an idea."

More recently, in 2009, Deeda Seed and Terri Martin of the Southern Utah Wilderness Alliance led an initiative called *Faith and the Land*. They held forums that brought together members of the Roman Catholic, Episcopalian, Islamic, Jewish, Latter-day Saint, Methodist, Presbyterian, Quaker, Unitarian Universalists, and United Church of Christ faith communities. More than 230 people took part. Participants discovered that, though their religious practices might vary, they stood on common ground in their respect for creation and the natural world. Whether they were from the city or the country, ranchers or suburbanites, man or woman, participants universally spoke of a feeling of being part of something larger than themselves; of healing, solace and renewal; of deepened bonds with their loved ones; and, finally, they spoke of feeling increased humility and sense of place in the scheme of things. What is that thing? What is it that everyone feels who spend some time in the solitude and grandeur of the natural outdoors?

Side by side with religion, science is also asking, "What is that thing?" Quantum physics raises very radical questions about the nature of reality. At the quantum level there is an unavoidable indication of consciousness or something of its kind playing an important role in shaping the ultimate structure of reality. In order to work the way it does, consciousness must have a universal aspect. Physicists call the place where physics encounters consciousness the "quantum enigma," and in order to avoid discussions of metaphysics and philosophy they often tell themselves to "Shut up and calculate." Nevertheless, in the science of the quantum it is as correct to hypothesize that the physical world springs from consciousness as the other way around. Holy smoke. It is at this point that science is observing the very nature of creation, and philosophy and religion come, ready or not, back into the picture.

In his seminal work, *The Idea of Wilderness,* author Max Oelschlaeger suggests that to protect wilderness we need a new story and that "if a new creation story is to ring true in a postmodern age, then it must have both scientific plausibility and religious distinctiveness." In the same vein he says that, "Crucially, the idea of wilderness appears to undergird a new paradigm for understanding humankind as embodying natural process grown self-conscious." He goes on, "What are we? Where are we going? Only when we are lost, Thoreau reminds, can we begin to find ourselves. Once we abandon the signposts, the directions that define the conventional world, we see wild nature, and there, in wildness, lies preservation of the world." Writers lobby Congress to protect the power of an archetypal idea, people of all faiths and political backgrounds go outside in silence and solitude for a while and universally feel a heightened sense of awareness and connection, physics unavoidably meets consciousness, and questions of the source of creation arise. Philosophy, religion, and science come together to answer the question of the value of wilderness. That in wilderness may lie the preservation of society is a story that, when examined closely, has a religious distinctiveness and a scientific plausibility.

Like Dora floating silently in a deep canyon pool, or Hyrum on a wild mountain peak, or the elegant and erudite Babcock twins at last reaching reconciliation and peace as they lie dying on the La Sal mountainside and their three consciousnesses merge, there are transcendent experiences available to all of us when we allow our natural selves—mind, body, and soul—to be most in tune with the wild places we come from. When enough of us individually grow from transcendent experiences, our collective consciousness can also evolve to a higher level. But only if there are wild places.

ABOUT TORREY HOUSE PRESS

Headquartered in Torrey, Utah, Torrey House Press is an independent book publisher of literary fiction and creative nonfiction about the environment, people, cultures, and resource management issues of the Colorado Plateau and the American West. Our mission is to increase awareness of and appreciation for the transcendent possibilities of Western land, particularly land in its natural state, through the power of pen and story.

2% for the West is a trademark of Torrey House Press designating that two percent of Torrey House Press sales are donated to a select group of not-for-profit environmental organizations in the West and used to create a scholarship available to upcoming writers at colleges throughout the West.

Torrey House Press, LLC
http://torreyhouse.com

Also available from Torrey House Press

Crooked Creek by Maximilian Werner

Sara and Preston, along with Sara's little brother Jasper, must flee Arizona when Sara's family runs afoul of American Indian artifact hunters. Sara, Preston, and Jasper ride into the Heber Valley of Utah seeking shelter and support from Sara's uncle, but they soon learn that life in the valley is not as it appears and that they cannot escape the burden of memory or the crimes of the past. Resonating with the work of such authors as Cormac McCarthy and Wallace Stegner, *Crooked Creek* is a warning to us all that we will live or die by virtue of the stories we tell about ourselves, the Earth, and our true place within the web of life.

The Plume Hunter by Renée Thompson

A moving story of conflict, friendship, and love, *The Plume Hunter* follows the life of Fin McFaddin, a late-nineteenth century Oregon outdoorsman who takes to plume hunting—killing birds to collect feathers for women's hats—to support his widowed mother. In 1885, more than five million birds were killed in the United States for the millinery industry, prompting the formation of the Audubon Society. The novel brings to life an era of American natural history seldom explored in fiction, and explores Fin's relationships with his lifelong friends as they struggle to adapt to society's changing mores.

Printed in the USA
CPSIA information can be obtained
at www.ICGtesting.com
JSHW012021140824
68134JS00033B/2801